SAVANNAH DOGS

SAVANNAH DOGS

MINNIE MCQUILLEN BEIL
EDITOR

FREDERIC C. BEIL

SAVANNAH

TO

OUR AGENCIES

Humane Society of Chatham–Savannah
Pet Assistance League of Savannah
Save-A-Life Animal Welfare Agency
Second Chance Dog Rescue and Referral

AND OUR
DOCTORS OF VETERINARIAN MEDICINE

Amy Ahles
Melanie Bevere
Richard W. Bink
Patrick Bremer
Al Camacho
Jerry L. Case
Kyle Christiansen
Ernest Compton
Max M. Cooper
James E. Ducey
Pamela Fandrich
Christopher Gall
Heather Gill
Alan C. Gross
Julie Harelson
Stephanie Hazlett
Don H. Howard
David Howes
G. Scott Hudspeth

J. Patrick Hudspeth
Karen Kane
David B. Kicklighter
J. Stanley Lester
Carla Case McCorvey
Lesley Y. Mailler
Steven M. Marlay
Joe Morris
Robert Pernell
Ann K. Rogers
Billy C. Sanders
Paul Schealy
Linda L. Scheller
Denise Schneider
John D. Schoettle
Terri Sparks
Michele Trammell
Christopher P. Wynens

Recollect that the Almighty,
who gave the dog to be companion
of our pleasures and our toils,
hath invested him with
a nature noble and incapable of deceit.

—Sir Walter Scott, *The Talisman*

CONTENTS

CONTENTS

CONTENTS

CONTENTS

CONTENTS

EDITOR'S NOTE

To the many dogs who inspired the stories in these pages, I thank you. Without your lives and the unconditional love that you offer to the members of your pack, there never would have been *Savannah Dogs*. I also want to thank the members of your pack who took the time to assist in writing some of the stories and in taking the photographs.

One of my goals in editing this particular canine collection was to acknowledge and express my gratitude to the organizations and veterinarians who have provided assistance in the Savannah area. Many of the dogs that you will read about in these pages were the beneficiaries of these organizations and doctors.

If you do not have a dog in your life at this time, it is my hope that you will find in these tales a compelling reason to bring a dog into your home and into your heart. In the end, that's the magic of the "tails."

MINNIE MCQUILLEN BEIL

SAVANNAH DOGS

St. Asaph Beardeaux ("Beary")

We have a Kerry blue terrier named Beary. In June 2000 I had the occasion to visit Kentucky, where I stayed with my former neighbor, Debbie. Beary went with me and remembered his old romping grounds. I took him for a long walk one evening, and we passed the brick wall at the entrance to the subdivision. A ten-inch pipe ran underground, across the road, and extended just beyond the ground surface on both sides of the road. You could see the edges of the pipe. That evening, as we were walking, Beary was snooping around the pipe. I just couldn't get him to leave the pipe alone. It was extremely hard to get him to move along; normally he obeys every command. He was very persistent though, sticking his snout into the outer edge of the pipe, but I finally got him to start moving again. I didn't really think too much about his interest in the opening of that pipe at that time.

I had an appointment at the courthouse early the next morning. I had to be there at 7:30 A.M. At 5 A.M. I walked Beary before going into town. Beary and I set out for a nice, quiet walk. It was a beautiful morning, but very dark. We came upon the same pipe that he had been interested in before. Beary immediately went for the pipe, whining and barking at it. He just would not leave it alone. I knelt down in the grass to see if there was something in the pipe, but I couldn't see anything at all. Beary just kept barking and whining, and that is when I heard a faint bark. It seemed to be coming from inside the pipe. I ran back to Debbie's house, got a flashlight, and tried to see inside the pipe. I kept talking to whatever was in there and kept hearing a weak bark and whine from a dog, trapped inside the pipe!

I called the sheriff's department. The sheriff, city police, fire department, animal control, and a big back-hoe came within minutes. They could hear the poor dog crying, and Beary wouldn't get out of the way for anything. He was going to help no matter what!

To make a long story short, they had to dig up the road and tear out the pipe, foot by foot, to try and reach the trapped dog. They finally reached the dog and were able to pull her out. She was a beautiful Siberian husky. I could not believe that a dog that size could get into the pipe in the first place. Had it rained, she would have died inside that pipe; and if Beary hadn't found her, she would have died anyway. This husky belonged to my former neighbor, Danny Huber. Since he could not find her the day before, he had hoped that his husky would wander home soon. Beary's persistence had saved this dog. Beary was the hero of the day! I just love my precious dog!

JOHN AND TRACY ROBIDEAUX

BENSON

When Sydney (my ten-year-old pug) died, I felt every emotion known for loss; but my overwhelming one was guilt. Guilt for not loving enough; guilt for not letting him off his lead and allowing him to roam the mountains around Highlands; guilt for not letting him spend his afternoons on my sofa; guilt for not letting him sleep at the foot of my bed every night—not just on cold nights. The list went on, and finally I thought I had come to agree with my mother, who said after the death of her pony that she would never have another pet "because you get so attached and when they die the grief is too hard." My sister then would ask, "What about your children?" There was never a reply.

Sydney was my first purebred, and the question came up—Should I replace him with a pug or another breed? Advice flowed in from every corner. Six months after Sydney's death, I decided to adopt. Mary Peabody volunteers at the Humane Society, and she said she would find me a new friend.

Not long after talking with Mary and telling her what I wanted—medium size, short hair, housebroken—I got a telephone call saying: "I've found the one for you." So time had come to replace Sydney, and,

3

oh, boy, did old R. E. Morse come running up the path. After giving myself a thorough talking to, I called Rae Harsch and asked her to go with me to meet Sydney's successor.

We arrived at the appointed time, and out came Mary and friend. Friend was half cocker spaniel, half Lhasa apso, who had not been groomed in months. He had been found on I-16, and appeared to be about two years old. Even before we were introduced, friend peed on one of the chair legs in the waiting room and gave a growl that sent shivers up my spine.

Rae looked at me, and I thought about Sydney and what a perfect pet he was—never made mistakes or unpleasant aggression. Oh, well, I had come this far, I might as well give him a try. So off we drove to Bryan Street.

As soon as friend marched into my house with his tail curled and head held high, he changed. It was as if he had said, "This is what I've been waiting for all my life—home and security."

Now it was time for a name. I believe in preppy names, not Spot, Spikie, and Buddy. So I decided on Benson in honor of E. F. Benson, the creator of the Queen Lucia series and a resident of Rye, Sussex, England, where I had spent two delightful weeks in a cottage just down Mermaid Street from Lamb House, where Mr. Benson wrote his charming tales of life in an English village. Not only am I an admirer of his characters, but Mary Aiken, who lived in Rye, was a friend of Mr. Benson.

When she and Conrad moved to Savannah, Mary said many times how much fun Benson would have had living in Savannah and writing about the people who live in the Historic District. They were so similar to the ones he immortalized in his Lucia books.

So, Benson it was. After grooming and lots of loving, Benson looked smart and began losing some of his fear that came out as anger. We have been together now almost two years, and his anxieties still come out when a stranger—animal or human—appears; but otherwise he has come full circle. By the way, he loves to sit on the sofa with me and lie next to me in bed. We'll have to see about running free in Highlands.

PORTER CARSWELL

Maggie Krajca
("Miss Maggie")

Thank you all for joining us here this day for the annual Savannah Junior League Dog commencement ceremonies. Our first speaker is Miss Maggie, a delightful purebred dachshund who has been with the Savannah Junior League Dogs for six years. You can't miss her glossy black-and-brown short hair and slender body (don't ever let her hear you say she needs to lose a few) with those petite perfect paws and that Southern disposition that puts all of us to shame. Now, without further ado, I would like to introduce Miss Maggie.

Thank you for the intro, Miss Muffy. Hello, everyone. I want to thank ya'll for comin' this evenin'. For all of those newbies out there, welcome. I thought I would start the day off with my success story in training my owners. We all need to understand the meaning of humility, and at times superior minds must digress to the human level to get their way. And, honey, if you're gonna be a part of this dog pack, well, you best listen carefully.

I don't think many truly understand the inherent responsibility of bein' a Southern socialite. When I adopted my owners, two Savannah transplants, I immediately knew I would have to train them in typical Southern hospitality. Of course, engagin' in conversation is a must, and this was to be my first task at paw.

I would gracefully lift my regal head, throw back my long black ears—ears even Scarlett O'Hara would envy—and begin a monologue on my need to meet my fellow counterparts in the neighborhood. At first my owners just stared with mouths wide open, then broke into laughter and disbelief. As if they had no clue as to the articulation of the canine language (humph!). But soon enough they began engagin' me in conversation on a daily basis. Unfortunately their favorite conversation consisted of three words, "I love you," and they would keep on repeatin' it over and over like they'd lost their everlovin' minds! Finally, out of sheer annoyance at their childish behavior, I gave in and repeated it back to them. Well, you woulda thought I'd thrown them a sloppy piece of fatback just drippin' with grease, they was so jumpin' around slobberin' and huggin' all over me. But, alas, I had a mission to meet my fellow furries, and my plan was now set in motion. Soon I was the belle of the ball as neighbors and guests came from all over to hear my rendition of the human words "I love you." You woulda thought you walked into a room where rabies was runnin' rampant, the way these two leggers were jabberin' an' foamin' at their mouths. In effect, I became the most adored in my social circle.

My owners now respond most expediently when I bark my demands, although at times I must improvise by simple gestures of charades to get my point across. For when my palate desires something tasty, I must put my perfectly manicured paw in my food dish and pull it around the room until they realize a meal needs to be prepared. Humility, darlin's, humility. Now, I assure you all that few know of this dirty and shameful act, and if you breathe a bark of this, I may have to seek

7

revenge. Believe you me, you will know the true meanin' of "Beware of the Dog" if you go yappin'. Anyways, (yawn) I am in need of my daily soak in the sun, so I must leave ya'll now. Do feel free to visit my neighborhood and pop your head in. It's the private doggie door with the white picket-fence ramp. I always have biscuits on paw for unexpected guests. And if you decide not to drop in, well, frankly my dears, I don't give a gosh dog! Smooches, everyone!

MISS MAGGIE

BRUNO BRIGHTWELL ("BOOM BOOM")

I was born in Stone Mountain in December 1998. My brothers and I were waiting to be adopted. I am a dachshund named Bruno, with reddish-brown hair, blue eyes, and a patch of white. In the white part there is a heart shaped in brown. Lucky me, in February I was adopted by Steve Brightwell. He brought me to Savannah and delivered me to my loving master and family for St. Valentine's Day.

It was love at first sight! What I didn't know was that my time with my new master would be so short. Unfortunately my master, who called himself Pop to me, had cancer. I was the size of his hand and was so very happy to be with him. He went to the hospital before he died. We missed each other terribly because we just couldn't be separated. I sent my Pop a card with my picture while he was in the hospital. I was pleading to him to please come home, and I even promised not to ever do potty in the house if he would just come back. I told him how much I loved him, and he cried so much that Mama had to hide me in her purse so she could sneak me into the hospital. We both were crying, Pop and I. We were so excited to see each other, but I could not stay too long for fear of being spotted by someone on the hospital staff. That was the happiest moment for both of us—to be able to reunite. Unfortunately my Pop passed away in July of that year.

I was heartbroken and I missed him terribly. What would I do without Pop? All I have is the wonderful memory of feeling his heart beat when I would sleep on his chest. We would take naps together, and his touch was so gentle when he would pet me and cuddle with me. Pop sure did love me! Now I live with my Mama, and we still talk about Pop. And I have a special feeling for all men because they remind me of Pop. So now I have to take good care of my Mama because it has only been three years since Pop went to heaven, and she misses him each and every day. I thought that this story could be a tribute to my Pop. One day it will be my turn to go to heaven, and then Pop and I can be together again. Until then I am going to be with my Mama so that she can love me just like he did.

I love you and miss you, Pop. Dream of me.

BRUNO

MAGGIE

Dear Minnie McQ,

When I heard that you were going to publish *Savannah Dogs*, I got so excited! I rang the bell with my nose, and as soon as my live-in opened the door I raced to tell Gus and Blue next door. Typical Labs, they were not impressed.

But Sadie, the cocker on the other side, said, "No way!"

"Yes! Yes! Yes! Yes!" I couldn't bark fast enough.

Stewie, the other cocker, had no idea I could write. Sadie told him exactly how many copies of my first book I had sold. "No way," Stewie growled, "you must be loaded."

"Well, not exactly," I said. "My live-in gives the money to less-fortunate animals, whatever that means. But I like going to schools. The kids all need kisses, and I sign their books."

"No way," growled Stewie again.

I tried to describe the nasty ink pad I step on to paw

11

the books, but he ran off to chase a squirrel. He'll never catch it. "Bye," I said.

I jumped on the door, and my live-in opened it on cue. Good girl. I got my chewy out of the toy box and began to think what I could write about. My last story was about the jobs I've had being a greeter at a tanning salon and a school crossing-guard. But since *Maggie: A Savannah Dog* came out, my full-time job has been fund-raising. At school fairs and library days I read to the kids and pose for pictures. At nursing homes I visit mostly old people. Even the ones who seem to be in another place will often say they used to have a dog like me and lean over for a kiss.

My live-in says soon we're going to take my friend Morgan along. She's a small black pug who likes to bite my ears. When her live-in, Gwen, brings her over, we tear up the backyard and then eat ice cubes and take a nap.

You don't think the public will like her better than me, do you? No. How could anyone prefer a Boston terrier? No offense, MMcQ, you're gorgeous too.

Did I tell you I have a purrperson? Her name is Liza, and she leaves my toys alone. But she always checks out my dish and sometimes even licks the food. I've gotten used to her. She likes to play hide-and-seek and tag, but I'd rather wrestle. She's getting good at it, but when she's bored she gets up on the piano to avoid a body slam! One day she sneaked outside. I barked and tackled her until my live-in came to get her. I got an extra biscuit. The biscuits are homemade by Daisy the dachs-hund and are yummy! My live-in sits up and begs me to eat them.

I've got a title for my story! What do you think of "Maggie Maggie Tail Waggie" or maybe "Maggie Makes Smiles"? I'll let you know soon. Save me a spot. I'll send you a biscuit.

Love to your live-in.

MAGGIE

PINOCCHIO LAZZARO ("BABY")

Hello! I'm Pinocchio. I was born in Savannah three years ago. I'm from a long line of miniature Italian greyhounds. Alas! I cannot be called "miniature." You see, I have this great passion that has taken control of my life—food. I love to eat everything. There is no food—explicitly, black olives, popcorn, and sardines—that I turn my nose up to.

For years my mommy looked and looked before she found me. I'm her first dog. She's a little strange, being that she had been bitten three times while riding her bike. She wanted a dog that did not bite, did not bark, and was not sensitive to loud noise. Also, she wanted a dog with short, light hair. This way she could see fleas and quickly kill them. We both are sensitive to fleas. She's been bitten many times.

Of course I had to be very friendly, which I am. I want to kiss everyone I meet in the car. A gentleman will not kiss a friend on the face. I also had to be very smart. Mommy does not do "dumb." And I can spell—dinner, eat, cookie, lunch, chicken—plus a few more words. My

14

manners had to be perfect. That was not a problem, since I am a gentleman.

As for barking, I had been in my new home for a few months and never had barked. One night, while everyone was asleep, I started to bark and bark and bark. Mommy ran to the kitchen, very excited because she had never heard me bark before. Mommy had forgotten to take a nice juicy ham out of the oven. I let her know that it was still cooking, and, boy, did it smell great. Well, she turned the oven off, and took that luscious ham out of the oven before it was burned to a crisp. Not only did I save the ham, after Mommy cooled it off in the freezer I was given a nice big piece of it. It sure was good. For a few days after that, I was called "Piggie"; but then Mommy went back to calling me "Baby." I do like that name so much better.

I never get to visit with other dogs, but I believe that I would love all of them. When we walk to Hull Park, near our house, I see many different dogs and I fall in love with all of them. Some don't fall in love with me.

One day a big black dog, who had an awful smell—I smell nice because after my teeth are brushed each morning my mommy puts a little Shalimar perfume behind my ears—anyway, this big hunk growled at me and showed his teeth! I gave him a long look with my ears pointed up, as if to say, "My goodness, you're no gentleman, are you. I can only assume that you must live a dog's life while I, Pinocchio Lazzaro, live the life of an Italian prince.

PINOCCHIO

SKIPPER MARCHANT

Etiquette and gentility require a well-learned "Savannah dog"—boastful and proud of his ancestry and rearing—to speak. And no story could be told more true than my reflection, beaming from the eyes of my Mamma and Daddy. No doubt—I am top dog!

In the Southern charm of a beckoning "empty nest," my dear Mamma is the undisputed clairvoyant whose maternal instinct joyfully takes credit for my "birth" into the Marchant family. After near-most nine months, Mamma and Daddy's tireless search throughout the Southeast ended in an abrupt maneuver into a convenience store many miles from home. Compelled by an intuitive urge to scan the want ads of one more paper, Mamma was disappointed to find only one promising ad. Ever confident, she made the call. "Yes, we have one 'baby boy' ready to go home." With intense excitement, Mamma could scarcely translate directions, asking repeatedly for clarification. Finally, in desperation, she was asked to clarify *her* present location. In doing so, our shared destiny was affirmed! Mamma and Daddy had literally stopped and were calling from a phone located directly across the street and in direct sight of where I was waiting to meet them, less than a hundred yards away. Love at first sight!

Until officially registered by the AKC/CCA as "El chico del bebé del oso de la miel de Skipper," my doctors knew me simply as Baby Boy Marchant, a pet name my Mamma finds "precious" and one that I found hard to shake as I grew up. One look at my bashfully handsome profile (see unretouched photo), and the girls quickly associate my incredibly rare pedigree with another good-looking young Latin heartthrob named Ricky. The boys, predictably, tease me sometimes with the nickname Grande Blanco Bandito, persuaded most obviously by my well-tailored, white-on-white suit worn proudly in the highest Southern tradition of a true Savannah gentleman, absent the cane and straw Stetson.

As a regular guy, however, I'm known best around town as Skipper, aptly conferred, as the commander of a sleek little Boston Whaler that navigates the oak-lined estuaries forming Savannah's island paradise. My little brother, First Mate, answers to "Matey," but instead of swabbing decks, prefers to search for sea critters, an entertaining pastime pursued unashamedly by a proud feline, who just happens to be three times my size.

Landlubber days start with an early morning potty break that conveniently coincides with Daddy's first cup of Java. This is a time to resurvey my kingdom—not to mention being rewarded my first treat of the day just for returning to the kitchen. This is no mere game, as it requires a vigilant watch performed throughout the day, but more vigorously discharged when my friendly adversaries change between day and nighttime shifts.

17

Nocturnal critters are led by a masked bandit I call "Wacky" (the waccoon). His platoon includes some unheralded cousins I call "Sammys" (rat-tailed possums). By day, my favorite trespasser is Ole Red Tail, a genetic flaw among a notorious family of rodents, raiders of the birdfeeders. Of course we're not really enemies, and in fact we have become rather unconventional friends. But the games are serious, and control of the family estate is no small mission for either side.

So that is my short story. I hope you like it and that we can be friends. By the way, you can call me what you like because I am the king of all I see! Just ask my Mamma and Daddy.

SKIPPER

BB

The floodwaters rose so high that we could paddle our canoe down the street. When the waters receded they left in their wake a morass of silt, broken branches, and life-less trash. Out of the midst of this sodden desolation trotted a black dog, stepping from the dark floodwaters into our deluged yard, tail wagging, begging us to love her. It was unbeknown at the time that the rain had tapped on the shell of an oyster awakening it to reveal a black pearl. Not so shiny, not so lustrous, just a damp and dirty dog.

The day after the dog's arrival we left for England and returned to find she had dug a hole three feet deep under the air conditioning unit, which was now "home." We had other commitments, so I made signs saying, "Black Labrador Female. For Sale." But my heart wasn't in it. In the yard I looked into her soft, brown eyes and felt great love to give and to receive. So, we gave her a bath to get rid of the cloud of insects that hovered in a per-petual shroud around her. We fed her, but she still ate out at every independent dog's diner in the neighbor-hood—fried chicken scraps, BBQ bones, and shrimp and crab leftovers. Whenever we pulled out of the driveway, she would chase us down the street, at full tilt, fading to a black apostrophe in the distance; and sometimes she would race so fast we would have to circle the block to bring her back home.

Then Hurricane Floyd paid Savannah a visit, so we left town with our black dog in the back of the jeep. The dog still had no name. No name meant no attachment. That was how it had to be, we said. We walked the dog around the hotel parking lot, around the railway lines and walnut groves of Cordele. She smiled at us so gently. Upon our return to Savannah, we decided to keep her and call her BB. So, Dr. Marlay spayed her. She bit her tongue during the operation and now has a hole in it through which her lower incisor fits. Dr. Marlay also treated BB for a life-threatening case of heartworm. But she is strong; and with good medical care, spiritual healing, and a lust for life she pulled through.

BB's passion is to chase things. A raised, pointing paw, a slinking body, and she explodes across the pampas of Forsyth. A hunter in full throttle, she hurdles the tall monkey grass, front paws reaching ever forward with hind limbs tucked in high aloft any obstacle; she is suspended above the world. It is total focus—total abandonment to the wild instincts so finely tuned in her species. People stop and stare at BB as she bounces like a Tigger beneath a tree. She is a unique sight. She is a wonderful thing, but she never makes her catch.

Now BB is a street dog that sleeps indoors, unless it is too hot, then she stays outside and digs herself a hole in the cool ground and remembers her oyster-shell shelter from before-the-storm.

STEPHANIE WOOD CALANDRUCCIO

BLUE ("BLUEY")

We named our girl Blue, because we think she is mostly blue healer. She looked a lot bluer before we gave her her first bath. Evidently life in the projects provides dogs with few opportunities to keep up on their hygiene. I met Blue while delivering the mail in the Yamacraw Village area of Savannah. Every day she would appear out of nowhere, follow me, mooch dog biscuits for a few blocks, and then disappear. This went on for a couple of months, and people in the neighborhood would ask me if she were my dog. I finally decided that I should get it over with and take her home. It was inevitable really; she was too irresistible. I hinted to my wife that it might be coming. She hinted to me that I might be sleeping in the garage.

On first impression, Blue is really much like a young child with ADD (Attention Deficit Disorder). But once you get to know her better, she is really a *lot* like a young child with ADD. I think it is fitting that my wife calls her Bluey. It rhymes with Sooeeey, like when you call a hog, which is how she eats, going from one dog's dish to another. It also goes with kablooey, as in when she is done with a room it looks like a bomb went off.

Whenever a new pet is adopted, one of the first things

21

that must be done is to make sure a good veterinarian checks it out as quickly as possible. Ours is a good old large-animal veterinarian with many years of experience with hundreds of hunting dogs. As I proudly introduced our vet to the latest member of the family, I asked him what breed he thought she was. Demonstrating his many years of knowledge and experience, he unhesitatingly told me he couldn't tell. Might she be a blue healer? Or maybe a German shorthaired pointer? And probably part black Lab? After debating her possible parentage and physical indicators, the doc said to watch her. If she seemed very alert and intelligent, she was probably German shorthair. If she was extremely hardheaded, strong willed if you please, then she was more likely blue healer. Hey, blue healer it is then.

The second priority of responsible dog ownership is to begin their training. Now that we have her house-broken, we are concentrating on teaching her to identify what exactly is food. She thinks that anything slower than herself is a candidate for dinner, including many non-food items. Road kill, cardboard, and things too unpleasant to mention have all been snacks for our girl.

Do all dogs watch television? Blue does. I think that she learned it from Toby, one of my other dogs. Toby and Blue love to watch television. You can't tell me that they don't understand it. Staring at the TV in rapt attention, they get excited when animals come on the screen, and even remember when the animals are about to show up in commercials. When they hear the right music and words, they get all aroused, ready to pounce upon the dog or cat as soon as it appears—more of those hunter instincts.

I don't mean to imply that Blue is not smart. She is certainly that. And sneaky. If one of the other dogs has a bone that she wants—other dogs' bones are always juicier—she will roll on the floor and beg them to play, jump over them, and do anything possible to distract them in order to snatch up their bone. If that doesn't work, she just runs to the door and starts barking. When they get up to investigate, she plops down and enjoys her feast.

Every dog, like every person, is a distinct individual. Blue is all of that and more. She is beautiful, frustrating, intuitive, and sensitive. She can tell when something is bothering us or when we are getting upset with her antics. If only I could just teach her to fetch the paper or, whenever I'm thirsty, an ice-cole drink . . .

ERIK GROSSNICKLE

KATIE GATENS

Katie is a thirteen-year-old bichon frise . . . and blind. It's amazing how our animals adapt and give us daily lessons on the attainment of happiness and contentment. Since she was a little puppy, Katie has managed to put a smile on the face of everyone she meets. We call her the "Hostess of Washington Square." She greets everyone with a wagging derriere and a smile on her face. Her entire backside swivels as she uses her hearing to zero in on your location and a voiceless command to "pet me, pet me." My husband and I have not moved the furniture since she became blind, and we take the same route for her walks. The way she tears out of the house when she hears "Do you want to go for a walk?"—takes a right down the steps, a left on the sidewalk, and the appropriate steps to the curb—convinces many tourists who roam our neighborhood that she can see.

She recently gave a scare to one of the haunted walking tours. It was time for a quick late-night constitution, which is conducted in front of our house. I was hoping that everyone was home in bed and took Katie out wearing unattractive pj's and a raincoat. As I opened the door, this little "Casper" flew down the steps into the middle of thirty tourists who were listening intently to a midnight ghost story, and scared the begeebers out of the group. Looking like a bag lady, I rushed to retrieve my whirling dervish, who was now receiving lots of hugs and labeled a "friendly ghost." I quickly returned home as fast as my fluffy slippers would take me.

St. Patrick's Day is another opportunity for Katie to show off. As we all know, everyone in Savannah is Irish, at least on March 17th. For that day Katie is no longer a member of the breed that used to occupy the French throne with Henry III, but an Irishman with the rest of us. Her white hair turns green (food coloring), and she wishes everyone "top o' the mornin'" with her smile and a bump into your legs when she misjudges your location. Her photograph is taken a million times that day, and she was even interviewed by WTOC and the Savannah News Press.

Katie came into my life the day I went to Candler Hospital to visit a good friend who just had a baby girl. I was now ready to be a "mom" to a dog. At the time I did not know that the puppy I chose was the victim of "puppy mill" practices of a pet store that has since been closed down. Katie lost her sight at the age of two, but through the talents of Victoria Pentlarge, a kind "doggie ophthalmologist," we were able to temporarily restore her vision. Over the years Katie has had numerous operations to buy her more time to see the world around her. We lost the battle last year, and now Katie has artificial eyes that sparkle with the reflection of her sweet disposition. We are truly fortunate for the love she brings into our home!   BARBARA GATENS

LADY
KATHERINE
OF CHATHAM
("KATIE")

Lady Katherine of Chatham was sired by Rob Roy, and the mother was Maggie Racket. Katie was born September 25, 1987, and came into our lives some eight weeks later. We bought Katie as a gift for our daughter, Jennifer, as we had just moved to Savannah from New Orleans, Louisiana, and she had always wanted a puppy, but our housekeeper there of twelve years was highly allergic to pet hair.

I named the Lady "Katie" as a tribute to one of Jennifer's friends in New Orleans. The name stuck, and Katie became a very special member of our household.

It was not easy for any of us moving to a new town, especially for our children, Jonathan, age fifteen, and Jennifer, age twelve. My wife and I opened our second restaurant, The Cock'd Hat, at 9 Drayton Street. When we returned home from the restaurant at all hours of the night and day, Katie was always at our front door to greet us with a loud bark, a wagging tail, and wet, licky kisses. During the night we could always hear her making the rounds to each child's room to ensure that all was well.

When Katie was two years old, I arranged a date with Spencer, a very handsome liver-roan springer spaniel

26

from championship stock owned by a local Episcopal priest. Katie and Spencer were close playmates from Forsyth Park. I will always remember Father Bill Willoughby yelling, "We have hook." A few months later Katie gave birth to nine beautiful pups. Katie was assisted by our daughter, Jennifer; my wife, Joan; Craig Lester, our friend and our vet's wife; and myself. I remember Katie giving birth to seven pups only to get out of her welping box to walk down twenty-one steps to greet Craig as she rang our front doorbell. Katie walked Craig upstairs, jumped into her whelping box, and gave birth to two more pups.

Joan and I own a bed and breakfast, Joan's on Jones, which is on the garden level of our three-story 1869 vintage Victorian home. One of the suites is reserved for clients with doggies. Katie gets a big thrill greeting her new and old canine friends and acts as a good host, showing them around the formal garden. Katie has gotten lots of gifts from repeat visitors, and daily we get phone calls asking us about the Lady.

We are very fortunate in having Forsyth Park only a few blocks away. It is the largest square designed by General James Olgethorpe around 1733. It is almost a mile and a tenth around, and has as a centerpiece a very beautiful, large, ornate fountain. For the past fourteen years Katie has been taking me for long walks there to meet her friends, both canine and human. There's Sam, the collie owned by Jackie and Ken Sirlin, formerly from Belgium; Max, the bichon frise owned by Fran and Larry Levow; Jack, a beige terrier owned by Caroline and Ed Hill; Elvis, a very large, overweight basset hound who always gets loose from her owner and shows up at our house; the late Blue, a blue schnauzer owned by Myrtle Jones; and the late Whitey, a white German shepherd owned by Emma and Lee Adler, who gave Katie fits. I believe that Barney, a large beige Benji dog, was Katie's secret lover. Many of the world's problems have been solved in Forsyth Park between cleaning up after our pets and untangling ourselves when the dogs' leashes get tangled.

Our Katie is fourteen years old now, and we do not get to Forsyth Park as often as we used to. We do make our early morning rounds to the dog friendly businesses in the neighborhood—Shavers' bookstore, The Market on Jones, and Home Run Video, where Katie is always welcome with a kiss and a dog biscuit.

Katie is not as active as she once was. Although the kids long ago left the nest, Katie still makes her rounds to their rooms. We help her up onto our bed at night and walk carefully around her as she sleeps almost all day on the floor. It is very sad to see such a grand lady grow old.

GARY AND JOAN LEVY

THE DUKE OF ALASKA ("DUKE")

My idea of having a good time is walking my property line. These aren't my words; I got them from an old Marshall Tucker Band song. They do describe me to a "T" though.

Today was a beautiful autumn Sunday afternoon at the homestead. I've been outside, not doing much, just piddling and spending some time with my dog. Thought about raking some leaves, but my back's still killing me from playing golf yesterday.

Someone's burning leaves in the neighborhood, and while I perversely enjoy the odor, I also worry about the dry conditions and the environment.

These are my thoughts as ol' Duke and I meander around our property. My significant, workaholic "other," who's had her nose in her work all day, remains inside and laughs at me. We only have a small house on less than half an acre of land, so I assure you she doesn't feel like the lady of the manor.

To me though it is the Ponderosa, and I'm Ben Cartwright. We're surrounded by people with similar lifestyles and homes, but I don't care, I'm still Lorne Greene when I'm on mine.

Duke knows his way around. Our backyard is fenced, and I've often watched him from the kitchen window as he makes his rounds. First thing he does after one of his many naps is to patrol the perimeter of our backyard. Once he is assured that all is copacetic, he comes up on the deck, peers through the window, and tries to lure me outside.

Duke is as big and as pretty a chocolate Lab as you've ever seen. When he bats his baby browns at me, I'm a goner. Grabbing a jacket and a beer, I go out to join him. He's ecstatic, and that makes me pleased. We make our way out front, where we can continue making our rounds.

"Kitty-cat chasing" is the first order of business. Our neighborhood is lousy with cats, and they seem to adore our yard. Duke is all dog, and it is his upheld sworn duty to give chase. At twelve years of age—though he runs like an arthritic, overweight linebacker chasing a Herschel Walker—he never seems to catch them.

When we moved to Savannah six years ago, I walked the boundaries of our property with him; and ever since, he's never set a paw over them without permission. These devious felines will escape his feeble chase, and then just sit there taunting him. Just beyond our borders, they know they're safe and that he won't leave home. To these conniving cats, he must seem like a dolt for his territorial instincts, but I know just where he's coming from and respect him all the more for them.

I've caught up with him now, and he proceeds to lead me around the lot. We've got this little feud going as to who's the boss around these here parts. Most of the time I'll let him lead, but sometimes my insecurity gets the best of me and I make him follow.

Today I just stroll, sip my beer, and let him show me any new developments. He points out where a branch is down. Moles are burrowing over there. Another dog has been over here, and "I'm not happy," he says. "See these deer droppings? Should we be concerned?"

He doesn't miss a thing, and makes sure I'm also aware of them. Myself, I see the camellias are budding and fixing to pop. Pine straw blankets the yard, and I'll be able to put off raking it for only so long. Both cars need washing and the shed needs painting, but that's okay.

Then we sit on the front steps as the sun sinks and the air chills. We talk a bit, groom each other, and enjoy the approaching evening together. Finally I say, "Come on, old man, it's dinnertime," and reluctantly rise. Of course he's off like a pup at the sound of his magic word, and I finally catch up with him by the back door waiting by his bowl.

I feed and water my best friend, then tell him it's bedtime. With his belly full and his ears thoroughly scratched, he contentedly curls up by the door. I enter the house, note its warmth, and hang up my coat. My baby is still immersed in her work, but she takes a moment to get up and greet me. She complains that I smell like the dog, but then hugs me and tells me how much she loves me.

Life is great, ain't it!

TOM PARRISH

 **MISSY**

Architect Eric Meyerhoff and wife Harriet have been living in the Historic District, on Greene Square, for the last twenty-eight years. We have always had a dog (or more) as part of the household. By design, our three dogs were all rescued from the Humane Society.

First there was Cuspidora, so named because she was mostly spitz. We called her Cuspi. She had many lovable traits. Among them was taking random socks left on the floor next to Eric's shoes and burying them in the backyard. Yet, after all these years, we have no argyle tree blooming there.

When we lost Cuspi, we selected a snow white (with a black ear tip) Maltese from the Humane Society. Our kids, enamored with the "Dukes of Hazard" at the time, named her Daisy. Daisy helped raise the kids, and vice-versa.

Harriet rescued Missy from the Savannah Humane Society as a young dog for her aging mother under the Pet Therapy Program. After her mother passed away, there was no question about keeping Missy in our

32

family. At that time she arrived as number-two dog, competing with Daisy.

While a mixed breed, and unusual in shape, Missy has the features of both corgi and shelty with a wonderful disposition, and we have never heard her growl. At the Humane Society she was known as "The Waving Girl," for her unique manner in greeting people. She would stand on her hind legs, waving both front paws. We should have taken her on the road with that act, but Missy was just not interested in a day job.

A close call with death occurred a few years ago when Missy ate something found on a walk. Thanks to a devoted vet who nursed her back to health after daily trips to his office, she recuperated beautifully, but not perfectly. She was left with damage to her larynx, causing her bark to sound more like a quack. Again, we thought about Missy in show biz, and again she refused to sign a contract.

One of the most incredible acts of love and devotion was shown by Missy toward Daisy, in Daisy's later years, when she was left totally blind and frail. On several occasions Missy would take one of her biscuits and carry it upstairs to Daisy, dropping it between Daisy's paws. We still look at the pictures, in fond memory, of Daisy and Missy cuddled up together in a corner of the room. Three years ago Daisy too passed through St. Peter's pearly dog gates.

Missy is now fourteen years old, with aging problems of her own. We find ourselves caring for her with the same devotion that she showed Daisy, however we have not yet learned to take a dog biscuit in our teeth and drop it in front of her.

For all the love we have given to our dogs, they have certainly returned in kind their companionship, faithfulness, and full devotion. We always have been and always will be true dog lovers . . . even though Missy refused to work for a living.

HARRIET AND ERIC MEYERHOFF

MATTINGLY

Okay, it's true that my name is Mattingly, and I am named after the New York Yankee, not the Georgia politician. But just because my owners chose to name me after a famous baseball player from the Bronx doesn't mean that I am a Yankee. The truth is that I was born and raised in Georgia. Now I might not have the so-called sophistication of my older sister, Justice, but in reality she is nothing more than a stuck-up snob who doesn't like to share her toys and is, as she calls it, "big boned." I say that she is just fat.

Now, as for me, I am a stud, if I do say so myself. I may just look like a small seventeen-pound dog. I am, however, a big dog stuck in a small dog's body. Justice says that I am crazy and out of control. Actually I am just trying to get out of this body and run with the big dogs.

I live on Wilmington Island with my parents, Marc and Pam, and my lazy sister. We take many walks around Wilmington Park. The problem is that nobody wants to walk as fast as me. If it was up to me, we would just run around the island; walking is for wimps. There

35

are lots of big dogs on Wilmington Island, and I am not scared of any of them—well, as long as Mom and Dad are around to pick me up if a really big dog barks at me. But that doesn't make me scared of them, does it?

One of my favorite things to do is to run around the backyard as fast as possible. Tybee, the Labrador that lives next door, can't even catch me. Then, when I am all tired out, I collapse on the tile floor in the kitchen with an ice cube to chew on. Ice cubes are the best!

As you may have already heard, Justice thinks that she is the boss of the family, and I am just some underling. I think Justice has been watching too much of the Sopranos. I let Justice think that she is in charge, but I always get my share of the treats, and I take any toy from her anytime that I want—well, unless she really wants it, then I graciously allow her to play with the toy.

When we are not playing, Justice and I both like to watch television. We really do watch, not like those other dogs who just sleep in front of the TV. We especially like shows and commercials with animals in them. Mom and Dad won't even turn on Discovery Channel or Animal Planet anymore because they got annoyed at me for jumping at the television. I told them that I was just making sure it was TV and not real animals. They get so aggravated, and all I am trying to do is to protect the house!

I really have a great life, and I love living in Savannah. Now, if only I could figure a way to get bigger.

MATTINGLY

36

JUSTICE

As a New York metropolitan-area pug transplanted to Savannah, my story is a unique one. I had a very stressful childhood. I began my life in Kansas, at a "puppy mill"—a very traumatic episode. I soon moved to New Jersey, where I lived in a home with several other dogs, who ate all of my food and bit me so badly that I required stitches on one occasion. Needless to say, I was not the beautiful pug you see today. (As you can tell, modesty is not my strong point.)

When I was eight months old, I was adopted by my family. Well, I actually believe that I adopted them. You see, Marc was in law school and he really needed some company, especially someone who would sit up with him during all of those late-night study sessions. That's how I got my name. Pam would come down to visit on weekends and would always give me extra treats. Pam really needed me to spend time cuddling with her, and of course I would comply.

Life was finally getting down to normal, and then one day Marc and Pam asked me if I would like to move to Savannah. Well, to tell the truth, I was skeptical at first.

Marc and Pam, however, assured me that life wouldn't change too much and that I would not have to slog through the snow in the winter anymore. Well, that sounded pretty good, and so off we were to Savannah.

Life in Savannah was very nice. I got to walk down the aisle at Marc and Pam's wedding. Really, I'm not kidding! Pam made me a special leash made of lace; I looked really pretty. So, anyway, things were going very well.

Well, now comes the big shocker. One year of living in Savannah—walking around Forsyth Park, the islands, and the beach—this is the life. Then one day Marc and Pam announce that Mattingly is coming to live with us. I thought, Mattingly, what is a Mattingly? Well, guess what! Mattingly is a wild, crazy, out-of-control pug! Marc says that I used to be the same way, but I don't believe him. After all, I am a very proper lady—well, I do get kind of excited over "good girl treats," but who wouldn't! Anyway, Mattingly comes into my neat, orderly home and proceeds to start playing with all of my toys and trying to take the prime spot, sitting on Pam's lap. He is just crazy. Marc and Pam tell me that he will calm down, but it has been two years and he is still pulling my beautiful tail and jumping on me to play with him. He's not too bad; sometimes he can even be fun. I especially like how he always follows me around, and he knows that I am the boss (and as we all know, the boss can steal the treats).

So, now here we are, the four of us, living in Savannah, walking around Wilmington Island, and life is pretty good, even with crazy Mattingly around.

JUSTICE

MURPHY

Shortly after the loss of my third golden retriever, I began a search for yet another. You see, I have eyes for only a golden as a companion.

I located one across the state bound for a rescue kennel. On the recommendation of a friend, I drove to see him. He was huge, untrained, headstrong, somewhat aggressive toward other animals, two-and-a-half years old, and weighed eighty-seven pounds. My first words were, "Look at the size of his feet, they are as big as saucers!" Then I realized his head was almost as big as a football, but both were in good proportion for his size. I took him home on a thirty-day trial.

He looked like a cur with a medium coat and floppy ears, and my friends questioned my knowledge of what a Golden looked like. Six months later he had developed a full coat and beautiful feathering, and was close to the desired appearance of the breed.

Murphy had been a yard dog, farmed out and returned, and in need of training. After three frustrating weeks I fell in love with this moose of a golden. We struggled with in-house behavior (he never went around anything, just over it). We spent hours bonding, including confinement to my bedroom at night, sharing my twin-size bed (it was crowded), and joining me on the sofa for TV-watching.

We went to obedience classes, and ten weeks later he graduated. Now he demonstrates obedience skills to novice handlers, has earned his AKC Canine Good Citizen medallion, and no longer demonstrates aggression.

Murphy has a comical side. He has done nearly everything you have ever seen in a Marmaduke cartoon. His first Christmas was a panic. I'd trim the tree, then he'd untrim the lower half by removing strings of lights and all the ornaments. The next year I had a table-top tree. A friend sent him a UPS Christmas package, which I allowed him to open—my gifts were on top of the desk for safety. He still thinks that any delivery truck that stops in the neighborhood has a package for him, and heaves a heavy sigh when the truck leaves and nothing was delivered to his door.

I've laughed myself silly watching this dog go through the puppy-hood he had never known. He has been excited about everything: boats on the river, horses and cattle in a pasture, ducks, chickens, joggers. He had to be taught to swim, learn to ride in an elevator, use stairs, find a specific toy or his collar when asked, and "bring it" on command. He has mastered the ability of balancing a football, on its end, on his muzzle!

Murphy has matured physically and socially, trimmed down to seventy-four pounds; and he has decided he prefers heat, air conditioning, and carpeting to living in a backyard. He never meets a stranger; and he stops traffic with his appearance, his ever jaunty swagger, and constantly smiling face.

I brought home problems; today he is a joy and pleasure. Murphy is a very special dog in my life.

LORRAINE A. BONNELL

JODY'S CAROLINA DREAM TO ("JODY")

My name is U-CD Jody's Carolina Dream To, CGC, CD, NA, NAJ, or Jody. All those letters before and after my name have significance, at least to my mom and me, but I'll get to that later. I'm a ten-year-old female fawn whippet, and I want to tell the story of my life to let the unfortunate dogs in the world know that there is hope.

I began my journey in an unscrupulous kennel in Atlanta, Georgia. Most of my world was cement with little change in the routine of feeding and cleaning. I grew up there, but at two years of age I was purchased by a woman from Savannah. She took me into her home and seemed to like me, but the man who lived with her did not share her sentiments. After a few days the woman took me to the most interesting place with lots of people and activity and dogs and beds. I love beds! The woman told the people there that she could not keep me because that man she lived with said I didn't have enough hair for a dog! Can you imagine someone saying that? One of the nice women at the interesting place said she would find me a home, so I stayed there for several weeks. It was fun, and I enjoyed myself every day.

I was resting in my kennel when the nice woman came to me and said, "There is someone here to see you." I didn't care who it was as long as I had the opportunity to run to the front of the building and crawl into one of the beds. I ran right past the woman who was there to see me and did just that. She eventually picked me up and put me in her truck, and I began my new life.

This new woman quickly became my mother. She cleaned me up, fed me, and gave me the best thing of all—my very own bed! Of course I slept on hers too, but it was nice to have one to call my own. There was also a man in this house. Fortunately he tried very hard to become my friend; and although I still don't like it when he wears a hat, I am proud to call him my father.

Mom decided some lessons would do me good. She and I worked together to become a team and to perform certain exercises. Mom calls it "obedience training." We did well enough to go to different cities and show off our work. Eventually we began "agility training" too, and this is where all those letters come in. They stand for titles that Mom and I have earned. It has been wonderful, traveling with Mom, staying in exciting places on different beds! I love it. Now I get to go and watch Mom work with the other dogs in the house. It is the best of all worlds: traveling, spending time with Mom, and sleeping on a variety of beds.

Just because your life started out poorly, don't think it will always be that way. I didn't think I was worth very much; being given away so many times tends to make you think you aren't special. Now I know I'm special because my family thinks I am. Don't ever give up hope. Your family may still be looking for you.

JODY

43

Patches Fishman ("Patch")

There was a minute I didn't think she would follow through. I could see the indecision in her eyes; I could read her mind. You don't spend nearly twenty-four hours with someone—over a ten-year span—and not know something about their psyche. She was nervous.

We've had this discussion for years. For years, I've gotten nowhere.

LISTEN UP. I NEED A HAIRCUT. IT'S 95 DEGREES OUT THERE—120 TO ME. I'M BLACK. I ABSORB THE SUN. CAN'T YOU SEE HOW MUCH BETTER I'D FEEL?

We'd talk about it some. I'd think I made some headway. Then, boom, she'd change her mind. Thought I needed all that hair for my identity. Can you imagine? Thought I'd feel naked without it? Come on! And all this time she's getting her hair cut shorter and shorter, wearing a WHITE shirt for tennis. Jeez Louise. I thought I'd lose it.

I'd say, "Why are we doing all this exercise if no one gets to see my figure? I mean, what's the point? I eat right, I do sit-ups, I brush my hair a hundred strokes each night. But with this winter coat, no one gets to see the real me? How am I ever going to find 'the one'?"

She'd say, "Just wait. You'll find someone who likes long hair."

Then she made the appointment. I didn't hear about the plan until the night before when I glanced at her appointment book to get a heads-up on the next day. See, I had a list of my own going, headed by a certain golden retriever. He's dazzling. But every time I see him I'm too nervous to leave anything behind for him to check out. Then I looked in her books, and I saw Carol's Pampered Pets.

All right! I've been waiting years for this.

That morning, she scoota-pooted me into the car, but she was nervous.

Get a grip, I answered. Change is good. Go out on a limb. All the things she always tells me.

When she left, the hair operator said, "We'd better do you first. She's scaring me."

Bzzz, errrgh, weehhez, snnnipp, clip-clip. I was right. I had a knock-out of a figure. I looked ten years younger. I was a babe.

When she picked me up, she didn't recognize me. She kept staring. Then she showed me off to Sparky and Ariel, took me over to Uncle Gene's, wrote "wait'll-you-see-Patches" emails to Aunt Carmela.

Enough of you, I said. I feel good. I look good. I smell good. I want to see some of MY friends!

It was great. I got the double-takes I dreamed about, the cat-calls, the whistling.

Then, my man appeared. Golden retriever. I cast my eyes down, wiggled my booty, and did something I was always too shy to do. I peed on an azalea bush ten feet away from him.

"Oooh, good looking," he said. "New in town? Too bad we didn't meet earlier. I've got my eye on a long, black shaggy girl. Only she doesn't know it."

Later that night, despondent, depressed, discouraged, I broke down and told her what happened.

"What does he know?" she said.

There's always winter, I thought.

PATCHES

SAGE

Sage was six months old when we found him at the well-run animal shelter in Ridgeland, South Carolina. He greeted us with a hopeful expression. His hazel eyes seemed to find us to his liking.

As we considered this stocky pup—his dense white coat, pointed cream-colored ears, tail curving over his back, and paws forecasting his large mature stature—we knew that he was to be our choice. One of his ears would require some treatment. There was a wound . . . a cut or a bite. Was he part husky or part Akita? The people at the shelter knew nothing of his origin. No matter, he was beautiful. We signed the required papers, paid the fee, and he was ours.

Our grandson, Lee, suggested that we name him Good—a noble thought, but hardly a name for a dog. Yet Lee's suggestion led us to the name "Sage," from the French, for good or wise.

Sage has two homes: our house in the city on Monterey Square and our farm, near Pineland, South Carolina. In the country he can run free under the good care of Randy Mason; in the city he has as much freedom as we can give him. The piazza looking out on the square is one of his favorite places. Here he rests his nose in the iron-work and watches the world go by. In our office he welcomes visitors, particularly the postman, who brings an anticipated puppy biscuit every day. Right away he chose my father's walnut youth bed in the hall on the second floor and sleeps there every night.

Each morning, at six o'clock, we walk around Forsyth Park; and in the afternoon Sage often plays in the park extension with as many as twenty-five dog-friends of all descriptions, or in Monterey Square with his good friend Nick Raskin, who, except for his brown coat, looks very much like him.

Sage greets man and beast with trust and enthusiasm and receives compliments every day. I am apt to say, "He loves everybody and thinks there's only good in the world." On one such occasion the reply was, "That's because he's blessed." His sunny exuberant nature has won us all.

Since they were young children, my grandchildren and I have composed a song for each dog that joins our family. I will conclude this little story with Sage's song, written to the tune of George M. Cohan's "You're a Grand Old Flag."

The Sage Song

Oh, the Ridgeland pound is the best one around
Because that is the place we got Sage.
We found him there, huddled in despair
On the floor of a big wire cage,

With a wounded ear, but with no trace of fear,
He looked longingly into our eyes.
So, we took him home, never more to roam
And Sage is our grand new prize.

EMMA ADLER

COUNT BERNARD OF BERKHOFF ("BARNEY")

My dad, Tom, had me hidden inside his shirt, and my little head was peeping out between two buttons. Born on Halloween 1997, I was both a Christmas present and a birthday present to my mom, Diane! She knew I was special when she first saw my face! She burst into tears, but I licked them away. Before I came along, my mom was very sad because her first dachshund, Berkoff, had gone to doggy heaven. I was determined to make her happy again!

I had to wait a long time for just the right name. My mom and I love to watch reruns of the Andy Griffith Show, and that is where I got my name—Barney! Sometimes I am afraid of my own shadow, just like Barney Fife, but I can be brave too.

My mom reminded me everyday that I had lots of potential and that I was a very special dog. She took me to places where I could be around crowds of noisy people so that I could get used to different situations. Once a motorcycle roared by and scared me, but I reminded myself that my mom said I was special and brave. Pretty quickly I got used to the strange machines and all the people. I found out that I like being the center of attention, and you can't be a scaredy cat—I mean dog—unless you are friendly.

I started school when I was only eight months old! It was called the PALS obedience class. I learned a lot of neat stuff, like how to get along with other dogs and to obey commands. I made lots of four-footed friends, and some of them even came to my house to play with me! I took a special test of simple commands at PALS and earned a Good Citizenship Award.

My mom wanted me to be a registered therapy dog. Did you know that pet therapy lowers blood pressure, decreases pain thresholds, and helps with motor coordination? I didn't either until I learned to be a therapy dog. I had to take a temperament test and a test for the obeying of commands. I wasn't worried. I remembered that my mom told me I was special.

Now that I am a certified pet therapy dog, I have a mission in life, besides being lovable and adorable! One of my jobs is therapy work at Hospice of Savannah. I love to greet the staff, who know me by name. I visit patients, kissing them under their chin or on their hand. We sometimes play and sometimes just sit and visit. Often, while patients pet me, they talk about their own pets. I just lie there and listen to these wonderful stories and enjoy the attention.

I like to go to the Hospice Children's Grief Camp. I also work with patients who are in stroke rehabilitation. When visiting schools, I wear my Barney Fife uniform. Mom talks to the students about pet therapy and dog safety. I show off by obeying commands.

To me, work is play. It's a dog's life!

DIANE BLAZER

BELLA
COOPER

After Sister died we chose to live dog-less for a time. Then, in October, we decided that while no dog could replace Sister, we missed hearing gentle snores at night from the plaid bed in the corner of our bedroom. So, Robert began to look. One Saturday he drove out to PETsMART, where different agencies bring dogs for adoption. He saw a small, black dog, happily situated at the bottom of a heap of children, and he said, "Hmmm." He traced the dog to Pam Cutting of PAWS (Pets Are Worth Saving), who said she would bring Mindy to our house for the afternoon. She came, we saw, and the rest is history. She came fully grown, spayed, housebroken, and with complete medical records.

Mindy became Bella and moved into our bedroom and our hearts. Her veterinarian, Dr. Steve M. Marlay (Eastside Veterinary Hospital), says she is part chow and part setter. She has silky black hair, a black tongue, and a golden disposition. Bella has been to training classes at Carol's Pampered Pets, where she graduated first in her class! She stays there when we go out of town and often goes on Thursdays for agility training.

Every afternoon, around four, Bella starts what we

call her "dinner dance." Her dinner is served around 4:30, to her great delight. After dinner she races around the house, notifying Robert through leaps and yips that it is time to go to Gordonston Park. Bella is one of the fleetest of the dogs who bring their owners to the park every afternoon, weather permitting. Bella's special friend at the park is Dodge Christman. When there are no children around, the dogs are allowed to shed their leashes and race around the perimeter of the park. Bella and Dodge are leaders in this expedition.

Bella seems fond of me, her adoptive mother, but she absolutely worships Robert. When I leave the room, Bella stays where she lies. When Robert leaves the room, she jumps to her feet and follows. She follows him out to his workshop in the morning, but she does not come in. She spends a great part of each day on "squirrel patrol." To date she has not caught a squirrel, but hope springs eternal. (Since one of my passions is studying the Italian language, Robert and Bella leave in the morning with Bella in search of *lo scoiattolo*, "the squirrel" in Italian.)

Bella loves to ride in our van. When I'm not along, Bella rides "shotgun" with Robert. When Robert goes without her, Bella paces the floor here at home, spending most of the time watching and waiting at the front window. Only when he's safely back at home can she lie down and relax.

While Sister will never be forgotten, we are so happy with Bella, who occupies a very important place in our house and in our hearts. We have a new friend in Pam Cutting of PAWS, who can be reached at 354-3308, in case you're looking for a canine companion.

Fond greetings to Minnie McQuillen Beil and her pack. We applaud this "doggedly important undertaking" and its dedication to veterinarians and all of Savannah's doggedly determined organizations.

ROBERT AND EMMELINE COOPER

POLLY PUMPKIN OF WINDSOR ("POLLY")

I have dictated the following short story about my exciting life to my mom, Carol Mett. I haven't been able to fit computer classes into my busy schedule, yet.

My name is Polly and I am the true, blonde bitch with an Attitude! I happen to have been born into the luscious body of a yellow Labrador retriever with brains included. I can read minds, put you in your place with a quiet stare, and adjust an attitude with a wrinkled smirk of my lips. I know I am really people because my mom daily reminds me of this.

My exciting life has been dedicated to helping Mom train dogs. I have helped her train, groom, board, and day care thousands of pups, and a few cats. I have worked hard to receive several obedience titles in four different registries so that my mom could qualify for an AKC Obedience Judge license. I also am a Frisbee and tennis-ball retrieving expert, lifeguard for the swimming classes, and number one "attitude adjuster." Since retiring four years ago, I work in an advisory position for the training classes. I lie in my desk on the sidelines during classes and respond quickly to any problems that Mom needs help with. I step out on the floor, check out the treats being used for bribes, and then give my "wrinkled smirk" to any of the young trainees that seem to need an "adjustment." Mom says I was born with a natural, invisible aura surrounding me that puts dogs in their place with a quiet stare and a quick lashing of the tongue. Once a dog has tried to enter my circle without being invited, he never tries it the second time. This natural aura is another reason to confirm that I am really people in doggie fur.

I finally convinced Mom and Dad to buy me a motor home so that my three sisters (Anna, Savannah, and Summer) and two brothers (Max and Sergeant) can travel together in comfort to all the dog trials. My siblings have plush crates, and I ride up front to help navigate while lying under Mom's feet and watching out my own side window.

I would like to express my sincere thanks to my two wonderful doctors at the Crossroad Animal Hospital: Dr. Billy Sanders, my pediatrician and family doctor; and Dr. Pam Fandrich, my gynecologist. They take excellent care of my family and friends. I will be celebrating the arrival of my teen years on September 22, 2001, with another "Happy Birthday" party at our training center.

I wish that all of the canine families could have the happy and healthy life that I am having. Please remember that "Dog" is "God" spelled backwards, and he loves us too.

CAROL METT

REMBRANDT ("REMY" OR "LUMPY")

Obsessed dog owners are well known for regaling each other with tales of the personalities, mannerisms, and antics of their pets. Only those equally devoted to their canines can relate and admire these stories.

One breed that seems to solicit cries of astonishment and beaming admiration concurrently is the Labrador retriever. Being the owner of a Lab (ninety-five pounds and counting!), I have often shared tales of the consumption of animal, mineral, and vegetable matter with other Lab owners. Add to that furniture and clothing, and you've run the spectrum of Lab calamities.

Allow me to expand upon some of the gastronomic feats of my dog, Rembrandt. As with all Labs, Remy (aka Lumpy) has an undying, limitless passion for food —ALL FOOD, all matter that once resembled food, all items that may have been related to food somewhere down the food chain, or anything that you find disgusting and wish he would never eat. As a vet once told me, "If it's totally disgusting to you, it's dinner to him."

Remy's best digestive effort was about ten pounds of gravel that had been doused with grease when a neighbor decided to clean his grill. The gravel, lightly smothered in steak drippings, was more than he could pass up. As he came wallowing into the house, I noticed his gait to be a bit heavier. Of course that night the gravel, a lovely pile of gray shale chips, was expelled onto my living room floor. I needed both paper towels and a shovel for the clean up!

The "disappearing dessert trick" is one that has me stumped to this day. I had baked a pan of brownies for a Memorial Day cookout with friends. Knowing the extremes that Lumpy would go to in order to share in these treats, I placed them high up on the counter, on top of a microwave, to cool. Leaving the house for only a half-hour, I returned home to find no trace of the brownies or pan. Like they had merely vanished! Of course not a crumb was to be found. But neither was the pan. I searched the kitchen completely and checked out the rest of the house in case he had decided to dine in another room. (Atmosphere is everything to a Lab.) Finally I gave up and chalked it up to early Alzheimer's. Days later I found the brownie pan in a rarely used kitchen cabinet, licked clean beyond the best forensic science. To this day I can't figure out how my dog managed this accomplishment.

Of course Lumpy has many other "achievements" about which I could brag—including the near swallow of a half of a large, dead bluefish, a pack of frozen chicken, and a five-pound bag of cat food. Regardless of their unsavory habits, Lab owners dote on their "hairy children" feverishly. As the bumper sticker on my car says: "My child drinks out of the toilet."

LINDA M. BRAY

SCOUT FINCH PRUITT
("SCOUT")

My name is Scout Finch Pruitt. I was born December
10, 2000. We live in Georgetown, sort of Savannah's
suburb. My mom says that I only stayed in the pet store
for three days before she brought me home. She said I
was really cute with my mismatched eyes and silver
specks and all. When I go to the vet, they are always
calling me the "dapple dachshund." I think "dapple"
must mean "really pretty." Mom says that all the time—
that I am actually the prettiest dog in the world. I was
born in Kansas, but I don't remember anything about
that time. Every now and then Mom says, "Just be glad
I didn't name you Toto!" I don't know what that means,
but I guess Toto must have had a tough life or something. Mom says a lot of strange things.

My best friend is a beagle mutt. His name is King's
Bishop Pruitt. We call him Bishop. He's from the
"outside," so he's always teaching me stuff about the
world. Sometimes at night, when we cuddle in our
crates, he tells me stories about his pack-family and how
wild they were. I think he makes a lot of stuff up though,
because Mom says he was adopted when he was a baby.

She said that a nice policeman found him with a makeshift collar around his neck that was strangling him. I'm not sure what that means, but it doesn't sound good. The policeman called a man named Lee, who volunteers with AWARE (Animal Welfare and Rescue Effort). Lee took Bishop to a nice lady's house, where he lived for a few months. Then one day Dad went to the "field" (he was in the military), and Mom said we were lonely in the house. So she went to see the orphans at PETsMART. Mom said she wanted to get Dad a "man's dog." I didn't know what that meant, and I wasn't sure whether it was good or bad.

We met Lee at PETsMART, and he took us to a kennel by a lake not far from our house. That's when Bishop jumped out of the back of Lee's van, and Mom said, "Is the beagle an orphan?" and Lee said yes. Bishop was just an awkward gangly thing, but I sure liked him 'cause he was different likc me! He had strange spots all over his coat, and his eyes didn't match either—one blue and one brown. Bishop came home with us that day, and Mom says we're not lonely anymore. I know she's right, 'cause Bishop's the best pal a dapple dachshund could ever have!

CHRISTINE PRUITT

CHEYENNE EVANS ("SUGAR BOOGER")

My name is Cheyenne; I'm a golden retriever. My pet names are Sugar Booger, Sweetie Pie, Angel, and Baby. I am never called "dog." I have not been raised as a typical dog. I live a plush life. I sleep on my mom's bed and sometimes on my own comforters and pillows. When I feel overheated, as I do often in Savannah's sultry temperatures, I plop myself down in the shower against the cool tiles and nap. I eat two meals a day and many snacks in-between. Whenever I feel a tinge of hunger, I stand in front of the pantry and bark until someone comes and hands me something to eat.

I am a very good swimmer. I swim often in the pond at Daffin Park. My mom throws the ball, and I retrieve it over and over and over. Many of the watering holes around Savannah have alligators, so I am very picky in choosing where I swim.

I take lots of walks in my neighborhood, where I encounter a few intolerable pests, including Chester, a white, yappy Pekingese whose master claims he has a Napoleonic complex. This little runt tries to attack me every time he spots me from a block away. The thought that comes to my mind is "snack time." The neighborhood's felines are other major annoyances on my walks. They all know how to irritate me. Knowing that I am on a leash and have no access to those arrogant little creatures, they slowly stretch their lithe bodies, all the while smirking and teasing me. Needless to say, they know how to push my buttons. And then there is Peter Cottontail, a precious little rabbit who makes his appearance periodically. He is always munching. Usually he has enough intelligence to keep his distance from me, but at times he will gather a little courage and dine near my pathway. Go figure!

My favorite vacationing spot is Melbourne, Florida. I have a younger brother named Bear, who lives there. I visit him a couple of times a year. We get along very well especially since he has matured some and doesn't pester me anymore. Sometimes we swim in the nice canal behind his house. It is a little like a spa—that is, a mud spa.

Every Thanksgiving my mom's parents, sister and family, and brothers and their families get together, usually out of town. My brother Bear; Toby and Lady, my biological parents; and Lucy, a cousin from the coonhound line, are part of this annual holiday-reunion gathering. We had so much fun last year in Myrtle Beach. Bear and I managed to escape the rooms a few times and race down the halls of the motel. Our owners thought we were a hoot. I don't believe the other guests felt the same. We also barked a little too loud at times. While we were napping, a guest knocked on our door by mistake and we heard an employee say, "You done gone and woke up the devil."

CHEYENNE

62

BEAU
("MR. SNIFFY")

Beau, a black, male, standard poodle, came to live with my husband and me on March 28, 1999, in our home on Charlton Street. He was a little over three years old when we got him. He had been living on the Isle of Hope in pretty much a country setting, sleeping outdoors in good weather and sharing the days with his mother, Belle, and an active family.

We were not really looking for another dog. We had two miniature, silver poodles, Basket and Tumbleston, sister and brother. We lost Tumbleston in July 1997 and Basket in August 1998. She would have been seventeen the next month. Our hearts weren't really into starting over with another dog. We had nursed Basket way longer than we should have, hand-feeding her spaghetti (the only food she would eat) and carrying her out to Troup Square, where she would totter along for a few minutes before we carried her back home. When we finally had her put to sleep, we were drained emotionally.

Out of the blue, a friend called in December 1998. She knew Beau needed a new home (Belle thought it was time he "spread his wings"!), so we drove out to see him and committed to him the next day. It was a big change for Beau, moving downtown, walking on a leash, seeing lots of other people and, of course, other dogs—and cats. He was pretty timid to begin with, but as he got used to his new surroundings, he became more assertive. Fortunately my husband works at home, so someone was usually with Beau all the time. He didn't like it when no one was there and would howl pitifully (we actually tape-recorded him!) until we returned. That stopped after a few weeks.

Initially Beau was more attached to my husband because they spent so much time together, but he grew fonder of me as I laced his dry food with bits of baked chicken and other treats, bought him three Orvis beds (one for the Jeep, one for downstairs, and one for the bedroom), and finally said it was okay to come up on our bed and sleep. My husband drew the line at getting up on the couch.

Beau is a strong walker and very curious. He loves to sniff along the edge of the sidewalk and under bushes (his nickname is "Mr. Sniffy"). For a while my husband would take him to Colonial Cemetery to let him run, but other dog owners were not cleaning up and the City made it known that dogs would have to be on leashes. So he has to be content with four walks a day and an occasional run on the beach at Tybee.

While he barks strenuously at other dogs, he's fine with them once they get acquainted. He's very affectionate, and easily meets other people and children. He travels with us just about everywhere we drive, and we wouldn't have it any other way. We hated to leave Basket and Tumbleston behind, and Beau is no different. He's family.   PATRICIA AND JOHN BISHOP

CAESAR PARKER
("CAESAR SALAD")

Caesar is truly the DOG with nine lives! His loving and loyal disposition and laid-back temperament have made him a pleasure to live and travel with, but his life with me has not been without crisis. When Caesar found his home with me, he was in terrible shape. Friends had found him in Forysth Park; he had come toward them, then turned out into the street, and collapsed. Local vet Dr. Stanley Lester examined Caesar and found that he had a broken rib, punctured lung, pneumonia, was starving and anemic, and had badly bruised hips and legs—all the result of horrible abuse.

The good news is that he had broken free of his captors! After more than a week in the hospital, I was asked to dog-sit for "a few days" and help find him a home. Of course, after a few days there was no way that anyone would ever pry Caesar away from me. He had a home! The next six months were tenuous. Caesar was back in the hospital three more times—twice on the verge of death, again with internal infections, bleeding, and pneumonia. He overcame all of this, and each day when I came home I was greeted by his "Caesar dance."

Standing up on his hind legs—his nose and eyes then were exactly even with mine—he would not touch me, but would always extend his left front paw as if to ask me for a dance. I would hold his paw, and he would do about five or six steps, then go back to all fours. Even today, seven years later, although he has trouble walking and can no longer dance, he still stands tall and proud of himself.

Caesar has been a very alert and protective companion. He often shop-sits with me at my antiques business; he loves the attention from the customers, and especially from the children. Once, however, I remember a man who wandered into the shop. Caesar began to growl. He had not done this before, so I immediately knew that something was wrong. As the man approached the counter, Caesar stood up on his hind legs, put his paws up into the air, showed all of his teeth, and barked. I'm not sure what the man's intentions were—he didn't stay around long enough to know—but as he flew out the door he was screaming, "Devil Dog!" I distinctly smelled alcohol as he left. Caesar had a steak for dinner that evening—medium rare, his favorite!

Caesar is aging, and because of the abuse he endured during his early life, he has difficulty in walking; but his spirit is young, and occasionally he can still give a squirrel or a chipmunk a scare. Shana, his girlfriend and companion, and Taz and Skeester, his cat friends, surround him; and then, of course, there is his loyal friend and servant, yours truly—all to keep him company.

NOREENE PARKER

MADRILENE
BLUE BOY COOPER
("COOPER")

Hi! My name is Cooper. I am new to Savannah. Well, I've only been here a few weeks and am only a couple of months old. My dad is a Georgia boy—Columbus, to be specific. My mom is a Clarksville, Tennessee, gal; and Clarksville is where I was born and raised until recently moving to Savannah.

I'm an English cocker spaniel in a very popular color called blue roan. English cockers grow to be larger as adults than the American cocker spaniel and are generally said to be a much more calmer animal. Both my mom and dad are show dogs as well as companions, and they both have earned their championships in the show ring. Although that makes me kind of proud, I'm not sure if I would want to follow in their paths. I think it might be kind of fun to be a fireman. I thought I would go ahead and tell you all of that because you are looking at my picture, and I am sure some of these questions are running through your mind.

So far Savannah seems like a good place to be. I like all the parks, and all the people seem so friendly and want to pet me and be sweet on me. My new "dad" seems to be a good guy. He makes sure I have plenty of food, fresh water, and exercise several times a day. He keeps telling me there are several rules I will need to obey, but that they are in my best interest and help with my safety in the long run. So that sounds fair enough, especially in a city the size of Savannah. I'll make sure to share those with you when I get them down pat.

The other thing people keep asking is if I have read "the book." Could someone please tell me what they mean by that. I haven't learned to read yet, but boy when I do, I am going to put that book on the top of my list.

Well, my attention span has been maxed on this. It's time to go and chase the cat. So if you're out and about and see me and want to meet, just yell "Cooper," or even "Coop" is okay.

Until later,

COOPER

SAVANNAH'S
MISS ASHLEY ANN
("ASHLEY")

So what do you call an elegant, voluptuous, ninety-pound, blue-black, female giant schnauzer? In Savannah she is called "Ashley"; on her registration papers, "Savannah's Miss Ashley Ann."

So now that you have been properly introduced, let me give the floor to her. Miss Ash, it's all yours.

Hello. It's a pleasure meeting all of you. Welcome to Savannah. When my dads bought me almost nine years ago, on New Year's Day, in Asheville, North Carolina—incidently, that's how I got the name Ashley—they told me all about my new home during the drive back to Savannah.

Well, after nine years I can tell you that, yes, Savannah is a unique city, as they had said it would be. Dogs here are treated as adopted or, should we say, chosen children for the most part. Well, at least I feel like a pampered lady. I receive regular brushing and grooming, an omelet for breakfast every morning, a special dinner mix, several good long walks each day, and many get-togethers with our neighbors and their "chosen children" on these excursions. It does get rather hot here

69

during July and August, so much so that on some of these days I do not go on the walk around Forsyth Park for fear of heat exhaustion. My dads always tell me that everyone asks where I am and if everything is okay, and I am happy for their concerns.

So if you're out there reading this and also happen to be considering a change of environment, please give Savannah some serious thought, especially if you happen to be a "chosen child" because I am blessed to be one of the "Savannah Dogs."

Sincerely,

ASHLEY

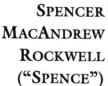

SPENCER MACANDREW ROCKWELL ("SPENCE")

I love life—catching butterflies and bugs, skipping and hopping, licking everyone's face, playing with all my toys, eating (boy do I love to eat), playing in the rain, digging holes, and chasing sticks. You see, I am only four months old and have a lot of living to do. Oh, where are my manners? (Mum is always talking about manners.) My name is Spencer; well, officially it is Spencer MacAndrew Rockwell, Lord of Diggingdom. My friends call me Spence. I am not old enough to have saved anyone yet or done anything heroic, but I'll work on it. I was sent to Mum by an angel dog named Sam. He was a West Highland white terrier too, and he went to dog heaven. Mum always said he would send her a pal when the time was right. Well, she walked through the door, and I worked my magic—licking and wagging my tail as much as possible. Next thing you know, I had adopted her. She even sent out announcements of my arrival.

I am very, very social. I already have lots of friends—Merlyn, Nicholas, Lampchop, Duke, Katie, and my brother, Wesley. Wesley adopted Mum's friends, which is great because we play together almost every day. I love to wrestle with my friends, especially in the flower beds. Mum usually raises her voice, but then starts laughing because I have dirt on my face and give her my cutest look. Boy, is she a pushover.

Thought for the moment: If there were a licking contest, I would win hands, I mean, paws down.

Walking on the leash is such fun. At first I was a little worried about this long thing being attached to my neck, but then I saw my friends Nunzio and Spike, and voila! They said you can't be a baby forever (I was only nine weeks at the time) and told me how much fun it can be to go for a walk, especially in Historic Savannah. You never know whom you are going to meet in the square, and sometimes people have treats. It's the niftiest! Back to walking. My brother didn't have anyone to show him, so I did! Now we both go to the square, chase pigeons, and greet visitors with licks. Maybe I'm the youngest four-pawed ambassador. My mum says I am getting a little carried away and to go play now because my friends will growl me in line.

Now I'm back. Whew. I ran and ran and ran. Mum says I have the life of Riley. Who's Riley?

Digging holes—my favorite. The muddier the ground, the better. Mum says I am a true terrier, but I think it's pride in her voice not anger. I try to be a good boy, but sometimes it is just too darn hard. All the good stuff—chewing shoes, digging holes, and running away when someone says "come"—gets me in trouble; but then again, I have time on my side. At least that is what I think when I overhear them saying, "Oh, he's just a puppy." That's when I turn on the charm and make everyone smile.

SPENCE

N. S. SHERLOCK KARLISS ("THUNDERPAWS")

It all started with a book about basset hounds. It referred to bassets as being "counter cruisers." Up to this point I had never displayed this behavior. I was just a year old, still somewhat of a pup. No one was in the kitchen except me. Being a scent-hound, my nose was twitching overtime. Before I knew what was happening, my front paws were on the counter and I was cruising. Boy, was this fun! Just as I was about to sink my lily whites into a big, juicy pot roast, my parents yelled, "No counter cruising!" I didn't think they were speaking to me, so I continued on my quest for food. You see, one thing bassets are driven by is food. So I couldn't help myself. It was one of those instinctive things we canines inherited from our ancestors. It was a canine buffet before me. Again they yelled, but this time they said, "Sherlock, no counter cruising!" Being the well-behaved dog of the family—and I use that expression loosely because most bassets think they are human, not canine—I had to respond since Sherlock is my given name. I turned and looked over my left shoulder just to make sure it was me they were speaking to. My father, the alpha of our pack, said in his deepest voice, "Sherlock, down," and pointed to the floor. For a brief moment I thought I could pretend I didn't understand

and just turn around and ignore him. You see, bassets do that very well too. Some humans may call us stubborn, but I like to refer to myself as determined. Then I realized that wasn't going to work. After all, they had paid for two behavior classes. Using my better judgment, my front paws dropped to the floor and I sat attentively looking up at him with the saddest face I could come up with. I knew that that had always worked before for food. He patted me on the head and said, "Good boy." Oh, of course, he cut me a big piece of that juicy pot roast still sitting on the counter. Now, however, it was pushed back so I couldn't reach it.

My parents had been enlightened! You would have thought my counter-cruising days were over. Well, not exactly. Whenever I think I can get away with it, and my parents forget to push things back, I go for it! I give it a hundred percent. You may be interested to know that my success rate is pretty high as long as I don't try it on a regular basis. I have to give my parents time, in-between attempts, to forget to push things back where I can't reach them.

I am presently teaching my new sister, Maggie Watson, about counter cruising. She's doing okay for a girl. Happy counter cruising to all you canines out there, especially to you bassets who are unusually successful at this. I think it's our long backs.

SHERLOCK

BOOMER

I'm a big dog. A really big dog. Most dog books and magazines classify dogs into small, medium, and large categories, the latter including those up to one hundred pounds. I hit that mark before my first birthday. My name is Boomer, and I'm an English mastiff. At almost five years of age I weigh in at a sleek two hundred pounds. Books talk about English mastiffs as being "grande of stature—bred to guard the homestead." Some describe us as "intelligent, but not excitable nor overly agile—reliable—a creature of habit." One word, however, you never see mentioned in the same sentence with our breed is "retriever." A case in point.

My best friend is a black Labrador named Wiley. We grew up together although he's a year younger than me. When we get together to play, Wiley always (I mean always) has a tennis ball in his mouth. The slimier the better as far as he's concerned. He has his master trained very well because every time he drops the ball at her feet she picks up the ball and throws it across the yard. Wiley dutifully runs after the ball and brings it right back to her feet. I was impressed the first time I saw this trick. It was remarkable how he was able to follow the flight of the ball in the air and then proceed to whisk it into his mouth as he was headed under a bush. He reappeared with the ball in his mouth, tail wagging, and a proud saunter as he made his way back to his owner. Nice show. But then he dropped the ball at her feet again. And with the same motion, she picked up the ball and heaved it across the yard. Guess what? Wiley repeated his quest for the flying sphere with the same panache he had shown the first time. The same catch, bush tumble, and tail-wagging return occurred right before my eyes. He received the praise of all around. Nice job, Wiley, but I'm not sure what the hubbub is all about. I thought, I'll give this a try if she throws the ball again. Well, like a well-oiled machine, Wiley dropped the ball at her feet and she scooped it up and heaved it across the yard. I had a head start of a few feet on the "Wild Man" as we darted toward that same bush, but his smaller size allowed him to slide under the bush and, you guessed it, come out with the ball between his teeth. I know he was going to go through the same process, so I hung back this time in anticipation of his master's throw. When she released the ball, it was clear the only hope I had was to catch it on the fly. Unfortunately my timing must have been off because it was a nose tip—you know, when you just don't get your mouth open early enough. I decided to watch this spectacle of canine behavior from a recumbent position. Occasionally I would escort Wiley back to his owner and cover his shiny black coat with some of my best slobber and then return to a cooler spot under a tree. After almost an hour of this repetitive play, Wiley looked over at me with a questioning look in his eye, and all I could do was respond, "Big dogs don't fetch."   BOOMER

MAYBELLE

Some years ago, more than I like to admit, I was abandoned on a country road under a mailbox. I lay beneath it, shivering and shaking. Would my owners return? Alas, no. My anxiety increased with every passing car. It was still early, when a tall man emerged from a lane. He looked at me with sympathy, secured his mail, and went off down the lane. Night was falling. Despair enveloped me. Then I caught a glimpse of a silhouette. It was the tall man. He came forward, gently picked me up, and took me to his home.

The lady of the house, three dogs, and two cats greeted me. Two of the dogs—Alfie, a shaggy white mix, and Dutchess, a shelty-collie mix—were friendly. They were older dogs. Missy, the third dog, possibly a Boston bull terrier mix, was much younger. She eyed me competitively. The cats, Leo and Suzie, were curious. My new-found mistress looked at me with pity. She associated me with the mailbox that inspired the name "Maybelle." Well, it was a better choice than "Freckles."

Whoopie! I'm an inside dog. Spaying was necessary in order to prevent unwanted puppies. I was agreeable to that. Life was beautiful. Good food, liberating walks in the woods. Everyone seemed to like me, except Missy.

Two female terriers vying for attention. We had one terrible fight, and our mistress was in tears. One of us would have to be put up for adoption. She discussed it with my rescuer, and the decision favored Missy. She was cuter, more appealing, and possibly purebred. All of their animals were originally strays. Missy's picture appeared in the Sunday paper as "Pet of the Week." Shortly thereafter she was adopted by a nice family with no pets.

In a few years life changed. Alfie and Dutchess, who regarded me as a "little sister," passed on. I became the only dog. Leo and Suzie tolerated me. We lounged inside and out. Then came the news of a move to a new home. Apprehension. Would they leave me behind? When the real estate lady offered to take me, the answer was, "No!" I was pleased by the asking and the answer. The moving van arrived. The house emptied, felt haunted. Suitcases filled the back of the car. They placed the cats in their carriers and me in the back seat. Savannah, here we come!

The long uneventful trip brought us to Savannah in the early evening. Leo broke the silence with endless meowing. The city was mind-altering. Sidewalks, buildings close together, cars, traffic, noise, people, distractions. Our house has an upstairs and downstairs. Might be fun! Dogs are on a leash and walk outside a few times a day. The cats are definitely inside. I can hear people talking as they pass by. From what I gather, I am one of the few mutts. Almost unique.

Well, that was ten years ago, and like the song, "I'm still here." It's been a wonderful experience. The beautiful squares, trees, the river, and the friendly people.

They remark how cute I am and pet me. What breed? Jack Russell terrier perhaps? Maybe a Dalmatian puppy with flying ears? Even the meter maids fuss over me. If you ask me if I love Savannah, the answer is "Yes."

MAYBELLE

GOLDEN HARVEST PHARAOH ("PHARAOH")

Our dog is a three-and-a-half-year-old Afghan hound named Golden Harvest Pharaoh. We initially got Pharaoh as a family pet. We had no plans to enter Pharaoh in dog shows, although he was a show-quality Afghan from a reputable breeder.

Pharaoh arrived home August 1999 at seven months of age. After his initial visit to our veterinarian, we were asked if we planned to show him. Our response was no; at that time the thought had not entered our minds. Our veterinarian replied that we should consider it, as Pharaoh was a very handsome dog with excellent features. Several others also suggested that we show him in dog shows over the next several months.

In the fall of 1999 there was an advertisement in the newspaper offering a dog clinic for people interested in learning how to show their dogs. We decided to attend to find out what was involved; and, needless to say, the prospect of showing our dog appealed to us.

Pharaoh's first dog show was held in Savannah in 1999. He did very well at that show. He has done equally as well at all dog shows in which he has been entered, bringing home many first-place ribbons and trophies.

In May 2000 Pharaoh broke his left front leg while chasing a squirrel. Upon arrival at the veterinarian's office, it was determined that this was a significantly complex fracture requiring surgical repair. We were referred to an orthopedic specialist here in Savannah for the surgery. Pharaoh spent four hours in the operating room for the repair of his fracture. His surgeon felt cautiously optimistic and believed that with proper rehabilitation our dog would regain full use of the leg. The rehabilitation process began as soon as Pharaoh came home from the hospital the next day. At first we had to passively exercise his leg to keep his range of motion intact without putting stress on the surgical site. As time went by and he had progressed to putting weight on his leg, his doctor wanted him to go to Charleston, South Carolina, to have water therapy at a rehabilitation center. At the center the dog is put into a swimming pool with a physical therapist. The goal is to allow the dog to swim and to fully exercise the injured leg without putting any stress on it. He also received nerve stimulation to his left front foot. His rehabilitation sessions involved driving him back and forth to Charleston each day for three weeks. We did not give all that travel a second thought. We wanted to do all we could to help our dog regain the full use of his leg.

After rehabilitation we continued to work with Pharaoh at home. Every day we exercised him and strengthened his muscles. Our greatest joy came the day Pharaoh ran for the first time since his injury. We knew then that all our efforts, love, and prayers paid off and that he was as good as new.

It has taken about a full year for Pharaoh to grow

back all the hair that was shaved for the surgery. We are planning to show him again beginning in the latter part of 2001. He does enjoy being in the show ring, and we are sure that he is anxious and excited to return.

In May 2001 the Savannah College of Art and Design Fashion Department held its Annual Fashion Show to present undergraduate and graduate fashion designs. Pharaoh was invited to the fashion show to accompany one of the professional models down the runway. This year's show was particularly special as Oscar de la Renta was presented with a Lifetime Achievement Award. The Savannah College of Art and Design was extremely proud and honored to have Mr. de la Renta at its school. You could literally feel all the excitement and energy filling the theater on this momentous occasion. What made the event even more stupendous for us was the fact that Pharaoh was included in this gala event. This was the first time that the Savannah College of Art and Design had ever had a dog make an appearance at its fashion show. Pharaoh enjoyed himself immensely at the show, and all those who participated in the creation of the show fell in love with him. Many people who had attended the show commented that Pharaoh stole the show.

We are tremendously proud of Pharaoh and overjoyed to have him as a member of our family. In our opinion he is the "King of Dogs" and will always hold a loving place in our hearts.

FRANK AND JANICE BYNES

JUSTIN BABST ("SWEETIE")

Fifteen years ago, on a beautiful May day, I was born on a basset hound breeding farm in New Jersey, one of ten puppies in my litter. The breeder did not think that I would make a good hunting dog, so he put me up for adoption. A nice lady rescued me, and named me Just-in-Time because Mr. Mean Breeder was about to put me to sleep, permanently. Anyway, Ms. Nice Lady told everyone she knew that she had a beautiful, lovable basset hound puppy who needed a home; and when Mr. Larry heard about me, he immediately decided to adopt me.

I was so excited! When Mr. Larry took me home to meet his family, I checked out the humans and the big dog house they lived in, and decided *I had it made*. My new family called me Justin—for short, even though I'm a girl. It didn't take me long to train my humans. They quickly learned that I was the queen of the house and that I was going to do exactly what I wanted to do, regardless of what they tried to teach me or of what they expected from me. They even hired a trainer when I was just a pup; what a waste of money. I failed the course because I am very smart, sneaky, stubborn, and spoiled—quite a combination. But I am awfully sweet, so my humans had to love me in spite of myself.

I was always getting into trouble, like the time I "ate" the stuffed reindeer. My lady-human collects dolls and stuffed animals. I especially liked the reindeer she got one Christmas. So one day, when I was home alone, I took the reindeer, pulled out all the stuffing, and spread it all over the house. Boy, that was fun! I don't understand why my lady-human was upset.

Then there was the time, when we were still living up north, we got a big snowstorm. It was so much fun that I kept asking to go out to play in the snow, but eventually my boy-human refused to take me out anymore. I sure showed him. I went up to his bedroom and left him a "present" right in the middle of his bed. Actions speak louder than words, if you know what I mean.

My jobs include greeting my humans excitedly when they come home, cleaning their dinner plates by eating the scraps, and giving them lots of love and affection. When my humans are not at home, I sleep on the most comfortable furniture and guard the house by occasionally barking at passersby.

I don't get into too much trouble anymore. I'm old now, my bones ache, I can't hear, and I don't see too well. But I'm still the boss of the house; I love my humans, and they love me. I'm so glad I didn't have to hunt for a living. So thank you, Mr. Mean Breeder, for giving me away. I've had a wonderful life!

JUSTIN

W.I.G.Y.
Betbeze-Powell
("The Big Wig")

They say cats have nine lives. Well, I think I'm working on at least my fifth! I believe I was born in downtown Savannah. Once old enough to spread my wings, I set out with collar and chain attached to a busy, yet independent, life. I found Victory Drive, where a nice man stopped traffic and scooped me up. I then became "Vicki"—for Victory Drive, I heard. For a few weeks I stayed with this nice man, who took me to a strange place where a woman did all sorts of things to me; some involved sharp objects. I've since learned the word "vet." He then took me to this big store with other dogs and people; it was "Adoption Day." A woman picked me up and exclaimed, "Pearl, you're the one!" I presumed she meant nothing less than the gem that I was. She proceeded to put me in a cart of some sort, and I acquired many a chew and toy. I went to her home, where I met the established canine in the family. That "life" didn't last too long on account of the previously established canine. I then became known as "Puppy" at this place, where I had my own space with a cool concrete slab, many new canine friends, and meals delivered—which was a long way from my scrounging independent days. I believe that this place was aptly called the "shelter." I was there, I've heard, "close to *the* time," whatever that means. I guess it means the time when this couple came by and met me. We visited. Then they came back and we played in the grass. It began to rain, which is something I do not like—a holdover from those independent days. Anyway, they decided to claim me. I heard one of my shelter friends say, "Puppy, you made it." So I assumed I was to make something of this new adventure. Unfortunately it started out at that big place again, where I thought I'd be another gem or something, but all went well and we left with many a toy and chew. Of course then I got suspicious as we visited that same "vet"; but then we were on our way, so I was okay. (These were coincidences, I'm told.)

We then went aboard this interesting vessel, a boat. I was a little leary, but I like the water, so I went along. We arrived at this place called the "island." What a place. I then began my current life as W.I.G.Y. ("Wassaw Island Girl Yarddog"), pronounced "Wiggy," I might add. Now, I do also answer to such nicknames as "Wiggles," the "Wigster," "the Wig," "The Big Wig" (my favorite), and "Wigwam." Now with this new life, there was one little glitch. I mentioned earlier the cat with nine lives. I entered the kingdom of "Maggie," who is sixteen and rules in most minds. I've even heard words like "Queen" mentioned. We have come to terms and, well, on with *my* life. I'm living this life to the fullest. I spend my days chasing ghost crabs, swimming in the ocean, and walking on the beach. I also play with my friend Shelby. She came to the island when she was one month old, so I practically raised her. She is something

I've heard called a "purebred," but all I know is that she is fun to play with. Well, that is my tale. I guess—as my Aunt Selena, Shelby's mom, said—"It is a life from skid row to Trump Towers."

All in all, I try to be friendly, for if it had not been for the nice friends along the way I would not be in this paradise. From my humble beginnings to the nice man on Victory Drive to the woman in that store (PETs-MART, how appropriate), to the "shelter" people, and now to the "island girls," I feel like the luckiest dog in not only Savannah, but in the world. I am W.I.G.Y.

W.I.G.Y.

TAYLOR

They say twins have a special bond. I wouldn't know. My twin sister, Troop, was given away just about the time that I came to live with my humans, and I haven't seen her since. That separation didn't hurt as much as the rejection of me by my mother. She conceived us when she was only seven months of age—another sad case of puppies having puppies. Motherhood is supposed to come naturally to every species, but Scout quickly tired of nursing us, and nobody was readier than she to see us leave. Perhaps we reminded her too much of our black Labrador cad of a father. She instantly resumed her easier role as puppy to Annabelle, a stunning golden retriever. Granny Annie, as I call her, still lives a few houses down, but we rarely speak. I like to think I have adjusted rather well in the four years since we all parted ways. Occasionally, however, something triggers my fear of again feeling victimized, abandoned, and unloved.

Take thunder, for instance. Distant rumbles make me restless, and nearby booms provoke real panic. Whimpering and desperately wagging my whole body, I seek immediate comfort at the hands of one of my people, preferably Mama. Her soothing voice and deep, slow scratches behind my ears dispel most of the fear right away. Then Daddy distracts me with a favorite crunchy treat, and I blissfully ignore the storm. He says I'm neurotic; he should know—he's a therapist.

Then there's the doorbell. I take my watchdog duties very seriously, so I do all I can to dissuade would-be visitors. Once they're inside the front door, however, my scare potential dwindles. I sit helplessly in the doorway—I'm not allowed out of the kitchen—and gruff under my breath from a distance. It's downright humiliating, and I wrestle with feelings of worthlessness for hours afterwards. Self-esteem, as any reputable psychologist will tell you, rests firmly on the foundations of early puppyhood, and my foundation has a major crack in it.

Most of the time my humans adore me, which goes a long way to ease the pain of that earlier rejection. I am docile and compliant, eager to please, and positively cuddly. I have to be; I can't risk further rejection. The potential is clear. Kika has pronounced that I am "un-photogenic" (whatever that is, it can't be good); Niko confuses me with his commands in French (if I were a really good dog, I'd surely be bilingual); and Andy strikes fear into my very soul when he comes at me with that "playful" look on his face. It takes real patience to refrain from biting when he approaches me from behind, scoops me up onto my hind legs, then drags me backwards into a sitting position cradled in his lap. It's not a pretty sight: a usually demure, eighty-pound lady sitting spraddle-legged on her haunches, pink tummy utterly exposed, and front paws awkwardly pinned in some variation of a half-nelson. I have learned that passive acceptance works best to shorten the ordeal. I sigh and wait until he tires of the game, but the old scars ache a bit. Meek and submissive as ever, I inwardly bemoan my further loss of dignity.

Still, my life is pretty good. I am well fed, occasionally walked, and constantly noticed by five wonderful people. They talk to me, see that I am clean and comfortable, and let me sleep under the kitchen table all day. I have a treasured red ball of my very own that I can catch in my mouth. What's best, they love me—neuroses and all. I may have lost a twin and a mother, but those ties were merely biological. I am blessed with a much more special bond.

TAYLOR

OSKAR AYCOCK

I came to live with Queen Gene in Savannah just last fall, shortly before Thanksgiving. My former master, Jonnie Jew, got real sick; and seeing how Queen Gene had taken a fancy to me when she first met me in Edenton, North Carolina, Jonnie Jew asked Queen if she'd like to have me when she died. Queen said of course, but much to her surprise, Jonnie Jew asked Queen to take me last fall—I think it was because I threatened to bite people, which didn't go over too well with all of Jonnie Jew's visitors and the help, even though Jonnie Jew thought it was hilarious.

I lived in Edenton a while and then moved to Pine Mountain, Georgia, with Jonnie Jew, who bought a dairy farm and converted the old barn into her home. I loved it there and had a grand time playing with P.B., Josie, and Little Bit, the horses, and George, Henny Penny, and Chicken Little, the rooster and chickens. I caught mice in the horse stalls for Jonnie Jew and entertained her by eating them at her feet. She got a big charge out of that and now does a very good imitation of me crunching mice heads.

So here I am in Savannah, spending my days with my friend Queen Gene. I'm enjoying being a town dog again, where I can find street morsels almost as sweet as mice in some of the squares. Oglethorpe, Wright, Reynolds, and Johnson squares—they're the best, and Chippewa's not bad. My favorite finds are fried chicken bones and occasional rib bones that I find in York Lane in front of Walls Bar-B-Que. And once I found a ham sandwich on Abercorn Street under a bus bench, some Chinese broccoli in Greene Square, and some really fresh bologna in Columbia Square. Queen's not too keen on this activity, however, and if her eyes are quicker than my snout, she snaps me right up into the air and I don't even get to eat what I find.

My days mainly consist of my scavenger hunts with Queen Gene, and then napping and waiting for Queen to come home to play. She worries all the time that I am bored, but I am okay. I get a carrot chunk in the morning, a slice of apple at lunch, and a biscuit before bedtime; and then in-between I have to eat these brown pellets that my doctor says are good for me. My latest entertainment has been racing down to see my friend David on Broughton Street. I can knock on the door and let myself in, and he always gives me a jerky stick. And I like seeing my friends Baker, Gracie, Cookie, Mac, and Maya (David's pal), and my new French friend, Hercule, from Cincinnati. I'm Australian myself, a little Aussie terrier.

Jonnie Jew is now doing much better in Pine Mountain, and Queen Gene and some of her buddies and I try to visit her once each season. It's great to see her and my farm pals. I miss being there, but I like living here in Savannah and with Queen Gene, too.

OSKAR

GRETCHEN CLARK ("GRETCH" OR "GRETCHIE")

I don't exactly know where Gretchie came from or how old she is. Some nice ladies rescued her when her original family moved away and left her behind. She ran the streets for no telling how long until the ladies took her in. They didn't have room for another dog, so she had to stay at Dr. Bink's. That was a nice place to live, except she had to stay in a crate most of the time and got lots of baths. She didn't socialize with the other dogs much. All she wanted to do was climb in people's laps.

Kathrine brought her home because she thought I needed a dog. Gretchie's pretty okay, though, if you have to have a dog. She isn't hoggish about food. She's scared of the chickens and won't chase ducks with me. Her goal in life is to become a full-time inside dog. She wants to sleep on a special cushion or up on the chair, at least.

Gretchie is the worrier in the family. She came to live with us not long before hurricane Floyd. I remember that because she didn't have her tag yet when we had to evacuate. We almost got into big trouble because of it. Actually, we kind of did get into big trouble over it and ended up in a faraway city wondering where in the world Kathrine was, and how did we end up in jail?

It's all Gretchie's fault. For starters, she chewed my collar off during one of our daily wrestling matches, so it was lost in our yard. Kathrine didn't have the time and energy to dig around in the dirt to find it, so we left without it.

At first we had a marvelous trip. Kathrine drove slowly and rolled the windows all the way down. I hung out the window and talked to some other dogs whose owners were also driving slowly with the windows down. Gretchie slept like a zombie with her head hidden under the backseat. After a while we got to drive faster, and there were no more cars around. All of a sudden a cop pulled us over. Gretchie jumped up into Kathrine's lap so she could have a talk with him. She's very protective. The cop was nice about it. Seeing how hot and tired we were, he sent us on our way with a warning.

When we finally got to the faraway place called Athens, Kathrine took us to the community dog lot and left us there. Gretchie just about lost her mind. She barked and barked. People came out and looked at us. The next morning a lady in a truck came. Gretchie wouldn't let her lead her away. She rolled over and went limp. Finally the lady got brave and carefully picked her up and took us off to jail. They gave Gretchie a special collar that said "Skippy." Gretchie was convinced she'd been abandoned again.

At long last we heard our jailers talking about "hurricanes" and "poor refugees." The lady put us back in her truck. She took us back to the dog lot, where Kathrine was waiting. We stayed in a fancy garden after that and slept in the garden shed at night.

GEORGE CLARK

SUNNY ("KNUCKLEHEAD" OR "BIG 'UN")

A few days before St. Valentine's Day 1997, I was at the Savannah Humane Society working on a story for the *Savannah Morning News*. That's when I saw her. I thought, What a good-looking dog. What is she doing in here? My girlfriend at the time had been encouraging me to get a dog, so I asked a staff member there what was involved in adopting the dog. After filling out a short questionnaire, I left to go back to the office. By the time I got back to work, there was a message from the humane society saying I could pick up the dog on Saturday.

I realize now that giving a pet as a gift is not the best idea, but at the time I thought it was brilliant. That Valentine's Day I bought a dog leash, a food bowl, a silly card with a dog on it—oh, and of course, a dozen roses (red). My girlfriend was delighted. Saturday we went to pick up our new dog, Sunny.

Everything was wonderful until one day I received a call at work from my girlfriend. Sunny couldn't walk. Her hind legs were completely paralyzed. She and my neighbor rushed Sunny to the vet, where I met them.

Sunny had a ruptured disk in her back, which was crushing her spinal cord. We were both crushed too.

The veterinarian said some anti-inflammatory drugs might cure her, but it would be the next morning before we would know. We both thought we would have to put her down if the medication was not effective. Then the vet told us about an operation that might work.

He called the next morning with the bad news. The medicine had not worked. Though the vet estimated only an eighty percent chance of success with the operation, we decided to go for it.

Several hundred dollars and a few months later, Sunny was about eighty percent better. In the beginning we both wondered whether we had made the right decision. But after weeks and weeks of carrying Sunny in and out of the house, holding her back end up and praying she would just stand on her own for a few seconds, helping her to walk up and down the sidewalk in front of the house, and, finally, watching her chase the tennis ball (however clumsily, she never was that graceful anyway) in the backyard, I knew we had done the right thing.

The former girlfriend is long gone, but Sunny and I are still best pals. She watches the house while I'm away, and I scratch behind her ears when I get home. When we go for walks, I don't know who's the bigger klutz, me or her. And when she steps on my feet or muddies my clean pants, I think of the time she was unable to walk, and I'm grateful that she had the determination to go on.

JOHN CARRINGTON

SADIE
CLARK

My name is Sadie, beta female of Pack Clark. My exact birthday and lineage are unknown, but I am about ten years old, and my mom and dad call me a "rare breed." I am quite beautiful, with a white coat and big brown eyes. I don't look anything like Mom and Dad.

They say that they adopted me. Actually I picked them out. A bunch of us were waiting at the Atlanta Humane Society and checking out potential packs. I knew as soon as I smelled them that I had found a home. Dad was a bit of a bozo, but Mom was an alpha female extraordinaire. They needed me. So I humored them. Okay if they think they adopted me. Okay if they think they trained me. It makes them happy, and that's good enough for me.

We have good times together. When we were younger we would go hiking. Mom and Dad carried all the stuff we needed and I just ran. I'm still a good runner. We play with tennis balls now, but I used to be a genius with the Frisbee. Mom never got the hang of throwing very well, but Dad could really make it fly. I was poetry in motion—a natural athlete.

Playtime is great, but what I really like to do is go to work with Mom. I used to stay home all day with my sister, Muffin. She is furry, but definitely not fun. She has these really sharp claws that can scratch you pretty bad. Good thing she's dumb. I like that in a cat. Going to work is fun. There are so many smells from the food store next door and from all the friends I have made. If I had thumbs, I'd pinch myself to make sure I'm not dreaming.

I know I do a good job because people are always giving me food. My parents say it's because I beg, but that is just not true. When you are good at what you do, you get rewarded for it. After all, do you work for free? I hate to state the obvious, but people give me food, and Mom and Dad get none. Enough said.

Oh, but I do love my pack, even Muffin. We all had to make some adjustments. There are some things I don't understand, like the bathroom thing. I say take it outside a long way from where you sleep. Or bathing. Just when I smell perfect like a dog, they drag me into a tub full of water and wash it all away. I wonder, Why did I bother to roll around on that dead bird? They also have this thing about curbs. I don't get it, but if I don't stop and stay until they say "okay," I get yelled at. It's the only thing that they yell at me about, and I don't like it. So I stop at each curb. No arguments. Period.

On the plus side, I do get to sleep in the bed, and I am in charge of the kitchen floor. If food hits the floor, I clean it up. Clumsy parents, gotta love 'em.

Overall, I'd say life is good. I don't understand some of the little things, but the big ones I get. We have enough to eat, have a warm place to sleep, we look out for each other, and we love each other. If this is a dog's life, I'll take it.   SADIE

99

 **CHUTNEY**

Benign creature; outgoing, good natured, playful—capriciously mixed with the breed's agile sparring instincts and natural wariness.

"The shar pei is a vet's dream," cautioned Kyle Christiansen, DVM, but that darling, copper-colored, fluffy beastie had captivated me. AKC-unacceptable, chow-like coat—the "bear coat"—a recessive gene results from an ancient relationship between the two breeds. She isn't the fearsome-looking dog I'd imagined.

So we amble along—she with her compromised immune system due to inbreeding, ongoing allergies, and I, her elderly owner, with all the accompanying indignities of aging.

Her cat-like tidiness and independence, her thoughtful intelligence is combined with an impulsive tactical-animal sense. The combination seems to create a paradoxical, *usually* careful, adventurousness.

Chutney, who loves company (people and dogs), has a sense of poise. Since she was a puppy, she appears to be up to social situations.

One spring morning I decided to let her take me for

a walk beyond Monterey Square, our usual turnaround point. Moving north along the west side of Bull Street, she crossed Liberty, turned right across Bull—not to Home Run Video, where we go for movies. (This dog friendly store not only offers movies, but also biscuits and, sometimes, if he's not busy, a teasing, affectionate, brief tussle with Alan, who is a special dog person.) No—she was going to the Gallery Espresso, where she gets not only my version of biscuits, but can sit outside, greet people, and enjoy watching the scene. A café dog who brings life and structuring responsibility to my daily existence.

JOAN COBITZ

My owner is an old lady who moves slower than than I do, except when she wants to be fast. She dawdles when we're going to go out, wanders around the house saying: "Where's your leash?" "I don't know where I left the keys." "I forgot the plastic bags." "Do I have a paper towel?" This last for when I embarrass her by shaking my head with drooling, floppy lips, slinging slobber about. Of course with her as a model I get to wander a bit before I answer her calls.

Keeping house doesn't suit my owner. She makes nests—one in the kitchen, another at the studio table, *and* in her bed. I have nests too. A not-quite-large-enough pillow, which I've had since a puppy, and which people trip over; and two pillows in the parlours—one of these by the window where I guard the house. I bring toys and chewies to my nest; she brings books and magazines, which she doesn't chew.

Sometimes, when I want to play, she doesn't. But we share dinner at home. When we eat out, I mustn't beg, even when meat-smells make me forget myself and groan. Oyster roasts are the best as the shells on the ground are for me and my friends.

She needs me for company and exercise; I take her for walks. So we lead our days—me on the leash mostly. I'm quite attached to her. She's all I have.

CHUTNEY

DUNE CORTESE ("DUNIE")

It was the worst of times.

My story begins six years ago in London, England. I've blocked out most of the details of my early years, but bear the scars of the abuse across my belly. At three, I left home and roamed the streets of London. I don't know how long I was on my own before I was picked up by the Battersea Dog Home. They took me in, fed me, and were kind.

I had just settled into the "adoption section" when a lady and her husband stopped to pat my head, but they quickly moved on. My hopes were dashed. Maybe no one would adopt me; all I could do was sit in the corner and whimper. The next thing I knew I was placed in a pen where that lady, man, and a black Labrador were waiting. I overheard them talking and discovered that they were looking for a companion for the Lab, a one-year-old girl named Spice. The lady and man, soon to be Mommy and Charlie, seemed kind enough, patting me and talking softly. After one or two cursory sniffs, Spice ignored me. Before long we were all driving away.

My new home had soft beds, good regular food, and lots of treats, but most importantly, love. I was washed, given a new collar, and checked by the vet. Time flew by.

In less then a month I had gained five pounds and was fashionably skinny instead of scrawny. I realized that I wasn't brown, but a beautiful creamy yellow. At night, watching TV, I'd snuggle and cuddle with Mommy while Spice lay down next to Charlie. Life was grand.

Then one day Spice and I were packed into crates and driven away. Could it be that they were getting rid of us? Hours passed. First, a ride to the airport, then we were put onto an airplane for a long time. Then we were in Atlanta, where Mommy and Charlie were waiting! After bowls of water and food, we were on our way to our new home in Savannah.

We arrived at night to a big old house with a garden. We ran outside and inside and wondered at all the new smells. The house was dark and empty, but before long our beds and bowls appeared. The next morning we woke up to glorious sunshine; it still amazes us that it's sunny and warm almost every day in Savannah. We were so accustomed to dark and rainy days in London that we can't seem to get enough of the sun. Now every day Spice and I lie for hours on the warm bricks in the garden soaking it in. We enjoy our morning and evening walks in Forsyth Park, where we meet lots of other Savannah dogs. Everyone is so nice and friendly and makes us feel so welcomed.

In my youth I never had much time for hobbies, but since moving to Savannah I've taken up chasing squirrels and birds. Despite the fact that I never catch them, I enjoy the chase through the grass, trees, and azalea bushes, all the while breathing in the sweet smells of the flowers.

In May we went to the Blessing of the Animals in

Troup Square. During the service I said a prayer of thanks for Mommy and Charlie and for the privilege of living amidst the beauty and serenity of Savannah.

It certainly is the best of times.

DUNE

SANDY DALES

I couldn't believe how lazy my owners were. It was 6 A.M., and they were *still* asleep. I was ready for some company after a long, lonely night outside, but I wasn't going to risk visiting the neighborhood until they had left. Finally, at 7:30, they stumbled out of the house for that horrible place they always talk about—school. As sad as I was to see them go, inside I was trembling with anticipation for the day ahead. Freckles, my best friend, and I had planned it all out the day before. The plan was foolproof; we could never get caught.

Once the car turned the corner, I prepared myself for the escape. At a dead sprint I approached the invisible shock. A jump into the air, a twist for the discomfort, and I was free! I set off at an easy lope to Freckles' house. By the time I got there, she had almost worked her way out. It was a bit trickier for her; she had to unlatch the gate to her pen. Standing up against the fence to make her short basset hound body taller, Freckles nudged the fastener on the gate up and out. One shove and the gate was open. We dashed away together, thrilled that we had another joyous day ahead.

On our way to the marsh by the pond, we stopped to

visit Buddy, a black Lab. As usual, he only tolerated us, not wanting to play. I didn't understand why he wouldn't play like all the other animals. Confused, Freckles and I headed on anyway to the mud and reeds.

We frolicked around in the black, smelly muck that we loved. The two of us wrestled around, getting thoroughly coated. Then we just sat there for a while in shallow water, enjoying its cool temperature compared to the blazing sun of Savannah's climate. At long last, we forced ourselves up and crossed the lane to the pond. I swam around a little in the shallow water while Freckles howled with envy on the side. The swimming served two purposes: to wash off the mud and for my enjoyment. Being a golden retriever, I am a natural born swimmer, so every once in a while I jump in to marvel at my skill. I could take about five minutes of my buddy's persistent whining, then I drew myself out of the water. Freckles can't swim, so she hates it when I leave her all by herself. To try and make up for my act of unfaithfulness, I curled up with her for a nap on the grass. Before I knew it, I had drifted off.

When I awoke, the sun was considerably lower in the sky. With a jolt I realized that my young playmates would be getting home soon. I had to welcome them as usual, and they certainly could not find out what we did each day. I roused Freckles, and we tore off in opposite directions toward home. Right after I reached home, the car pulled up by me. The little girl got out when she saw me outside the electric fence. As she took off the shock collar to let me back in the yard, she said, "Sandy, you got out again. You silly big baby, you must have had a busy day." She had no idea.   SANDY

JIFFY WYLLY

Okay! So I have a funny name! Jiffy! Well, wanna know something? I like it. I'll tell you how I got that name. Here's my story.

First, let me say I'm a pretty cool dude. I'm white, curly, and cuddly, and have a healthy hooter—in other words, a big nose. My former owners didn't love me. No sir, they didn't. Otherwise, they wouldn't have dumped me off at the Jiffy Mart. I was barely eight months old.

Well, when I realized I'd been abandoned, I started begging for cookies or bagels, anything, 'cause I was mighty hungry. My spirits were crushed. I was scared too. I slept in an old inner tube behind the Jiffy Mart and hoped the rats wouldn't hear my rumbling stomach. I hate rats. I was filthy, and my coat was snarled and tangled. What was to happen to me?

I felt discouraged, rejected, and depressed. Maybe I should throw myself under a car. Panting and lost, I trotted off down the median of a busy road. Cars whizzed past me. I felt a frightening gust of wind as each one sped by. Horns blared. I dodged. Sitting down to rest, I hung my head and closed my eyes. I missed home. I needed water. I needed a welcoming lap and a soft hand smoothing my back. "Get up," I told myself. "Keep going!" It was dark now.

I became aware of voices. "Come here, puppy. Good boy," said a smiling lady who had stopped her white Jeep.

"Come on, feller. You're not hurt, are you?" inquired another nice lady who'd also pulled over. They conversed, and soon I found myself being driven off in the Jeep. Where were we going? She seemed to be a caring person, so I settled down on the leather seats.

We pulled up to a large white house. Gently I was lifted onto the grass for a piddle and then carried inside.

A tall sunburned man looked down at me. "I don't want a silly little mutt," he said. "I need a strong hunting dog." My heart sank. "Maybe the neighbors will take him." Nobody wanted me. The nice lady made a bed for me in the corner, and I whimpered myself to sleep. The next day she had me groomed, which felt sensational. I had no more itchy fleas, and I was given a new collar.

A few days later I sat meditating through the screen door. "Come on, pup," she said, picking me up. She plopped me into the big man's lap. Nervously I licked his nose.

"Hey! Hey! What's this?" he blurted. His hand rested on my back. Slowly it began to stroke. I wriggled with joy and licked him again. "What's his name?" he called to his wife.

From the kitchen came the reply, "Doesn't have one. You can call him Jiffy if you like. I found him at the Jiffy Mart. By the way, the neighbors may, after all, take him."

There was a long silence. The stroking continued.

"Maybe he doesn't have to go anywhere. He's not such a bad pup," said the big man.

That was it! I knew I had a home. That was eight years ago. My life today is blissful. I go fishing with my tall master. I chase sand crabs on deserted beaches. I ride in his air-conditioned truck. They even put me on their Christmas cards 'cause I'm an important member of their family now. I tried quail hunting with my master once, but the loud gun scared me so badly that I fled for miles. They even bought me a little Harley Davidson leather outfit complete with a black cap.

My coat is dyed green with food coloring on St. Patrick's Day, and I'm taken to the parade. Again, my white coat is dyed red, white, and blue on the Fourth of July. Everybody knows me. I'm never left at home.

I'm spoiled rotten. And do you know what? I love the name Jiffy. Oh, excuse me! I'm being called for my brushing.

JIFFY

DAISY FORD ("DAISY MAE")

We picked Daisy up from the Humane Society late one afternoon a few days before Christmas 2000. We took her straight to Dr. Joe Morris in Rincon to be spayed and to have her shots. It was late the next evening before we got her home. We decided that since it was so late and cold, we would keep her inside for the night so we could get used to each other. We needed a big dog with a good bark to stay in our yard and help protect us. We had had a break-in at our home a few nights before, and we'd rest better with a dog to stand guard.

Daisy was named Cindy when we got her, but she just never looked like a Cindy to me. We renamed her Daisy in memory of our daughter, who died in 1994 from cystic fibrosis. Carol had always wanted an animal named Daisy, since she read a story I once wrote about two kids and a cow named Daisy.

Daisy was frightened and timid for the first few days after we brought her home. I'm sure that her previous owners had used anything they could to discourage her habit of digging, opening gates, and destroying everything in sight. Every time I turned on the hose to water my flowers, she tucked her tail and ran. She soon realized I wasn't going to spray her, and now she follows me around and drinks from the hose without a worry.

We've had numerous battles over my pot plants. She gets upset every time we leave her, and sometimes she'll destroy my plants. I come home to find my plants and potting soil strewn over the driveway. I hated to resort to spanking her, but after exhausting every other tactic, I gave her a couple of scoldings, and now she rarely bothers my flowers.

Daisy is a German shepherd mix. What she's mixed with I couldn't say. But to me she's beautiful. She's mostly black and tan, with two white toes. She has the warmest, most intelligent eyes, and they're usually looking for mischief. I can't help hugging her and telling her how much I love her. She'll give me kisses if I beg long enough. She tries to ignore me and walk off. But if I keep making kissing sounds and asking her to give Mama a kiss, she'll finally give in. She's a sweetheart and I thank the Doggy Angel for leading us to her.

I am also grateful to her previous owners for taking her to the Humane Society and not putting her out on the side of the road somewhere.

She loves coffee. When I have a cup, I save her a few sips when I'm done. She's my walking partner when the weather isn't too hot. She enjoys being out with me now, but it took her a while to understand walking with the leash. She fought it at first, then she gradually got used to it. Opening a gate is child's play to Daisy. With absolutely no effort, she flips up the latch with her nose. We at first tried putting a screw through the lock slot, but she soon learned to pull that out. So now we have to keep a lock in the gate. She's bad when she wants to be, but mostly she's a barrel of fun, and I love her dearly. That love is returned tenfold. LILLY FORD

Max Fagan

Hi! My name is Max, but my dad only calls me that sometimes. Other times he calls me Maxie Pad, Mad Max, or Max Factor. I don't know why? We live next to the big park in Savannah. It's my favorite place to play because it stinks like birds and squirrels, but I can never find them; and if I do find them, I can never catch them.

My second favorite thing to do is swim. I love the water, for drinking and for swimming; and I'm pretty good at swimming too, because I can swim faster than my dad. My favorite treats are cheese-filled beef sticks. I don't know where he gets them, but they are the yummiest. I can't seem to get enough of them, but my dad is always asking me to do stupid stuff—for instance, "Roll over!"—in order to get the beef sticks. How is that going to help me survive in the world? So I do it for *him* to make *him* happy. But most of the time I just ignore him until he gets mad. He just doesn't understand that I'd rather focus on the many new smells out there.

My other favorite thing that my dad and I do is drive around town. I stand on the window. All of those smells at once is wonderful, but he always has to hold onto my leg for some reason. He says that we are gonna go around the world together, and then I can find new smells. But I think that his smell is the best of all.   MAX

113

ABBY DAUENHAUER

I'm not really from Savannah; actually I hail from Rincon, and I've lived in quite a few places besides Savannah—Madison, Georgia; Durham, North Carolina; and New York City, to be specific—but when my immediate family decided to move to London, that's when I put my paw down. I mean I loved them and all, but really, how much could I be expected to take? So I demanded to return to my favorite place of all, Savannah. My grandmother responded appropriately, rented a car, and chauffeured me the eight hundred miles from the Upper East Side back to Ardsley Park, which is where I belong.

My grandparents and my aunt adopted me mid-November, almost eight years ago. I spent the whole day playing with them, but at 9:30 that evening they tied a big red bow around my neck and took me down the street and deposited me on a doorstep. They knocked on the door and then hid around the corner of the house. I had no idea what was going on. When I looked up, I saw this girl peering down at me through the window.

"There's a puppy out there!" she cried, swooping me up in her arms. "Merry early Christmas!" everyone shouted, and Ansley and I became pretty much inseparable.

Shortly after that we got introduced to Mark, who was to figure pretty prominently in things as time went on. We went to visit him in Athens one time, not long after I had arrived. I had a pretty good time chasing my tail, jumping on and off his sofas, barking furiously at the other dog in the mirror, and generally exercising my puppyhood. Unlike Ansley, Mark didn't do too much to try and stop me, which raised him significantly in my esteem. That morning, after trying in vain to lift yet another spoonful of Cheerios to his mouth, he very calmly looked at Ansley and said, "Is breakfast time always like this?"

The people in my life tell a lot of stories on me. They especially love to recount all of my eating escapades. To be fair, I will tell their side of the story, but before I do, let me say that I am a *very* active black Lab–boxer mix with a lot of energy. I'm not the least bit fat, so obviously I needed those calories!

They love to remember the two platters of Saran-wrapped tenderloin I consumed three hours before a catering job. Thank God for Johnnie Ganem; fifty dollars later, and Ansley and I were almost out of trouble! The hunk out of Albertha's Christmas pound cake, still warm from the oven—my granddad was thrilled; it wasn't Albertha's any longer! Two dozen chocolate chip cookies straight from the pan. An entire stick of butter left low enough for me to sample. Half a platter of brownies an hour before a party—I paid for that one; I was sick all night. Twenty-five dollars worth of salmon marinating on the kitchen counter—gone without a trace. But their favorite eating escapade was when I helped myself to the Thanksgiving turkey and fixings left in the kitchen. That was the first time Maggie, my grandparents' old dog, would have anything to do with me. I managed to scrape some turkey and gravy over the side of the counter for her too. Of course, it dripped off her back, but at least she got some. We hungry dogs have to stick together.

They also like to recount my experiences with camping. There is nothing I like more than a day spent hiking in the mountains, but when the tent comes out at night, well, that can be a different story. If you surveyed your options and realized you were either going to be out in the cold at the end of a sleeping bag, or a little crowded by burrowing head-first into your person's mummy bag, which would you choose? I really couldn't help it that my tail stuck out of the top; it just didn't fit.

When Ansley told me we were going to have a baby, that was fine with me. So far all of the many changes we had gone through had turned out to be for the better. I loved to curl up next to her and rub my head against her belly. Sometimes the baby would even kick back! We also moved to the Big Apple during this time. It was all right, but not as great as some of the other places we had lived. I had a hard time making dog friends there. The worst of it was that no matter where we were before, we would always make periodic car trips back to Savannah. Now we were, or at least I was, almost always stuck on the Upper East Side.

Then London came up for my people. I knew something was going on because they kept shooting me these looks. Quite frankly, I didn't even look back when my grandma put me in that car to take me back to Savannah. Sure I miss Ansley and Mark and the baby (well, maybe not her too much). I miss all the things we used to do, like running, swimming in the lake with my buddy Porter, hiking, and long early morning walks. But I don't miss the city one bit, and I still get to see them fairly frequently. Besides, Ansley sends me postcards, and I talk to them on the phone all the time.

If you'll excuse me now, I have to go see if someone left some food out on the counter.

ABBY

MR. BEAUREGARD EVANS ("BEAU" OR "BO BO")

I believe that every creature is special (even some humans). But my bassett hound Beau is particularly individual. Unique even. And I'm sure you will agree.

Just days after being discharged from a lengthy hospital stay, where my life teetered in the balance, Beau came into my life. Quite unexpectedly. A friend who has bassetts woke up to find him in his fenced backyard. But this sweet, lovable stranger had no collar or ID. It seemed obvious that this little canine had been purposely abandoned. Someone must have put Beau over the fence, figuring these people have bassetts, so they're good candidates for foster care.

This strikingly handsome muscle of a four-footed variety was in the right hands. A great home would be found. Of course, my friend did the right thing. He advertised in the lost-and-found section of the paper, and checked with local vets and the humane society. But to no avail.

Knowing of my present condition—convalescing, I suppose, one would call it—my friend immediately thought of me for Beau's new companion. Well, except for the stray my dad brought home when I was about eight or nine, I had never really had a dog. But Shaggy didn't stick around long. You can rescue a dog from its stray but, with some dogs you can't seem to take the stray out of 'em.

Don't get me wrong. I've always been a real animal lover. I've raised and offered convalescence to everybody from owls to raccoons. I once nursed a gannet back to health. North Atlantic seabird. Watching his glorious eight-foot wingspan lift him into the Tybee beach winds was as good as it gets. But I digress.

The moment Beau and I first met eyes we both new. He's home. This royally bred being ran up to me, raised his comically stout front paws, and with the joy of a child on Christmas morning licked his way right into my heart.

As I eased back into work over the next few weeks, he accompanied me daily. Always at my feet, his upward glances shined not just doe-eyed brown, but utter love and contentment.

To say that he aided in my speedy recovery would be an understatement. Laid out on my sofa together, snuggling and hugging almost seemed to heal me from the inside out. The bond was magically supernatural. A vibe, if you will.

Needless to say, Beau has become my constant companion. I even had a spare key made for my car, so when I have to run into some place real quick, I can leave the car running with the air conditioner on and him safely locked inside.

Together we often take to the wildwood trails, which is especially adventurous with a scent hound. Beau sniffs out everything, even little intricately woven rabbit nests hiding baby bunnies. He once led me to a box turtle that was depositing her eggs in a shallow excavation of her making. What a sight! And Beau is ever so gentle around any wildlife he comes across. He'll show me a brooding mallard on the banks of Casey Canal and never move in close enough to cause her alarm.

Of course he sleeps with me every night. So human-like! He puts his head right up on the pillow next to mine and stretches out like a snake on a rock on a warm sunny day. When the alarm clock goes off, I awaken to the most beautiful brown eyes looking into mine. Then he slaps me with a warm, wet, good-morning kiss. How can one have a bad day with such a beginning?

BERNIE EVANS

BEIJING BANDIT ("B.B.")

I'm a survivor.

When I was born I was given the name Beijing Bandit. My lineage is more impressive than most humans, but I'm not like one of those fancy-schmantzy Shih Tzus that just sat at the emperor's feet. I'm just a plain fun-loving pet who goes by the ordinary name B.B.

I was born on the 22nd day of May 1985, making me sixteen years old. Can you believe that? I guess that makes me one of the oldest dogs in Savannah. I don't feel that old, and everyone says I don't look it either. Of course some days I feel older than others.

My first owner died when I was four, and I was given to my current owners, who had lost their last dog only months before. But I didn't replace her—after all, I'm unique.

We lived for two years in the suburbs, where I had a huge yard in which to wander. I was really concerned when my owners moved us to a house in the historic district, because they expected me to be happy in a teensy-weensy courtyard. But I showed them who was boss. I insisted upon taking long walks several times a day, so they had no choice but to give in to me.

As much as I enjoy my family, I always had wander-lust. A few days before we moved downtown, we were there getting things ready. While my owners were busy, someone left the back door open and I wandered outside. When they realized I was gone, after they panicked, they posted signs all over and sent out a search party. Several hours later I was found at a nice man's house. I had crossed many streets by myself for the first time, and luckily wasn't injured. My owners became much more careful after that.

My favorite spot used to be right inside the front door. My owners had a glass storm door installed so that I could survey the outside. When our new house was built, they had a door designed by a famous local black-smith just for me.

I used to be much more sociable than now. When my owners had company, I enjoyed being right there with them. But most of the time now I prefer staying on the second floor, where I sleep wherever I want. No pet bed for me—I'm the king of the entire floor.

As I got older I lost most of my sight and hearing, but my owners have done whatever they can to help me. I also acquired what is known as "cognitive disorder," which caused me to be very confused. Now that I take an anipryl tablet each day I seem to be better.

Throughout the years my owners have traveled a lot, but they've always found wonderful sitters for me. Several times I stayed with a couple who loved me dearly—they even let me sleep in their bed with them! But they weren't too careful about keeping their doors closed, and I wandered out on more than one occasion. The last time this happened was this past December on an extremely cold, rainy day. They and their neighbors searched for me all day. It wasn't until the next morning that I was found, in a nearby marsh, nearly frozen to death. After a few hours at my doctor's office, bundled in blankets, with a heat lamp nearby, I was well enough to go home to my owners who had returned that day. That's when Dr. Amy, my wonderful doctor, gave me the nickname "Timex" because no matter what happens, I keep on ticking.

Only a few weeks later I suffered a major stroke and was at the hospital for days. Before long I regained use of my legs and was as good as ever. Since then I've had some pin strokes, but they haven't kept me down for long.

As Dr. Amy said, I just keep on ticking!

B.B.

LADY DAPHNE
BEAST OF LEDLIE
OUT OF GARBAGE
ON GORDON
("DAPHNE")

Hi! My name's Daphne, and I'm a very lucky girl. My first week on this planet was spent in a garbage can with a hole somebody put in my head. When *she* found me, I was a palm-size clot with no hair and no skin and a very big smile! I still have the big smile, and I'll never forget the sweet smell of *she*. *She* gave me vitamins and fed me, and introduced me to my dad. Even when *that* vet said I didn't have a chance, *she* took care of me for my dad. He had to be in California for a little while, but when he came back he took me in and introduced me to Rufus and Oliver. Oliver was my size 'cause he's a cat, and we were best playmates.

Dad thought I'd be a little black-and-white dog to accompany his big black-and-white dog, but I had a large surprise. From that little clot I started blowing up like a balloon. I grew at the same rate all over, so my feet never were bigger than the rest of me, or my head, or my ears. Of course he didn't care if I was big or little 'cause we had too much fun! I'm very interesting.

In my youth I could catch the squirrels in the park,

much to Dad's dismay, and to the dismay of most people watching. If Dad was paying attention, he would usually distract the squirrel first, and I just had the fun of the chase; but sometimes people who got mad at me would distract Dad, and that's when I got my squirrel. Some bitchy blonde was yelling at Dad one day about the dumb squirrels, and I killed one right in front of her. Well, stroke city, get the oxygen, and call the ambulance 'cause she was critical. We went home and had din-din.

Unlike most dogs, I have a bank account. Sometimes I have to stare down Dad in order to receive my deposit, but he doesn't forget very often. Every morning, in from the park, I receive two bones, for whatever reason I don't know, but I just do, and I hide them. Of course I think they're hidden, but Dad doesn't tell me when they are just lying in plain sight on top of the floor. He does tell me when I dig in the sofa and push them under the cushion. Once a week he cleans them up and makes a deposit and I keep receiving dividends.

Now that I'm older and lovelier, and no longer murder little things in the park, I've begun to enjoy the more sedate things, like licking my toes and lounging in front of the fan. I like my downtime, but when Dad comes home I always have my big smile and a really loud bark to greet him. I can remember when I could just walk through a room and inadvertently snap at a pillow, and it would fly across the room, and with effortless grace I could destroy it in a second. Of course Dad usually saw this about to happen, and the blast of his voice hurt my ears so badly that I stopped. Shucks!

I have wonderful friends in Savannah, and I've traveled the country and buried my bones in as many places as I could, so that my deposits are varied and widespread. Thanks to *she,* who found me, and I still know her scent. Thanks to Dad, who kept me, for we are very mistreated by many. Still smiling.

DAPHNE

JAKE ALEXANDER ("JAKEY," "BUDDY," "WHITE LIGHTENING")

One lucky Easter weekend I found the place that I now call home. After many long days on my own and without anyone to love, my best friends in the whole wide world, my mommy and daddy, took me in. They thought that I was brown when they took me in, but quickly realized after I had a long bath and a close shave that I was indeed white. They decided to call me Jake. My favorite nickname is White Lightening.

I love to run and jump and when I do, I run fast and I jump very high. Running in my backyard, chasing after my daddy, and then leaping from the deck onto the grass are some of the things that I have perfected. I like to play Frisbee too and have learned how to catch it in the air with no problems. My best buddy from next door (a terrier named Bailey) comes over to my yard, and we run, run, run. We now have a game called "Indy 500," where I run circles around the entire yard and Bailey tries to catch me. She is too slow for the White Lightening. We have a lot of fun together in my backyard. One day, when it was really hot outside, I taught her how to bury herself in the cool mud. My mommy didn't find this an amusing game, and Bailey had to go home.

Weekends are my favorite time, as Mommy and Daddy are with me the whole day. During the week, however, I am on my own during the day and find ways to keep myself busy. Most of the time, I am sitting upstairs, looking out the window, watching neighbors drive by, and anxiously awaiting the arrival of my parents. Sometimes, when I get bored of watching out of the window, I like to go into the kitchen and see what there might be to eat. Sometimes Mommy and Daddy forget to secure the lazy-susan (where all of the goods are kept), and I have a wide selection of foods to choose from. One day I decided to press my luck and found Mommy's Bisquick mix. Unfortunately I should not have drank my water right after finishing the Bisquick because by the time Mommy and Daddy arrived, my whiskers were a little stiff and crusty. Oops, busted!

I love to go on walks and do so every day, sometimes two and three times a day. My neighborhood is always full of surprises. One of my favorite things to do on my walk is to go duck hunting. When I see the ducks, I get into the crouched position, carefully, but quickly, tiptoe upon the ducks, and when I am close, I lunge at them in hopes of catching one. My daddy and I have so much fun at this game, and he lets me get close to catching them, but not too close. Although one morning on our walk, White Lightening prevailed and caught one by the butt. I had a good grip until my daddy shook me loose. Oh well, maybe next time.

I could not have asked for a better home and look forward to many more days of fun—running, playing, and, of course, duck hunting.   JAKE

CAMDEN

It was twelve years ago when I met my friend Camden. I learned what it felt like to have ten wiggling pups crawl over me as I lay in the grass enjoying my neighbor's good fortune. I remember it vividly. It was a clear December day. I could feel the warmth of the sun on my skin. Getting caught in the excitement that one can only feel in a moment like this, I noticed a small, honey-colored wanderer. He was off by himself studying a dandelion. I picked up my camera and steadied myself on my elbows. Just as I took the shot, tiny pounced on the flower and looked at me with a mouth full of fluff. I was in love.

This was the beginning of the years in which we would teach each other about life. Initially I thought I was the one wearing the trainer's hat. I must admit I was wrong. My first lesson was about choice. I looked at the fattest, and the cutest, and the most gregarious. I held the sleepiest and the smartest. I even snuggled the softest, but I chose the one who walked away from his group and found a moment to enjoy his own flower.

The second lesson came quickly. We headed to the store to "pick up a few things." It was then that I was confronted with responsibility. Working with a college budget, I purchased dog food and the things I thought

129

I would need for my new charge. I also bought groceries. Since there was so little money left, I bought soup. It was inexpensive and nutritious. I also found it was easy to stay slim when that's all you could afford to eat.

As Camden and I spent all of our days together, I learned of friendship. We were inseparable. We enjoyed bike rides to class as he fit nicely into my backpack. He slept through art history lectures hidden away in the cool, dark room. We swam and played Frisbee in the sun. We smiled and laughed and knew how lucky we were.

Camden did not like the days when I would leave him. He hung his head and shook while standing at the door. I would lean down, kiss him, and assure him that I would be home as soon as I was able. I would leave each day feeling his loneliness in my heart. When I returned he would greet me with happiness and summersaults. One day I came home and I was not met at the door. Worried, I wandered the house with an unusual feeling. When I found Camden, I thought he was sick. Sadly I went to the kitchen to get water for him. There I found garbage smeared from one end to the other. The only thing clean was a can of tuna. I marched into the other room, took a deep breath, and was ready to explode. Something stopped me. I thought of all the days my friend waited alone wondering when and if I would come back. I also thought of how each day he would greet me, jumping, licking, and giving his best hello. I became aware of his fourth lesson, forgiveness.

Over the years Camden's teachings were great in number. He taught me of fierce loyalty, giving, and trust. He showed me sunbeams for napping and took me for long walks. He even taught me how to play. Most important, he taught me the meaning of love. I am honored that Camden chooses to walk with me each day with the same enthusiasm as the first. And I am thankful that he picked me on that warm December day.

JENNIFER BEAUFAIT

MERCER BOWYER

Well, I'll make this quick because if my mom finds out I can type, she'll have me vacuuming in no time. I came from Miami with about two hundred ticks, a sore eye, and a coat of grunge that would embarrass a cat. I had just been pulled from the Miami Dade Shelter by Neapolitan Mastiff Rescue and was scared to death when I met Mom. Luckily she was looking for a lucky star, and that's what I have on my chest, so we were a pair and hightailed it away from the streets of Miami. On the way home she realized that I needed a new name since I was pretty closed lipped about my past. When she realized that we were both enjoying a Johnny Mercer CD during our journey home to Savannah, we decided that Mercer would be my new name.

Once home, I did a little remodeling, got my sea legs, and decided that a pouty lip will get you almost anywhere in life you need to go. Being a lover of small dogs (and small people), I love to attend dinner parties and don't mind at all when the little guys hang on my lips. Mom keeps promising to get me a saddle so I can go to birthday parties too, but no luck yet. She also promised to get me certified as a therapy dog so I can go cheer up older people (they are about my speed). I guess I need to remind her.

My favorite thing to do on the weekends is to ride out in the boat to Wassaw or Ossabaw and hang out in the water. Mom's got a big straw hat, and I just hang on to her shoulders and keep my face in the shade—I have enough wrinkles! When it's too hot, I retire under the Bimini for a quick rally nap, cool water, and a little snack. This really is the way to ride—I have my own space in the car, but it doesn't get the wind through my ears quite like I like it. I'm always up for a ride, even in the car, because it always leads to an adventure. Mom can't understand why I can jump in myself when we leave home, but won't even try when it's time to go home. She thinks I'm just lazy, and she's right! I love to play, but 9:30 is my bedtime, rain or shine!

The parks are also a fun place to visit, especially Forsyth. I don't really know what "tourist" means, besides a whole lot of love. They stop us all of the time just to love on me, especially when my coat is clean. This is one of the things I consider when Mom tells me to get in the tub. Baths are secretly really wonderful, but it's against a puppy's honor code to admit that. Ear cleanings are somewhat less fun, but I know there is a rawhide somewhere at the end of that deal, so I manage to endure. Mom thinks I don't know about the allergy pills she puts on my cracker with peanut butter, but it does help keep my feet from itching, so I just go along with it. Wouldn't want to hurt her feelings!

Nap time is upon us, so I must go. Please come to visit anytime, and remember, if anyone asks, I never typed this! XOXO,   MERCER

LAZARUS CHRISTIE ("LAZ-LAZ")

My wife, Cindy, and I first heard of Lazarus on the local evening news in June 2000. We heard that he had been set on fire intentionally. We both commented how horrible an act of cruelty and cowardice this was, clearly gross neglect by the owner. As avid local news watchers, we kept up with his recovery process, but only in a nonchalant way. You see, we recently had to put to sleep our American Staffordshire bull terrier, Mike the Dog. That was June 10, 2000. He was a great dog, and his passing left me very sad and melancholy.

Some weeks passed before I became aware of Lazarus' progress in recovering. It was the last week of July 2000, following my forty-eighth birthday, that through the grace of God I heard on a local radio station (Q-105) that Lazarus was now healthy enough to find a new home. Amazingly, only a short twenty to thirty minutes later, I was at a customer's home discussing some billing problems with her. While there, I was greeted by her young dog. As we chatted about pets and my recent loss of Mike, she commented that the cure for the loss of a pet was to find another to fill that void. That thought stuck in my mind the rest of the morning. Shortly after lunchtime I again heard on the radio the call to find a home for Lazarus. Jerry Rogers of Q-105 was telling his story and saying how important it was for this dog to find a good home and giving the particulars of how to apply for his adoption. I just found this to be coincidental—that in the same morning I should learn of his need for a home and of a way to ease the passing of Mike! I immediately went to a phone to call Save-A-Life, Lazarus' caregivers and benefactors after his ordeal. Well, their answering machine was full of messages, and I could not leave one. I recognized the phone number to be at the Landings on Skidaway Island in Savannah. As an employee at the Landings water company, I was able to get Ms. Deborah Friedman's address. Ms. Friedman is an officer in the Save-A-Life foundation. I just decided that I would go to her home and introduce myself.

Ms. Friedman, I believe, was surprised that someone would come to her door to inquire about Lazarus. I told her of my failed attempt to leave a message and how compelled I was to apply for a chance to adopt him. Ms. Friedman was so nice to me and listened about Mike passing away. I think she knew that I was the kind of person who would be good for Lazarus. She told me to come to the adoption center on the following Saturday to fill out the adoption application. When I went there, I carried photos of Mike the Dog, family grandkids, and pictures of our yard to show that I had the right kind of home for Lazarus. I gave her the name of my veterinarian as a reference. I don't know why, but at this point I had not even seen Lazarus in the flesh. And yet I just felt—no, I knew—that Lazarus and I were meant to find each other.

It was at this time that I thought that I had better let

my Cindy know that I was trying to adopt Lazarus. As you can imagine, it took Cindy by surprise as we had said, "No more pets . . . just too painful when they pass away." She initially thought that I was just being emotional over our loss. During the next few days I tried to persuade her, and I think she saw that it was a need I had to fulfill. She agreed to proceed with the adoption application. Save-A-Life had some definite criteria that had to be met by anyone adopting Lazarus. The most important expressed to us was the need not to leave him alone for long periods of time. Because Cindy works at home in her own beauty salon, we easily met that main requirement. With our large backyard and a home already doggie-proof, with three grandsons for playmates, and a privacy fence with a second four-foot chain-link fence behind it, we were leading the list of candidates for Lazarus.

Ms. Friedman called the following Tuesday to tell us that yes indeed we were chosen to welcome Lazarus into our home. With a great deal of excitement, we met Lazarus on the day he came home with us from Dr. Terry Sparks's veterinary office. When Cindy saw Lazarus for the first time at the vet's office, it was love at first sight for her and Lazarus. They bonded instantly. He took to Cindy like they were old friends. After some TV interviews and last-minute paperwork, we were finally a family. We were asked by the media if we were going to change the name Lazarus had been given. Of course we said no because "Lazarus" is the perfect name for him after surviving his near-death trauma of fire and several operations to remove one ear and several to save his right eye.

Lazarus was rather cautious of me for the first few days, and I didn't rush our relationship. Within a week he was greeting me at the door when I came home from work. He has a job in Cindy's salon—he meets and greets her clients with unbridled enthusiasm. He loves to show his tricks to all. He can shake and speak and roll over and even count to five—all taught by Cindy. She taught him to do the stop, drop, and roll, and then took him to our grandson's first-grade class to show them how Lazarus had put out the fire on himself that fateful day. The kids loved his tricks and made a giant thank-you poster signed by the class; my wife proudly displays it in her salon.

On Christmas Day 2000 we gave Lazarus a six-week-old mixed-breed female puppy. You would have thought that he was the parent of her the way he cared and cajoled over her. Miss Belle, only a fraction of his size, is his best friend, and they spend endless hours of playtime and companionship. Cindy and I have laughed so long and hard over their antics that our jaws have actually ached.

Having this dog come into our lives at that time is a gift of immeasurable value. Lazarus came into my life at a time when I needed him the most. I think that it was Lazarus who rescued me from my grief, and he always puts a smile on my face as he greets me every afternoon.

CHARLES E. CHRISTIE

Fraser Molly Rose Duncan ("Rosie")

To begin my life at the beginning of my life, I was born on March 24, 1993, on Betz Creek, Wilmington Island. I was the most petite of the litter, but it was I who became the celebrity of my Cavalier King Charles family. While still a pup I moved downtown and became director of public relations for an antique map and print business on Monterey Square.

You are doubtless wondering how I became famous, but first, in true Savannah style, let me tell you about my ancestors. My earliest forbears evolved in ancient China. From Spain we acquired our family name of spaniel, but it took a Cavalier king to bring my breed to court. Both King Charles I and II doted on us, and on our collars at one of the royal estates was the couplet:

I am King Charles' dog at Kew

I pray thee sir, whose dog are you?

It was the Duke of Marlborough who developed our beautiful color and named it Blenheim after his famous palace. He carefully trained his dogs to sit at the feet of the best-dressed, a tradition I faithfully uphold.

138

In 1996 I gained national media exposure on the CBS Evening News during the Summer Olympics, and my first international exposure was the German travel book *Georgia*, in which I posed for a centerfold. I must confess that I owe my celebrity not only to my own charm and beauty, but to a thing everyone calls "The Book," written by my old friend John Berendt. When movie director Clint Eastwood visited my folks, he promptly sat down on the parlor rug and petted me. (Eat your heart out, girls.) I sat at his feet for the remainder of the evening and won a non-barking role in *Midnight in the Garden of Good and Evil*.

Along with my half-brother Toby Karp, I appeared in a scene with John Cusack, and we became good buddies when we watched the Bulls playoff games on TV in my den. Actors Jude Law, Jack Thompson, Kim Hunter, and Kevin Spacey all stopped by to scratch my ears and pay their respects.

Savannah soon became the center of a media frenzy, and I made appearances on the "CNN Travel Show," "BBC Savannah Special," "Dream Drives" and "If Walls Could Talk" on HGTV, and the "New Yankee Workshop" on PBS. I was photographed for *Southern Living*, *Traditional Home*, and *Travel & Leisure* magazines, and for more newspapers than I can name both here and abroad. Historic Savannah Foundation included me in two beautiful picture books, and I appear with my folks on the cover of the CD-ROM "Savannah Armchair Tour." Admirers from Canada to Florida send me birthday cards, and my fan club includes Pat and Sandra Conroy, Governor Jerry Brown, Margaret Whiting, Robert Altman, Julius LaRosa, Kenneth Branagh, a

Venetian contessa, a cousin of Flannery O'Connor, and an eighth-generation descendent of Peter Tondee.

Although I have no offspring, I have had a lifelong flirtation with Cavalier Wills Cunningham, and I take pride in my namesakes Savannah Rose in Michigan and more recently Ashley Rose in Kentucky. My parents say I am very smart since I know fifty-two words or names, but "no" and "come" are not among them. Like Lassie and Rin-Tin-Tin, I have my own postcard, which I pawprint upon request, and continue to enjoy minding the store and meeting new people every day.

ROSIE

RANSOM'S CHESAPEAKE CHANEL ("CHANEL")

"You're cuteness gets you everything!"

That's what my mom always tells me. Regardless of what I want—a hug, a treat, a rawhide, a cow's ear, popcorn—it doesn't matter what it is, because I get it if I put on my "cute" face. It is no trick, and it's so easy for a Lab. Hey, all you Labs out there, listen! You have an inbred face that gets you whatever you want (at least that's what your mom and dad think). Use your face (and floppy ears too) to bribe them for anything you want. It works!

Speaking dog to dog, can you, in your wildest dreams, imagine anyone naming their dog Chanel? That's me! I mean really, Chanel? What happened to Rover, Spot, Brute, Champ, King, Queenie? No, nothing but the best for Mom. She even thought about calling me Chardonnay or Chablis! How weird can you get? But alas, and I quote, "Because she is so cute and beautiful, we are naming her after the number-one designer, Chanel." Yep, my cuteness even got me my name! Please, Mom, don't make me wear Chanel's signature pearl necklaces!

141

Actually, I kind of like "Chanel." After eleven years, it has grown on me. I am an eighty-pound, beautiful, black Labrador retriever. Although I was born in Baltimore, my roots extend to Canada and England. That is why I have such a big, flat head. (No, I am not stupid!) I'm stocky too (versus sleek), but of course my mom tells me and everyone else that is because of my lineage. You should have seen her when she discovered that all of my relatives were mentioned and pictured in the Labrador retriever book. She stuck those stupid post-it notes on nearly every page; and if that isn't enough, she gets it out and shows it to all of our visitors. Then they "Ooh and Aah" me, pet me, play with me, and naturally, once again, I get spoiled and more treats. And when our little grandchildren come and play with me, they give me lots of treats because they love to spoil me!

You see, my goal in life is eating and sleeping. I'm truly a resting refrigerator. I just have to exist, and Mom and Dad tell me how cute I am. I whimper a little, and "Yippee!" I get either a treat or they let me swim in the pool. Don't let them fool you, they are strict and I have to obey, but what a piece of cake. Did I say "cake"? Love it, and popcorn and pizza crust! Those are the only people-foods that I get. Dad often says, "Not a lot of light under that stomach." Can't he understand that I am just solid beauty?

Now, we all have "pet" names. For me, it is Miss Piggy or Pumpkin Face. Why they call me Miss Piggy is beyond my comprehension. Pumpkin Face originated because my mom thinks I am so cute. But why Miss Piggy? How about "Babe"?

On to how I spoil Mom. I love it when she comes home from work. She kisses me before Dad! And, of course, if I lick her enough, I get a treat or my favorite, Denta Bones. They think they clean my teeth, but those bones are delicious. And the large ones are great!

I have a great life at home. As much as I didn't like Puppy Kindergarten or Basic Obedience, it was worth it. The praise and treats were the best part. And eight weeks of following commands is really nothing, compared with a life of being spoiled. My mom and dad are the best parents in the world. I know they love me because I am such a good dog. Let them think that I am cute. Let them call me Chanel or Miss Piggy. It doesn't really matter, as long as I get my treats! What else is there in this dog world but treats, and more treats and more treats!

CHANEL

COOKIE HAYWOOD

It started as a typical Saturday morning. We were up and out for my morning walk, which is usually shorter than my evening walk simply because my mom's not a morning person. We returned home, and I received a treat as I always do after each walk. After my mom fixed my morning breakfast, she was off to the shower. She does the shower thing *every* morning—whew, I'm glad that's not a canine kind of thing.

I was relaxing under the sofa while she finished getting ready. I wasn't sure what the day held because my mom's a pretty busy person and is always off and running. Me, I'm a laid-back kind of dog. I just lounge around most of the day and wait for her to return so that we can play in the afternoons.

As I was about to doze off for the second or third time, I heard Mom on the phone explaining to someone about my "not-so-calm" behavior when I'm in strange surroundings or around strange people. I began to sense a red flag as I heard her explain repeatedly my excitable nature when I'm around other animals. She requested a wider time span between appointments. I knew something unusual was up. After she finished her telephone conversation, she hollered for me. As I lay under the sofa, I debated whether I should come out. I was starting to get a little nervous, but knew she would find me eventually. I slowly crawled out from under the sofa, and with the saddest face I could possible muster, I came and sat at her feet. She motioned for me to jump up on the recliner. I obeyed. Mom sat down beside me with a very serious look on her face as she tried to explain the day.

"We are going to have our picture made today," she said. I wondered why this was such a serious event. I mean, my grandmother snaps pictures of me at every event; and since Kara, my cousin, came into this world, the pictures are twice as bad. No big deal, I thought. I've taken thousands of pictures over the years, and I'm quite photogenic. In a nervous voice she continued, "We are going to a studio for these pictures." "Studio"—hmmm, that's a big word. I'll have to took that one up. "I want you to be on your best behavior," she explained. "No running or jumping, and you must do what Michael tells you." I will admit I was confused. First of all, who was Michael and, secondly, why would taking a picture be such a big deal that it would warrant a lecture?

At this point the phone rang, and I jumped down off the sofa. I had to find a dictionary and look up that word "studio." Well, the dictionary mentioned something about a room with a television. Now I was really confused. I hang out in the studio every day while Mom's at work. Of course, we don't call it a studio. We just say living room. But to each his own. So my mom was stressed out about taking pictures in the living room with Michael. The only thing I could figure is that there must be something up with this Michael person.

145

We left the house shortly after that and arrived across town. My anxiety was starting to build as my mom slipped my harness on me. We entered a big room with lots of plants, lights on tall polls, a platform that extended out from one wall, and a long table with papers, toys, and some tasty-smelling pastries. I imme-diately noticed the smell of other dogs, cats, birds, and some smells I could not identify. My mom made small talk with Michael. Ah, so that was Michael!

She sat on the platform and called for me to come. I obeyed. Michael snapped a picture just as I leapt from my mom's lap. Too much to see, too much to smell. She called me back. I jumped into her lap, and within a split second he snapped another picture. This happened about half a dozen times. Then the disaster began. My mom wanted me to sit on the platform by myself.

She was standing over by Michael. I was not sitting up there by myself. The lights were bright, and Michael kept sticking his head under this black cape. He tried to squeak a toy to draw my attention. I ran to the toy, and he snapped a picture. But he appeared unhappy and very frustrated! His assistant took me back to the platform and tried to hold me there. Oh no, I couldn't stand to be pinned down! I began to squirm, to jerk . . . anything to get out of her grip and back to my mom. Michael recommended that my mom leave the room. Oh no, she's not leaving me! I bolted! Out the side door and into the fresh air I went. I ran to the car and waited. My mom found me and was most unhappy. She lectured me and sent me back in. I was not staying in here without my mom! I bolted again. The assistant tried to catch me.

146

The lights fell over, the food spilled, the papers scattered, and everyone wanted to blame me.

Michael explained to my mom that he had done the best he could do—several good shots of the two of us and one "wait-and-see" shot of me alone. The proofs would be ready in six weeks.

I'm happy to report that the picture of Mom and me turned out really great! The one of me alone was wonderful, too. I looked calm, collected, and very well mannered. A little advice to all my friends out there: Don't ever go to a studio to have your picture made. It's not like being at Grandma's or in your living room at home.

COOKIE

BONNIE KRAFT ("BOO")

A big hello to all my fellow dog authors!

My real name is Bonnie, but I like my nickname, Boo, much better. I'm a Cairn terrier, and I'm seven years old. I was born in Warner Robins, but I've lived in Savannah since I was three months old. I'm black and silver with a gray beard. I admit I might be just a tad overweight, but I am on a diet.

There are three other members of my pack. There's my Daddy-Dog, the pack leader (and my best friend), though I believe I run a close second. Then there's Mommy-Dog. I still haven't figured out her order in the scheme of things other than to feed me, give me treats, and meet my every desire. I'm still trying to train her to obey me. You know how stubborn some humans can be! And last, but not least, is Maggie. She's a four-year-old Cairn terrier. She came as a complete surprise to me! She was seven weeks old when I first met her. She was so little I could barely see her, and I didn't have a clue as to what kind of creature she was! Then, of all things, she decided to bond with me, instead of Daddy-Dog and

Mommy-Dog. Can you imagine that?

I still had all the toys that I had had since I was a puppy, and they were in perfect condition. She had her own toys, but she stole all of mine too, and systematically destroyed them all! The only things I have left now are a few balls that must be Maggie-proof. And she considers those hers too.

When Maggie was little, she used to have to stand in her bowl to eat. That was really funny to see. When she got bigger, we had a few fights over food, so now she eats on the porch; and I, of course, still eat in the kitchen. I'll protect her, but I will also steal her food in a heartbeat!

Because our house is so close to the river, we bark at all the boats that go by, but haven't gotten a toll out of one yet! We also like to bark at all the squirrels that are right outside our fence. They don't pay much attention either. My goal in life is to catch one of the helicopters that fly real close to our house! If the army is ever missing any . . . well, need I say more?

Basically I'm pretty much of a couch potato. Eating and chewing on pigs' ears are my favorite hobbies. I also love to nap, and, more than anything else, I love to kiss my Daddy-Dog—face, ears, and feet, but not necessarily in that order. When he lets me lick his bare feet, that is heaven! I can do that all day long! Even Mommy-Dog has started letting me lick her feet. She tells me it makes her feel relaxed, now that she's getting used to it. What to lick next?

Humans always seem to wonder about the meaning of life. We know the secret. It is LOVE.

BOO

MAGGIE KRAFT
("THE BAGSTER")

To all my fellow dog authors:

Hi! I'm Maggie, and I'm a four-year-old Cairn terrier. I've lived in Savannah since I was seven weeks old. I'm supposed to be brindle, but I've turned almost black, with gray in my beard. Not to brag, but I'm also very intelligent. Once I got to my new home here and found out where the porch door was, I knew to go there when I needed to go out. Of course I still had little accidents when I was too busy playing to get there in time, but I astounded the rest of my pack!

Speaking of my pack, there are four of us in all. Daddy-Dog is the pack leader and a really cool guy. Mommy-Dog is my best friend ever. And my big sister, Boo, is a Cairn terrier also. She was very good about me moving in here, once she figured out that I was a dog too.

I love to play and I love toys, especially stuffed animals. When I was little, I thought the object was to kill them. I used to tear off their ears, feet, arms, eyes, etc. until their insides came out. Then Mommy-Dog would have to sew them back together. She's a great surgeon, but she had to be with me around! I don't do that so much anymore, but I still bring one to bed with me at night. We have a very tall bed, so first Daddy-Dog puts me up, then he puts my animal on the bed too.

I have very gourmet tastes, unlike my sister, who will eat anything that doesn't eat her first. I must have canned dog food, heated exactly to my taste, and mixed with dry food, or forget that! I also like herbs sprinkled lightly on top, like a dash of garlic, some basil or sweet basil. Luckily Mommy-Dog grows herbs, which I sometimes get caught munching on. I love pigs' ears too!

I enjoy life, and I make a game out of everything, even having my feet dried! After that's done, I like to "Rrrrrr" and take off running around the house, chasing my sister or "attacking" Daddy-Dog. I love being out-side! I like to examine everything I see, and every day I find new surprises. I enjoy lying on my back in the grass on sunny days, getting a tan on my belly year-round. Then there's always the chance I might get to see my boyfriend, a Jack Russell. (I can't have babies though.)

Besides playing, I have a very important job too. I have to be the protector of my pack. I'm always on guard and very alert. I stand with my feet on the brick part of our glassed-in porch and keep watch out the window. When we go out at night, I run out the door first, barking to scare any bad things away from us. I'm only afraid when it rains really hard on the skylights. Then I lie on Daddy-Dog's shoulders while he sits on the couch. I can hide my head then.

My motto in life is—Always have fun!

THE BAGSTER

MAGGIE LOW ("MAGGIE")

Distinctive and appealing, with a wide-eyed look, my name is Sacha Marie, and I am an orange tabby. My job is to lounge in the Georgia sun and scrutinize my best friend, Maggie Low. And I would love to share some of her remarkable qualities.

Seven years ago we started searching for our special dog and finally ended up at the Hilton Head Humane Society, where I also had come from fourteen years ago. Mom selected Maggie first from all the other dogs, probably because of Maggie's large brown eyes that followed her constantly, Maggie's happy face that said, "Pick me," and her spontaneously wagging tail. After she had been found roaming the beach, she spent more than a year in the kennel. They guessed that she was about two years old and that she was a black Lab, with maybe a little hound for good luck. The staff at the humane society were diligent. They insisted that Mom walk five other dogs, but she always went back to Maggie. So, after a few hours and some heavy deliberation, adoption papers were signed and home Maggie came. Needless to say, she had a personal hygiene problem, so her first stop was a long bath.

Maggie was jubilant about her new home. She had people to love her, and she was inseparable from Mom. At bedtime she was so afraid of being abandoned that she would hang over the side of the bed and whimper until Mom would go in and go to sleep with her. Gradually Maggie became confident that this was her true home.

While we were restoring our house, Maggie took over the job as personal supervisor. You had to pass the sniff test—a little sandwich graft did help—and since she was seventy-five pounds, she was the boss.

One of Maggie's favorite trips was to the paint store. She made friends with the design staff and would head for their biscuit stash behind the counter.

For weekend fun she would go boating with Rosie, a standard poodle. Maggie would swim from the boat to the shore for a picnic. Later, back on the boat, with ears flapping in the breeze, Maggie was in complete enjoyment with her day off.

When we moved close to Forsyth Park, she was in heaven—squirrels to chase, new friends to play with, and, best of all, her personal dog-bone delivery service (dressed as Eric the mailman).

Maggie is now the concierge for the Garden Inn Bed and Breakfast. She often runs to greet guests at the door with a ferocious bark and finds them hiding behind the door until they see her wagging tail.

Once she makes the acquaintance of the guests, they become her ward. She shows them around, stopping wishfully by the cookies, sizing up the guests to see who is a soft touch, and then convincing the guests to bring back leftover dinner and, on return visits, presents.

Other duties are morning trips to the grocery. While waiting for Mom, she socializes with the shoppers and staff who know her by name and lavish her with love.

One night, when Mom was gone, Maggie felt abandoned. As each guest came in, she followed them to their room, sat outside their door, and moaned until they invited her in. Three times she did this. Finally, when Mom got home a few hours later, Maggie flew down the stairs to the security of her arms. As you can tell, Mom and Maggie have a special bond. They spend twenty-four hours a day together and have a strong commitment to each other.

One day, while coming home from the park, a very tall policeman was passing out flyers. Mom went to take one from his hand. All Maggie saw was something going toward her mom, and she went after the policeman. Totally shocked, Mom yanked Maggie's leash and apologized profusely, stating that this had never happened before, meanwhile waiting for the handcuffs. But the policeman tapped Maggie on the head and said, "Lady, you have a great dog." So, Maggie even has prevailed over the policeman.

As age creeps onward, Maggie is becoming quite gray, but is in wonderful health and looks forward to her next adventure.

SACHA

PEARSE HAROLD ("PEARSE PUPPY")

How does a ninety-five pound, eight-year-old male golden retriever become a mother? In my case it was by default, not by choice. But I'm jumping ahead in explaining how I had my only child.

My name is Pearse Puppy, at least that's what I'm called on my "good dog" days. Not being your typical golden retriever, I hate petting, especially "forced petting sessions," when humans follow me into my secret lair. I try desperately to become invisible under the dining table or melt into the rug whenever I hear that call— "Peeeaarssse!" Yuk, I know what's coming—hugs, kisses, grooming, ear cleaning, and, worst of all, the dreaded bath.

Born in Savannah, I moved to Tybee when I was six weeks old to live with Clancy Powell, an ancient golden known as "Mr. Sweetness," and five, semi-wild, saved-from-the-dunes cats. Sadly, my old friends have moved on to the great hunting ground in the sky only to be replaced by a new crop of misfits and throwaways. Dad would bring home every homeless animal in Chatham County—if Mom would let him; if we had a yard, which we don't; if dogs could run on the beach, which they can't; and if they could afford the vet bills and food.

One day Dad began a "Can we have a new pet?" campaign. "May I bring home two kittens?"

"No! Remember? We *have* a cat, Buster Hogan! He'll beat them up or worse."

Call number two: "They are only three weeks old. They're so precious. You'll love them. How about a trial run?"

"No! You know what happens with our trial runs, they come to stay!"

A few more calls wore her down. "Bring them home. You were going to anyway."

So Ozzie and Harriet, formerly known as the Nelsons, came to live on Tybee with me; my sister, Niamh the Weave, a seventy-five-pound "gold-a-dor" (combo black Lab and golden retriever); and Buster Hogan.

The twins weighed a half pound each, and hadn't been weaned from their mother. Cats choose you, and Harriett decided on day one that I was, and forever more would be, her mom. I was under my dining table when she approached crying and hungry. She moved straight to the crook of my neck, nuzzled into the mane of hair under my ear, and began making a "kitty pet nest." Mom kept going on that I was going to "roll over and crush her!" All that kneading of fur, and sucking and slurping had me terrified! I couldn't imagine what this mewing little thing hoped to find buried there. All I know is that she attached herself to my neck for all she was worth, and she's been there ever since. As for me, let's just say, I've gotten used to it over time.

Years later Harriet still seeks me out when she's

156

feeling anxious or lonely. Every night she sneaks into my bed, does her nesting thing, and curls up in the familiar spot by my neck. My secret confession, and I'll deny it if you tell anyone, is that I'm a big dog who loves his cat and believes that motherhood is grand!

PEARSE PUPPY

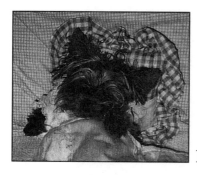

BEBA

Hello. I think your idea of publishing our story of our dogs is very sweet and of course very entertaining, but have you thought of the very deep meaning of their love to us? I believe that this is the very basis of creation—unconditional love. "Dog" spelled backwards is "God." How very interesting isn't this observation! Why is it that we feel so overwhelmed by the unconditional love that we receive from our dear friends? They always are there for us no matter what we do or how we treat them. They are always beside us, if we allow them to be. They try their best to call our attention so we will show them a bit of kindness, and the more we share with them our love the happier they are! How very little they are contented with, yet how ready they are to give to us their all.

Even when we go away for some time, they patiently remain waiting for us. Patient, kind, gentle, long suffering, joyful, and loving they are, but then so are these the "fruits of the Holy Spirit." Do you believe that perhaps God made these beautiful little friends as a true reminder of how God loves us and that He is with us no matter how we are to Him. His love is truly too unconditional. Our God finds many ways to find us, and this may be just one of them. God's blessings to all of you.

Now I will tell you the story of our sweet and loving little Yorkie, Beba, which means "baby" in Spanish. Beba soon will be two years old. From the time she came to be with us, she was like a little baby we so missed, since our four children (Lisa, Sean, Mercedes, and Maureen) were almost all young adults. A gift from Heaven, Beba came to us giving so much love. As everything in life, nothing is a coincidence. The Lord knew her timing was perfect, for she would be my companion to help me put together our beautiful store, Faith, Hope & Love. It is our store because this is truly His store. He named it, put it all together, and blesses it every day. Beba and I get to work for Him, and I do say this in the most humblest way.

Beba is our greeter, and she ever so gently goes to each person to welcome them. She is so loved, and many people come just to see her. I believe that she is the most loved dog in all Savannah. She could not be cuter or sweeter. She weighs four pounds, her hair is shiny (not long), her eyes are like the twinkling stars, and she also understands English, Spanish, and French. She will let you hold her and loves for you to play with her and her little toys. Her special place in the store is the Pets' Corner and the Babies' Room. We even sell in our store a tiny little Yorkie toy puppy that looks just like her.

Beba has won the hearts of many who have come to visit us, and we thank God for giving us this, His reminder, of His unconditional love for us.

MAUREEN VICTORIA HUEYO

159

Miss Yo-Yo Maya Cain Kaminsky ("Maya")

Hey, Poot-poot, you want your DINNER? It's TUNA night! Good stuff. Mmm-m.

Little miss, what d'you know? You want to go in the CAR? In the front . . . in the back. You want to go to the CEMETERY? LOOK! There's a PUPPY over there. Hey, Boojer, you wanna go for a WALK?

Where's your LEASH? Let's go to the STUDIO. Let's go to the SQUARE. (Wright.) Not NOW, LATER. NOT for puppies.

STAY, stay, STAY! SIT, sit, SIT! Closer, come CLOSER. We have to go see Dr. Joe. (All vets are Dr. Joe.)

That's ENOUGH. Kitties are EATING your dinner. PRETTY girl, sweet girl, priss-priss. What a sweet belly. It's DAVID! HUP! HALT!

What d'you WANT? In or out?

You wanna go to the BEACH? And see OTIS puppy? And ANDY and DEB? Who you barking at? LEAVE it! Let's get in your BED. TREAT! This way! NO kitty food. B-A-T-H.

Do you want to go in the BOAT? Look, FISH! (Dolphins.) There's BUCKY! Stay with the kitties. GET that bone. HOLD it! Let's go for a SWIM! In the CREEK. Oh, Pobracita, Poor BABY.

160

Let's go see OSKAR! PATCHES! BISCUIT PUPPY! LUCY! ANGELO! ROWDY! LADY! HAPPY AND JOY!

Kiss, Kiss. Sweet BABIES! CUPCAKE'S here.

CHUTNEY puppy and JOAN are coming to Maya's HOUSE! YES, they are! CHICKEN! CLAMS! OYSTERS! SHRIMPS! Easy, easy.

Oh, GOOD girl! What an excellent DOG! Good BOY!

Be sweet to the KITTIES. I'm going where puppies CAN'T GO. I'll be BACK. Squirrels! NO COONS! Move it! Pee and Pooh. Maya, we're HOME.

All I can say is that I am glad I'm not a bunny. But that is another story. My story is that I'm a Save-A-Life pup with a large vocabulary, as you can see. (I actually understand more than I am given credit for.) My breed is "mixed," a special breed, which leads to lots of speculation on the part of everyone we meet. I take pleasure in this attention, although I am not a snob.

I live with two perplexing people, two cats, and, for a while, a rabbit almost as big as I am. The cats are okay. One is very sweet and likes me to groom her; the other likes to go on walks with me, but also has a behavioral problem I find intolerable. She swipes at me when I walk by her, and I keep forgetting she is going to do this. Ouch! Misdirected play aggression, they say. Will someone please *do* something about it? I just ignore her and slink by. I'm not going to tell you what I particularly enjoyed about having the rabbit running around.

My greatest accomplishment is having spent no longer than four hours "staying with the kitties." I get to go everywhere. My life as a dog is very good.

MAYA

161

PRINCE MAXIMILLIAN LVOV ("MAX")

Max! That's me! I am a little ball of fluffy white fur. I'm cute and so lovable. Maybe we should start at the beginning. I was born three and a half years ago. My mother picked me over all my brothers and sister because I was so adorable. She said I was to be all hers. She and my father had lost a big black Lab that they refer to as "the great one" and wanted to replace him, so they chose me! I mean, isn't that a scream? I was to replace such a big dog. Well, I was going to try. And try I did. Not only did I replace him, I took over their hearts. They called me Max even though a friend of theirs said to call me "Bruno." Ha, ha, ha, that's not funny. I would have had to act like a nasty old Bruno if that was my name, but instead I get to act like a cute little ball of fluff, and I like that one better. My dad told Mom that I was going to be the grandchild that she didn't have, and I am; but now they are going to be grandparents. What am I going to do?

I like to do everything, but drive in a car. I get so scared and shake all over. That's not a fun thing to do. One day my mother took me in the car for a two-hour drive to Amelia Island. By the time I got there, all I wanted to do was get out of that moving thing. I went into the house of her friend. After they had lunch, they thought they'd get me back in the car for a drive with their golden retriever. I ran back to the door of the house and cried. My mother said that I would be happier in a strange house than in the car, and she put me back in the house. Boy, was I happy.

Another car trip was the day hurricane Floyd was to hit Savannah. I drove for five hours and didn't think I would ever get over the shock. But I stayed with a very nice family and their dog. The best part of the whole trip was that I got a chance to play in the red Georgia clay, and my parents took home a pink dog at the end of the trip!

My very best friend in the whole world is Joey, a dog who lives down the street. Joey looks just like me, and I think I'm looking into the mirror. I love him so much that when I see him we kiss each other. It's so nice to have a friend. I also love the horses that pull carriages around my historic home. My daddy lifts me up, and I kiss the horse on his very large face.

I'm just happy and love living here in Georgia. I play with all the tourists on the street, and they love me. I also play with all the dogs, and sometimes I even growl at big dogs, just to show them who's boss. You know, I come from a long line of tough dogs, just look up my history. I'm a bichon frise, and my kind won the best in show last year at the Westminster Kennel Club Dog Show.

MAX

SNIPER PARKER

My name is Sniper. I am a German shepherd, born on the July 4, 1998. They (my caretakers) were first going to call me Yankee Doodle Dandy, probably because my birthplace was in New York State. But I am now a resident of Georgia. My home is not in Savannah at the present time, but I am a frequent visitor. Sterling, my adopted brother, lives in Savannah. He belongs to my people's daughter. I love coming to Savannah. It is a lot of fun, especially Forsyth Park, directly across the street from where Sterling lives. Now that is a fun place—lots of dogs and people, I love it. The tourists, they are nice. They take your picture and you get petted, and that always feel good. And sometimes you are covered with children. It's the best! The dog owners like to get together in the park. They can brag about us dogs, and we like that.

Now, there is River Street. Woof! I really like going down there! You know you can make money off tourists if you know how. My friend Sterling and I had our Irish T-shirts on for St. Patrick's Day. There where a lot of visitors from England and Ireland there. Sterling and I are good at "singing." We make a nice duet. On the way to the river we walk past several parks called "squares." One of them had a group of people singing and playing songs from Ireland. We helped them, and got applause from everyone.

At the river we did another concert and made some money. An English tourist took our photo and put a dollar under Sterling's T-shirt. It really would be nice to have a doggie pool in the park. A dog could have a lot of fun shaking water on everyone. Dogs and their caretakers really miss meeting in the cemetery downtown. That was so nice, and safe. The fenced area made it good. You did not have to worry about getting hit by a car; the fence prevented us from running too fast and ending up in the street. But I guess someone did not behave properly, and the city told our people we could no longer meet there. But besides all that, I do have a good time visiting the nice city of Savannah.

One evening, while going out back to conduct some business, Sterling and I saw this suspicious person lurking about the trash dumpster. Well, that was a call for some good barking. The person suddenly disappeared. Our human went looking for what we had barked at, and out of the dumpster peaked this poor man's face. He thought we were killer dogs. It was funny—to us, but probably not to him.

The good part of Savannah is that there are so many dogs here. It is similar to England; maybe it has something to do with the heritage of the city. Dogs really add to the charm of Savannah.

I think they need to put up a wash-your-dog facility in the park, like they have car-wash places. That could be a lot of fun for everyone.   SNIPER

165

TRUVY
MOORE-
ELLISON

My name is Truvy Moore-Ellison, and I am your basic Heinz-57, mixed-breed dog (with lots of Beagle), residing in Savannah's Historic District. My two dads, Jack Moore and Rick Ellison, own and manage the Green Palm Inn on President Street.

I have the great fortune of being a "bed and breakfast dog," which means that nearly all of the guests at the inn do whatever it takes to spoil me rotten. In fact, many of the inn's guests have sent gifts to me after their vacation in Savannah. Unfortunately I have to share the inn with Pixie, Jack and Rick's stupid cat. Pixie, however, keeps a pretty low profile when I'm in and schmoozing around with the guests.

Although I love hanging around the inn, my greatest enjoyment in life is the squirrel hunt (also known as a walk) that I go on four times a day. The squirrels of Greene Square are absolutely terrorized by me, and I also make the squirrels of Columbia and Washington squares very nervous.

My second greatest enjoyment in life is riding in Dad's car around town. He enjoys going out to Tybee, but I must admit I found that route fairly boring, since it appears that the marshes are devoid of squirrels.

You may think my life sounds pretty easygoing, but it hasn't always been that way, not at all. When I was a mere six weeks old, a truck driver with a big heart found me walking along Interstate-20 west of Atlanta, obviously lost. He rescued me from the highway and took me to the Fulton County dog shelter in Atlanta. The next day I was adopted by Rick. Cool, huh!

As a puppy, I was truly "bad to the bone!" Since "Daddy Jack" was out of town during my adoption process, I knew that he was the one to pick on during my puppyhood. Accordingly I ate two pairs of his loafers, his wallet, his watch, and his boss's high heels! I guess you could say I have a penchant for leather.

During my puppyhood I also suffered from an identity crisis, and kept thinking to myself, "What am I? Who am I?" There were no other dogs in the household, so I learned about life by watching Jack and Rick's two cats, Nigel and Pixie. Basically I considered myself to be an odd sort of feline! Accordingly I tried unsuccessfully to clean myself the way a cat does. I also tried to walk gracefully across the top of the sofa just like Nigel and Pixie did. Needless to say, I fumbled and fell off the sofa every single time that I attempted this feat! Still there were times that I truly thought I was a cat, like when all three of us pets would sit in the window staring anxiously at the birds and squirrels climbing the trees just outside of Jack and Rick's home. At other times I bonded so well with Rick and Jack that I thought I might be human. What I didn't know until later was that I was a D-O-G.

It took a few trips to a mountain cabin in North Georgia for me to learn my true identity. All of the neighboring cabins had dogs around, so I was finally able to experience hanging around my "own kind." Unlike the cats, these animals wanted to play just like I did. We chased each other, growled, got dirty, and otherwise had loads of fun. I became Truvy, the D-O-G!

Three years have passed since then, and I have become very much at home here in Savannah since we moved here in 1998. 1 love the squares as much as the tourists do (for different reasons, of course), and I must admit that it's a great life being able to meet so many different people all the time who stay in the inn. If only we could do something about the hot "dog days" of August in Savannah!

TRUVY

MAGGIE METTS

I was born on Tybee Island in early November 1996. I did not have a name then, but I had a pretty happy life with my mother and two littermates. Since I am a fawn boxer, I am not a really big dog, but I look mean and scare people sometimes.

Destiny had a plan for me that ensured the wonderful life of a city dog. Little did I know there was a home on Whitaker Street that needed me to come and complete a family. The mom of the house, who really did not want the responsibility of a dog, had a list of stipulations that were especially designed for me: (1) the dog must be quiet and not bark all the time; (2) the dog must have short hair because there is not enough time to groom a dog; (3) the dog must look as though she will protect whoever will be walking her in the park, so Mom does not have to worry about mean, nasty strangers; and (4) the dog must like children since there is a three-year-old in the family. Mom thought she had this all sewn up. No canine could have a résumé to fit these criteria.

Well, little did Mom know that Tori, the three-year-old, asked Santa for a dog! Santa knew right where to go to get me; and I was ready, I thought. When Santa picked me up on Christmas Eve, I was scared, but this looked like an adventure that would last a lifetime. So a little elf put a big red bow around my neck. I jumped in the sleigh and away we went.

Wow! What a big house this was. When Santa and I came down the chimney, we landed by the Christmas tree. I knew at that moment that I was finally home. It was not long until my new family woke up to see what Santa had left behind. The little blonde-haired, blue-eyed girl walked into the room. When she saw me she exclaimed with excitement, "This is what I have always wanted!" Everyone laughed because Tori was only three years old, and her excitement seemed as though she had been waiting a lifetime. The elves in the sleigh had already given me the name of Maggie, and that was the best Christmas ever at the Metts residence on Whitaker Street.

Since that day a lot has happened. I did prove to everyone that I could live up to their list of expectations. The only one I am a little weak in is number three. My papa (Jimmie Metts) says that I am like the lion in the *Wizard of Oz*, and I must say that describes me pretty well.

I have many canine friends downtown that I meet in Forsyth Park and run and play with. But my best friend lives next door on Whitaker Street. His name is Hampton Smith. He belongs to Mark and Kim Smith. We love each other so much and we share everything. When Hampton's mom picks up the phone, Hampton knows that I am coming over to play. He starts barking and usually does not stop until I get there. But I can get there in no time because they only have to ask me once and I am ready to go. I take off running, and no one even has to escort me.

Although my family life has been stable, it has grown quite a bit in the past few years. There have been several new additions to the household. We now have a cat named Purrball; a turtle named Speedy, two bunnies (Midnight and Nibbles), a guinea pig named Chocolate, two fish, and two finches. My human sister, Jennifer, and her fiancé, Wes, adopted a Boston terrier named Daisy, who comes to play with me most every day. I have a very happy life in the city, and don't think I would change a thing.

Another human sister, Holly, is currently in veterinary school. The way this family is growing, we'll be glad when we no longer have to make trips to the vet's office.

MAGGIE

CALHOUN ("TOONS")

It wasn't that I really wanted to move to Savannah. I was having a perfectly grand time living on Horse Island. South Carolina island living suited me. No fences, just nose to the ground, and I'm off for the day! What could be better for a basset hound? Think of it—marsh and river at my doorstep. Plus I had friends. Hannah, my German shepherd sister; Fairway, my golden retriever best friend; and C.B. Mom gave C.B. his name. She said it stood for Calhoun's Buddy. Mostly I hung out with Fairway and C.B. Hannah sort of thought of me as a jerk. She hated it when I'd have a surge. When I'm surging at full force, I'm invincible! No one can stop me, and no one (except Hannah) could make me behave. I could wear her down though. By the time she could catch me by the neck and throw me down, she was pretty overheated. She would have to dive in the pond to recover.

Mom says I'm incorrigible. Dad calls me his Son. Mom has one of those weird psychic minds. She does *not* trust me. I remember once when there was a large, perfectly great, dead animal (skull and backbone intact) that washed up into the marsh. Mom told Dad that I was going to drag it home. So Dad threw it back into the marsh along the river so that the tide would take it out, only the tide brought it *in*! My legs are short, and that's a handicap in shallow, muddy water. However, I have great upper body strength, and I managed to drag it in. This took me quite some time, given the tide and my vertical challenge. It took me so much time, in fact, that Mom saw me from the kitchen window and sent Dad to snatch my prize.

It became clear to me that we were going to move. Dad said he was tired of boarding up the house every time there was a hurricane alert, and Mom said she was ready for civilization. They liked a place called Savannah!

We moved to a part of Savannah called Ardsley Park. At first there was a great deal of consternation about my yard. Mom said I had no brain for traffic or city living. She and Dad had brick walls and iron fences built so I wouldn't get "flattened." In my own mind there was much more angst than was necessary. I understand my neighborhood perfectly. I have all the parks well marked, and I have a definite schedule. I don't really vary my routine if I can help it. I have a very high-pitched, nasal whine, and my parents will do just about anything not to hear it. We walk promptly after Mom finishes her breakfast.

One very sad thing happened after our second year in Savannah. Hannah died. Hannah was Mom's dog, and Mom's heart was broken. I really think that's the reason that Lucy came to stay. Lucy is one of Mom's rescue basset hounds. Mom told Dad that Lucy is old, and old dogs are hard to place. She said that Lucy has arthritis and that she is a WONDERFUL, SWEET, LOVING dog with Bette Davis eyes. Now, I want to clue you in to Lucy. She is old, but she *can* move when she wants to. She bothers my stuff and steals my bed and my couch whenever she gets a chance. Dad says I should share the couch, but I can't stand to have Lucy touching me. If Dad sits in the middle, it's sort of okay. I have to watch Lucy *all* the time. I just don't trust her.

Then to complicate things, Gracie arrived. She is another one of Mom's rescue dogs. She was only supposed to stay for a couple of days, but Mom said she was too frightened to be sent to a new home. Gracie is a small gold-colored cocker spaniel. She has totally convinced Mom that she is the *most* precious dog around. Mom even carries her around. I personally think Gracie's ridiculous in that emotional way cocker spaniels have. She's clingy and has a nervous bladder. Every time she's excited or scared, there's a puddle. I'm here to tell you that if I did that I'd be in deep and serious trouble. I really don't mind Gracie as much as Lucy though. She's so neurotic that she never leaves Mom's side, and that means she has no time to touch my toys.

Now Plum is another matter. Plum Purrdy is one of Mom's foster cats. There have been many foster kittens. I happen to like kittens so I get to be in charge of them. I have raised a lot of kittens. I let them eat out of my bowl, and I let them sleep on the couch with me. Kittens don't bother me one bit. Anyway, Plum is one of the kittens I raised. Mom didn't try to find a home for Plum because Dad thought he was cool. He's a big orange, long-haired, tabby cat. He's gigantic and he's only ten months old. Plum and I are the best of friends. We understand each other, and we have Lucy and Gracie figured out big time. Lucy pretends to be so sweet, but whenever Plum gets near her she barks at him. Dad says he enters her force field. The force field used to be about two feet around her, but I think it's growing. I know for a fact that Gracie chases Plum, but since it's Precious Gracie no one seems to be too bent out of shape about it. The really beautiful thing is that Plum is fearless. There is nothing they can do to make him afraid. I love that!

CALHOUN

PRINCESS

Hi. I'm Princess, the cocker spaniel, and I live on Tybee Island with my family—two grown-ups, a teenager named Lindsay, and a couple of cats that I have to keep in line.

The cats are Saffron, an orange tabby, and Savannah, a tortoise shell. They are fun to hang out with and really fun to chase around the house.

I don't chase my people much, but I do love them—a lot. Sometimes I have to jump on them. Most of the time I follow them around like a dog—upstairs, downstairs, over to the food bowl, down to the yard. Wherever they are, you'll probably find me. But then, I'm always working hard, protecting them twenty-four hours a day.

It's a big responsibility. But then, you never know when a burglar might leap out from behind a bush. I may look like I sleep a lot on the cool hearth in front of the fireplace. But don't be fooled. I'm working. If the UPS man comes, I bark! If the frogs in the swamp get too loud, I tell them to pipe down. And if the cats get

176

uppity, I have to jump at them and chase them under the couch.

I also have a special security function: Every day I have to poke around in all the waste baskets, pull out used Kleenexes, and tear them into shreds. GRRRR. (After all, these are Killer Kleenexes; if you don't watch them carefully, they could climb out of the wastebaskets, sneak up behind the cats, and attack them. And I have to protect my cats.)

All this security work can be exhausting. So after I chase the cats, I may have to take another long rest in front of the fireplace. Sure, my eyes look closed. Sure, my feet are spread out behind me. But I'm alert. Watching. You never know when a rabid pelican or a flying tuna will attack the house. And I'm there, 24/7.

Well, I do leave the house once in a while. I have to ride in the car a lot to make sure my people are safe. Sometimes I go downtown or to the mall, but usually I go to the Tybee Market or over to Wilmington Island to supervise the grocery shopping.

I'm working hard in the car too, of course. I sit in the front seat and watch stuff: Traffic. Other dogs. (I can tell what a dog looks like a hundred feet away.) And when we go by Jaycee Park, there might be a fat squirrel in the road or a duck sitting on the grass, and I might have to try to throw myself out the window and pant and bark and make a big effort to chase it. All this is just part of my job, protecting my people, of course.

Also part of the job—making sure the teenager gets to St. Andrew's School on time. We have to rush through breakfast and race to the car and get to school by eight

A.M. Fun! But I am sad when she gets out. Why does she leave me? Why can't I come too? But then we pick her up in the afternoon and she is fine, and I am *so glad* to see her. I wag my huge tail. (Some cocker spaniels don't have tails anymore, but I have a bushy white one!)

I also like to help with the afternoon carpool, greeting the teenager's friends, Michael and Kory. I am the official carpool greeter! (Sometimes the carpoolers pat me. But sometimes, when I haven't had my weekly bath, they say I smell like a dog.)

Though I go to school nearly every day, I'm not much of a student. I flunked obedience school. I sit when I feel like it. Sometimes I come when people call my name, but mostly I don't. The teenager complains that I am not very smart. She says I will come when she calls me any old name, like "Rocketship." But who needs smart when you've got a terrific dog like me, protecting her people and keeping those cats in line twenty-four hours a day?

PRINCESS

SHAWNEE
PERKINS

If my memory serves me correctly, and I have no doubt
that it will, the experience of the last several weeks has
been the most terrifying of my life. I've enjoyed pleasant
surroundings, plenty of delicious food, and a warm and
cozy home, so a major collision with these conditions
was nowhere to be found on my to-do list.

The last run of the day is an enjoyable event. So began
my evening. After tending to my outside practical
matters, I approached the steps and slowly collapsed to
the ground.

"Shawnee, Shawnee, come on girl," Miss Jewell
called.

"I'm trying to get up," I thought, "but I can't."

There I was, lying a few feet from her. Seeing the
sudden anguish and surprise in her eyes, I tried again.
My body could not respond to the dictates of my mind.
"Why can't I move?" Pain invaded my body, and at that
moment we each knew something serious had taken
control of our lives. Her first thoughts were that a spider
or a snake had bitten me. Desperately she tried to help
me stand. It was futile and the struggle ended. Realizing
the apparent seriousness of our situation, she knew
assistance was needed. A call to 911 gave us the name
and number of the animal emergency hospital.

It was 10:30 P.M., and a call to anyone meant that we would disturb their sleep. Thank goodness for her caring grandson, who came quickly and struggled to lift me into his truck. Away we went for perhaps the most fearful and eventful weeks of my life.

I was so scared. My teeth were clicking, and a constant shiver rumbled through my body. My eyes, with pupils enlarged and glassy, revealed my throbbing pain, and I could hear the drum-beat sounds of my heart.

Suddenly there were bright lights, voices with directions, and orderly movement, which now are meshed in my memory. But that night, unbeknown to me, I was on center stage.

Examinations, blood tests, and X-rays were extensive. Finally we learned that there was no spider or snake bite, but rather an unusual condition of a blood clot on my spine. No wonder that I was affected so quickly. Wham, there I was, unable to stand.

A serious recovery regimen was adopted and the medical assistants began therapy. It was essential that they gain my confidence and respect in order for there to be positive results. With gentle voices and pats on the head, they endeavored to proceed. The reassurance and concern that they demonstrated allowed me to submit to the conditions of my treatment.

Grasping the fact that I was paralyzed in one leg did not come readily. Once, when my family came to visit, I was resting on a sheepskin blanket and taking my intravenous lunch. When I saw them, my eyes lit up and I tried to get up. I did scramble about somewhat, and so did the stand and IV bags. Wow, what a commotion I created. Learning a new life-style was to be a challenge.

Advanced therapy was offered at the veterinarian hospital in North Charleston, South Carolina. So off I went to begin another stage of recovery.

Stretching exercises and massages were a daily encounter, but swimming in the warm water became my favorite. At first I wore a life jacket, which helped reassure me of my ability to stay afloat. Slowly I began to walk with assistance, and as the days passed, my body and mind responded to the healing.

Then the day came when I was released to go home. Home—what a sacred word. It was hard leaving those who had given me another chance to walk and soon to run again. They had become my friends.

Maybe by telling a little of my experience others will realize how important our relationship is with humans. We each have a gift waiting for someone to accept. So, remember, best friends always come in pairs.

SHAWNEE

 **TIA**

Until the day my precious Chinese Shar-Pei, Tia, ran away, I was fairly well entrenched in agnosticism, or at least on the fence. But everything changed the afternoon following a sleepless night that she slyly pushed open an unlatched door of a friend's business in Savannah and sprinted across the parking lot toward busy Johnny Mercer Boulevard.

Chasing her on foot would be futile. Though petite for the breed, she is a lean, well-muscled, and elegant mass of wrinkles in a rich sable-toned bristled fur. And absolutely schizophrenic. By that I mean that she twice graduated top of her class in obedience training, and made me proud when she was on a leash. She snapped to attention, kept her eyes trained on me, and responded sharply to every command. An absolute angel.

But, Sister, let me tell you! Off the leash, she's a headstrong problem child who runs away from me, rather than to me, when I call. After the first unheeded command, it's useless to try anymore. It's as if she's crying out, "Free! Free at last!" To Tia, it's a big game, and she's running the show.

The funny thing is, she loves people so much, she'll go to any strange adult or child, and if they can discern my problem, they'll hold her for me. End of problem.

On the day Tia ran away, though, it was the first time she had done so in busy traffic. So I immediately abandoned the foot chase; she was way ahead of me. I jumped into my old Toyota and headed in her general direction toward a neighborhood of suburban homes.

Then I spotted her hanging out with some other juvenile delinquent dogs, and I resorted to the only thing in my bag of tricks. Since she's allergic to every common dog food and treat, I train her with French fries, and I just happened to have some with me.

I pulled up to a house just in time to be embarrassed by her "soiling" a homeowner's lawn (what a brat!). Then I opened the car door and started waving French fries and calling her so sweetly. She bounded to within a couple of feet of the car, paused as if thinking it over, and obviously decided the price of freedom to be much higher. Hence, she bolted, but this time I lost her for good.

This is when my hysterical thinking took over. "She's going to die. . . . Someone will find her and keep her, but not give her the medicine she needs. . . . I'll never see her again . . . I'm going to die." And on and on until huge tears were rolling down my cheeks and I was sobbing uncontrollably.

Now here's where the shift in my spiritual values came in. I'm driving up and down the street of this subdivision through blurred vision, sobbing, calling, and thinking, "Oh, my God, what am I going to do?" After an hour or so, confused and heartbroken, it somehow

183

occurred to me to actually let the scales of spiritual pride fall away from my eyes and humbly ask God for help.

I cried out to the traditional God of my childhood, "Dear God! Please help me! I'm so powerless. I don't know what to do. Please don't let anything happen to my baby. Please tell me what to do next!"

This was spoken aloud with heartfelt earnestness. And I got an answer almost right away, but not aloud. In a still, small voice that I heard in my head, I was told to keep doing what I was doing. Keep driving up and down neighborhood streets, stopping residents, grown-ups, and kids, asking if they've seen a wrinkled dog.

I really couldn't think of a better idea, and I was still crying (I get that way sometimes), so I followed instructions and kept going up one street and down another for at least another hour.

Randomly I turned down a street, saw a man standing in his yard, and said to myself, "Are you going to ask every person you see?"

Without waiting to answer myself, I parked haphazardly near the curb and approached him. Before I could open my mouth, he took one look at my stricken face and said, "I think you're looking for something wrinkled."

I had no more tears, but I practically collapsed in his arms.

"Yeah," he said, "she just came up and started playing with my kids. I figured she didn't look like the kind of dog that should just be wandering around so I tied her up in my backyard. I've been trying to reach you for about two hours."

I no longer believe in coincidences. I firmly believe

that the kindness of that man finding Tia and the unlikely event of my finding him was divine intervention. My faith has grown since that day.

But Tia, lovely princess that she is, at four years old, still has that rebellious streak. She sneaks through my gate and runs away from time to time. But I just drive up and down streets asking strangers if they've seen her, holding on to the faith that I'll get her back—and I do every time.

PATRICIA PHILLIPS

Scout Phillips

Six days a week, always about midafternoon, I hear the whining squeak of brakes. Then I hear the side door of his van roll open and roll shut.

He's coming soon. I don't move yet, but I sit up on the honey-colored wood floor. My ears perk up. It takes about ten minutes for him to come around to my house, and to get his nerve up to step on the porch. I know he's checked out every house on the block. But this house is where the good stuff is—a refrigerator full of chicken, a cupboard of bread, and cookies. Plus, this is where my girl sits to scratch my head and cuddle me at night.

Suddenly I hear the heavy boot stomp on the first step. I leap to my feet. The metal door slot slams shut, sending a clanging echo through the house as I charge the door. With chocolate brown hair bristled, I pounce. I bare my teeth and bark at him to go away. My paws press against the glass. At eighty pounds, I look ferocious.

As he flees to the safety of his van, I bite the papers he shoved in my house. I shake them to send a message. Come inside my house and this is what I'll do to you.

186

One day he left my girl a note. I bit it too. The white form listed twenty possible problems with mailboxes. Number 20 read "other faults," and he scrawled this inside the blank box: "Your dog is hampering the delivery of your mail through door slot. Please provide higher slot or outside box to prevent any safety hazard to carrier."

Weenie. I can't hurt him through a slot. My girl said I should stop the game. But it is no game. This is serious. Each day a stranger comes to my door. I charge. I bark. He leaves. Everyone knows those lazy cats aren't going to do anything about it. The way I see things, that's my job and it is well done.

SCOUT

JACK AND J.T.

Jack and J.T. are a father-and-son Savannah dynasty. Jack is a Snoodle (full blooded), and J.T. is a Pek-a-snoo (his mother was the Pekinese, Princess Poo Poo). He was the pick of the litter.

Jack is fifteen and deaf, except he can hear crackers being opened from two floors away. Jack, who is a bit of a chow hound, will eat *anything* at any time. No one can stop him once he's started. Don't even try! All that bread the woman with the cornflower hat leaves in the square for the birds is "Jack food." Jack eats what bums leave, what cats leave.

J.T. is Jack's one-eyed son, who suffers from a very bad back. He is thirteen and has to be carried up and down the three flights of stairs four times a day to walk in the square, which is owned by Jack, his father. Some day it will all be J.T.'s if he lives long enough. Meanwhile, he handles the aggression part of being a "square owner" since his father is interested only in the scrumptious repast to be found there.

Together Jack and J.T. have almost enough parts to make up one whole dog. It is their delight to be served by their masters, who have kept them ignorant of the horrors of the world and even of their own names, for it is the masters from whom they take no crap.

ED AND CAROLINE HILL

188

NUDNIK ("NICK")

If my Yiddish were better, I would have never named him Nudnik. It means "pest," and he is anything but. I thought a nudnik was kind of a hapless person and had an affectionate connotation, so our sweet and utterly self-contained pet is hung with this unfortunate and inaccurate moniker.

I call him the mayor of Monterey Square. Twice a day he can be found (leashless, usually) aimlessly grazing, greeting old friends and strangers with such a diffident manner that only rarely have we heard a complaint and then from the most dogophobic. This in spite of a shepherd look and a black muzzle that can be misread as menacing.

We found him of course. After he came to live with us, we heard from three different "downtowners" that he'd been in the neighborhood for two or three weeks, staying in this yard, being fed by the occasional benefactor. We met him through the hairdresser across the street. She told us he'd been in her shop all day, and she'd assumed that he belonged to *someone*! After her last appointment, with no clients in sight, there was this dog. So she called us, and in her usual overwrought and

189

breathless voice told us exactly why we had to adopt this utterly amiable beast. My wife and I were newly married with an enormous tyrannical cat, and we were not at all sure we wanted another pet; but we let our neighbor bring the dog over and we put him—safely, we thought—in our yard. He got out. We figured that was that, but decided that if he returned it would be ordained—we would keep him. The next afternoon, Halloween, punctually at mealtime, I heard my wife exclaim, "The dog's back!" The rest, as they say . . .

ALEX RASKIN

CHRISTY LEIGH
PLASPOHL

Being true to my breed as a golden retriever, I love the water. I consider myself lucky because I live across the street from Silver Lake, and can go swimming just about anytime I want. Whenever I am hot from working out in the yard (on squirrel patrol) or have just finished a run with my humans, I love to cool off in the lake, which I consider to be my own personal swimming hole.

I have gone for many a swim during my eight years, but none compares in excitement to one particular dip I had the misfortune of taking a few years ago. We had just had a big rain that seemed to last forever; and when it finally came to a stop, the water level in Silver Lake was much higher than normal. It was so high that the excess water flowed across the road at the low end of the lake into a concrete culvert, which was designed for instances such as this. The water cascaded swiftly down the culvert into what is normally a little creek. On this day the creek was so swollen with rainwater that it looked like another vast lake.

Spillovers like this always draw a crowd of curious onlookers in the neighborhood. I went over to the scene of all the excitement with my humans, happy to finally

191

be out of the house. I wasn't too sure about that swift current crossing the road, and kept my distance at first. We explored all around the area, checking out the community dock that was totally submerged. Our attention kept coming back to the gushing whitecaps making their way down the long cement basin into the creek below.

I watched my dad slowly walk through the rapids until he got to the other side. I thought, "Hey, don't leave me over here. I can do that, too!" I started wading across the swift current. This turned out to be a little harder than I thought. I was halfway across when a big wave came along and knocked me off balance. Instead of continuing my trek, I crouched down low into the water, thinking this would help stabilize my balance.

The next thing I knew, the water swept me off my feet and I was being pulled amidst the waves down to where the water dumped into the creek. I couldn't stand up because the current was too swift. I was totally out of control, and there wasn't anything I could do about it. For the first time in my swimming career, I was scared. My human sister, Libby, was standing there watching the drama unfold, and called out, "Dad, Dad, you've got to save her!" I remember thinking, "Yes, please save me!" My human dad wasted no time. He jumped into the water and let the rapids carry him along as he followed me down the culvert. I know his arms and legs must have taken a good scraping along the rough cement.

I got to the bottom of the culvert; the current then launched me into the swollen creek. The water level was way over my head. There were stumps and limbs sticking out, and I wasn't sure which way to go or what to do. I felt a big push and turned around to see my dad right there, trying to move me toward the land. The water was so deep that it was over his head, too.

I was happy my dad was there to save me. He gently guided me out of the water over to the bank, making sure I was safe. Libby came running over to both of us, not sure whether to laugh or cry. We must have been a sight! The three of us made the short walk back home to tell my human mom about the big canine rescue of the day.

Now, every time I swim in Silver Lake (which is at least once every weekend), I remember that day when my stealthy swimming skills were put to the test. The next time we have a big flood in the neighborhood, this is one golden retriever who will not test the waters!

CHRISTY

GROMMET
("GROM," "GROMMY,"
"RAMEN NOODLE,"
"NOODLE," "OMELET")

Grommet, a clumsy pup with huge paws and soft black coat, ended up at the Humane Society after experiencing more "lows" than any puppy in the Low Country deserves. One look into those big brown eyes, so wide the whites were showing, and we were goners.

At home in the comfort of our living room, Grommet remained petrified. We could only imagine the abuse he must have endured in his three short months on the streets of Savannah to make him remain huddled in a ball, shying away from us and his food.

His indomitable puppy spirit, however, soon trumped. Grommet, a true child of joy, put aside his fears and bad experiences to drink in more of his surroundings. He started to romp and play, exploring the wilds of the backyard, and sniffing out the nooks and crannies of our old house.

Sadly, Grommet was destined for more pain. In a blur one spring night of his first year, he was struck by a speeding truck, which broke his hip in two places. But Grommet's fractured exterior belied his soul's immensity.

Even though now slowed with a slight limp, Grommet continued to bound into each day. The best philosopher, Grommet was beginning to teach me.

On his first trip to the marsh, Grommet feasted on all the splendid sights and fecund smells in the marsh grass. With his pal Bailey leading the way, Grommet forgot his mom and her companion walking behind as they bobbed in and out of the green and brown marsh grass, spraying mud—the kind of dog fun that makes you laugh just to see it.

When it got very quiet, too quiet, we turned back to see Bailey and Grommet mesmerized at the edge of the still water. "Look! Bailey is rolling in something. . . . Hah, hah, your dog is rolling in dead-thing!" I exclaimed smugly.

"Very funny," my friend replied, then hollered after Bailey.

A few moments later we peered back down the dirt road again and it was my friend's turn, "Hah, hah, Grommet is *eating* dead-thing!" Grommet feasted mightily before I could arrest his attentions. On the way home in the jeep, Grommet remained still and quiet until I pulled in front of the house. Just as I opened the back door and called to him, he looked over with a positively stricken face, then lurched forward to release all the marsh water and dead-thing his stomach could carry—right between the seats of my jeep!

Appalled, I almost started to fuss at Grommet for drinking the brackish water, and eating the dead-thing. Then it finally hit me: Grommet, a child among his new-born blisses, will not become jaded by this, or his other, experiences. Each day Grommet is reborn, and he will sport along the shore without a trace of cynicism, anger, or resentment at his lows.

Thanks to the puppy-hearts with which we live,
Thanks to their joys, tenderness and fears,
To me the meanest marsh grass (or dead-thing scent)
that blows can give,
Thoughts that do often lie too deep for tears.

MAURY BOWEN ROTHSCHILD

KING'S BISHOP PRUITT ("BISHOP" OR "BISHIE")

That is a pretty snazzy name, isn't it? I've been called many things. As a young pup I was what many would refer to as a "citizen of the world." That was a great life. Back then, people just called me "Puppy." I was one with Nature. Every time the rain fell, it fell on me! There was such a variety of foods in my world, that I ate something different most every day. The weather was usually nice and warm too, especially during the summer. I learned to love Popsicles in the winter months. I traveled most of greater Savannah back then. I stayed in the finest door stoops and pockets of woods that a canine could ask for.

Fine as it was, after a while that life began to close in on me. It was literally choking the life out of me. One day the cops appeared and picked me up. Puppy's reign as Prince of the Free Dog World had come to an end. It didn't bother me. As I said, I was feeling pretty drained by then anyway. Those police officers really changed my life that day.

After being "picked up," I felt healthy and invigorated with a new feeling of life. Maybe that was a direct result of the policemen removing the makeshift red rope-collar I had outgrown. I moved to a nice new home, where I

197

could sleep on a bed, play with other dogs, and did not have to fight for my food. It was a lazy life, but I learned to like it. After a while in that new home, I figured out that I had become "Bishop" when I was in trouble or "Bishie" when I was good.

I lived with a foster mother and several brothers and sisters. Every week we would board a van with A.W.A.R.E. volunteers and go to Heaven for a few hours. Heaven (PETsMART) was more like Hades because I was posted right beside *tons* of dog food and treats and permitted to sample *none*.

After a few visits the sheen had worn off of this new "situation." One afternoon my new mom came to take me home. She spoke with my kennel guardian for a few minutes then took me for a leashed walk. I gave her the slip, testing her reflexes and stamina. This girl would do just fine. She was pretty quick and smelled nice too.

Mom gave me my classy name, King's Bishop Pruitt. I found myself in a new apartment with a buddy named Scout Finch. She is a cute little "hotdog" with mismatched blue-and-brown eyes like mine. I played so hard that first night that I was sick all over the rug. I guess getting sick was okay in my new apartment because I didn't get into much trouble. Scout did punish me some by biting and hanging from my lip several times and then biting my tail, but it was a small price to pay.

We've recently moved to a new home, where I can run and play with Mom, Dad, and Scout. We have a magical house. I can make messes with my toys on the floor, and the mess quickly disappears. Food appears in my dish like clockwork and, soon after, *vanishes*, an act I have been working on for several years. Another trick

I can do is pass through doors without opening them. If I want to go outside, I simply walk *through* the wall. Can you believe that!

It is a good life—a dog's life. I'm going to enjoy my retirement as Prince of Savannah's Dogs.

BISHOP

KEA MANGO MAGIC ("KING KEA")

At the time of my birth, in the year of our Lord 1994, I was weighed, poked, and prodded; measured from head to tail; and had all the tests one must go through on one's way to becoming a king. At the light of the next day I received a regal tag on my tail. Surely now I would be sent off to the palace. You can imagine my surprise when I was rudely stuffed into a small crate, placed in the cargo hold of an airplane, and sent not to the palace, but to a place called Savannah, Georgia. The indignity. There I was transferred a few more times, and at the tender age of six weeks was adopted by a therapist and an attorney. At first I was delighted at the aspect of having an attorney in my house to straighten out this mistake of my royal destiny. The home I was taken to was comfortable enough, with down pillows, treats, toys, and the like. I decided that this would do quite nicely until the matter of my royal status was straightened out. During the coming months, I was introduced to meditation by my therapist. It was peaceful and calming, a good practice for a future king. She also insisted that I become a vegetarian. At first I was shocked. Can you imagine a

200

king not partaking of any meat! Why wouldn't anyone want to eat a big steak or at least a chicken? I am not even allowed to eat fish. There is a fish that resides in our house. I like to watch him swim in his bowl. I bet he would taste good!

Water plays a big part in our lives. We live on the beach. I, King Kea, however, am not allowed on the beach—a law, I am told, that was passed before I had arrived. When I have regained my royal status, I will have this law changed. I am confident that my attorney will arrange this. By the way, did I tell you that my attorney also thinks he is a king? I am not quite sure of the logistics of having two kings ruling from the palace! I will have to explore this when my royal status is regained.

I get to travel quite a bit. To be a good king, one must travel for education and culture. When I travel I stay in luxury hotels and shop in the finest stores. Naturally I travel first class in a "magical royal carrier." When I am placed in this carrier and settled down on my royal pillow, it appears no one can see me. I surmise that it makes me invisible. My royal subjects carry me. We have had many travel adventures.

Lately I have almost forgotten about the royal palace. My home here is ever so good. My therapist says we all create our own kingdoms. You know, she could be onto something! I am happy and loved. All is well in Kea's kingdom.

KING KEA

 **HANNIBLE**

My name is Hannible. My tale is about how I went from being a homeless stray to becoming a service dog.

And I am Hannible's partner, Art Saile. I was brought into Hannible's tale by a phone call from a Savannah Kennel Club member, Dianne Davis, who told me about a Shar-Pei that had been rescued from the Savannah humane shelter by a veterinarian at the Southside Hospital for Animals. The dog needed a home, and since I already had two Shar-Peis, I was asked if I could please help. So I drove from Hinesville to Savannah to meet the dog. What I saw was a thin, cream-colored Shar-Pei with sad brown eyes, wagging his tail and being too cute. So I agreed to take him home temporarily; that was three years ago, and he's still here.

Hannible, who was named by Alicia, my youngest daughter, became a member of our Shar-Pei family. After some small disagreements over sofa sleeping places, food bowls, and who goes through a door first, all soon was well.

Hannible's service-dog career began when Ming, my therapy dog, had to be retired on account of health

202

problems. Hannible began his training program in order to replace Ming. First came basic obedience class, then three months of therapy dog–training clinics. Hannible then passed the therapy dog international certification test and became a certified therapy dog.

Hannible makes visits to a variety of institutions in Savannah and nearby areas—including nursing homes, care facilities for Alzheimer's disease, youth shelters, mental health treatment facilities, and Hospice Savannah, where he and I are volunteers in the Pet-a-Pet program.

Hannible and the other therapy dog members of Coastal Therapy Dogs, the local chapter of Therapy Dogs International, take part in other activities in the Savannah area. These include public education events in the local shopping malls given by the Savannah Kennel Club; the Safe Kids Program of Savannah; special summer camps for kids given by the MDA chapter of Savannah; Grief Camp for Kids, given by Hospice Savannah; and the camp for children undergoing long-term physical therapy, held at Magnolia Springs State Park, and given by the Children Rehabilitation Hospital of Augusta. Hannible also does a good turn for Boy Scout and Girl Scout troops by helping give programs in safety and dog care. Just about every weekend he works in therapy and public education programs.

Hannible also participates in the St. Patrick's Day Parade, the highlight of every Savannah dog's social calendar. A few years ago at the parade, he was described by a local WTOC-TV anchorman as having a face that only a mother could love. For many years—right, Doug?

The impact of Hannible's therapy work was brought home to me by something that happened at a public education event held at the Savannah Mall two years ago. Hannible was about to go on a break from his meet-and-greet duties at the Coastal Therapy Dogs information table. While I was talking with our relief person, a member of CTD said, "Look at Hannible." As I turned to look, I thought: He is probably begging for some goodies from a child. What I saw was a well-dressed lady, kneeling down, hugging Hannible, and crying. I walked over and asked the lady if I could help. The lady said no, stood up, and then explained that Hannible's visits to her mother had been a source of joy during her last days at hospice. She said that Hannible and I had been her mother's last visitors before she had passed away. She had wanted to thank Hannible and me for the visits, but had been unable to contact us. She hugged Hannible again, shook my hand, and walked away into the mall crowd. I never found out her name.

The motto of therapy dogs is: "Changing tears into smiles and helping the forgotten to laugh." That sums up what Hannible does best.

The journey of Hannible from being a homeless stray to a therapy dog—giving unconditional love to all he meets—is surely a tale worth the telling.

HANNIBLE AND ART

HARRY BARKER

The origins of Harry Barker are lost in the mists of time. Some say I came on a Viking ship. Must be my regal bearing. Some say I was smuggled in a bunch of bananas from Central America. Must be my fiery temper. Some know the truth: I was born in my mother's heart as soon as she heard about Shetland sheepdogs.

My mother, Carol Perkins, heard about shelties from her best friend, Jackie, who had five of us by the time she was grown up. Yikes! Carol was skeptical, but did her research, and soon found me. I was an innocent ball of fluff. That would all change. Carol was just starting a company that made things for dogs and people; it was a company that cared a lot for dogs and people. And it needed a name, just around the same time I needed a name. What are the chances? And that is how I came to be Harry Barker.

What else can be said about the myth of *me*? Most shelties weigh in at about twenty pounds. Some are smaller, some are larger. I weigh sixty-five pounds. Why? No one knows. The food's not *that* good. I'm very big. Very large indeed. Most shelties retain their herding instinct and snap around the heels of people and dogs; I still actually nip. I'm not saying that's a good thing, but it does make me special, if not slightly feared.

Some people say that dogs begin to resemble their owners, or vice versa. I don't resemble Carol. I'm a boy. A big handsome boy. With my breathtaking bluish-gray ruff and my haunting brown eyes, I'm told I resemble Richard Gere. Again, I'm not bragging, but I understand he's considered quite a hot property among humans.

So that's really my story. I'm available for dinner and a show, but it's probably best for everyone if you just come by the store.

HARRY BARKER

Coco

You know the old adage, "The kids left home and the dog died." Well, it really happened to us. In September 1989 our last son went off to college at the University of Richmond, and we trekked to Costa Rica for a Labor Day holiday. Upon returning, we found that our beloved red dachshund, Jingles, age thirteen, had died at the kennel. We were bereft.

I came with a dog as part of the marriage package, so I naturally thought of a replacement after a decent interval. I really hoped for a chocolate dachsie and told everyone I knew about my intentions. My husband was adamantly against another dog.

Months passed—fast forward to Memorial Day. Both sons came home for the holiday. Our next-door neighbors, two young men, knocked on the door and handed me a tiny, sad-eyed, chocolate semi-dachshund. They had found this waif, who apparently had been abused, discarded downtown. She was frightened and without the copious AKC papers of former pets. She had a white fur vest, so she clearly was not a thoroughbred. It was love at first sight.

That was eleven years ago, and Coco (named for Coco Chanel, the only Chanel I thought I would ever have) has been a bright spot for all of us over the years. She is intelligent and sprightly, and she earned a gold star at obedience school in spite of her puppy diagnosis of ADD. I inquired facetiously of our vet if Coco needed to go for counseling. He said no, but she did need to take Ritalin. Having raised two sons without medications, I was astonished to now find myself popping pills for a wiener dog.

There have been many funny times with Coco. Once, while I was in Mexico, she was to take an antibiotic for some condition. She would only take it dipped in peanut butter. She managed to leave one pill on the fingertips of my husband (her father). He inadvertently licked the peanut butter fingertip and swallowed the pill. He called me in Monterrey to find out what to do. He said he felt fine; it was only when he passed a fire hydrant that he got the strangest urge.

Coco has matured to a gray-muzzled dowager and reigns as queen at our house, hopefully for many more years.

PAT SASEEN

DUCEY SCHULZE

Ducey Schulze started life as a very special fellow and a bit of a celebrity. His name comes from the fact that he was born on the millennium, and in fact was featured in full color on the front page of the Hartsville, South Carolina, newspaper with his littermates. At eight weeks of age his mother and I got him as the pick of the litter, and he then moved to his new home to begin a duel career as a hunting dog and retriever for his mom, and an adjunct ophthalmology dog for his father and uncle.

Quite early in his career as a tiny little fellow, Ducey began coming to the office to help entertain and manage patients. He immediately became a big hit with the staff and patients, and rapidly adapted to his role as an entertainer. In addition, his uncle, who performs LASIK surgery, was running an advertising campaign, and Ducey figured prominently in a television ad, barking on cue.

Once Ducey was about nine months old, he was sent off for three months to hunting-dog boarding school, where he excelled to the point that the trainers felt that he could make it on the professional field-trials circuit, but his mom really did not like the idea of his turning pro and preferred to have him at home working for her with retrieving.

Ducey is not the only golden retriever who comes to our office. His littermate, Millie, who is owned by his Uncle Richard, Jr., as well as Ducey's cousin, Marlow, are frequent visitors. Ducey's brother, Dingle, who is about six months younger, is following in Ducey's pawsteps. Interestingly each of these golden retrievers has their own style in dealing with patients. And just as interestingly, we have quite a number of people who schedule their appointments on "dog days." Having serious eye problems is quite stressful as one can imagine, and having a wonderful furry friendly little fellow come in to cheer you up often makes a big difference. Ducey has already had a very full, exciting, and rewarding life, and he has much more to give.

DR. RICHARD R. SCHULZE

Daphne Francis ("Daphne")

Tawny brown with white toes,
A bib and markings on my nose,
Ears like the pedals of a rose,
With almond eyes,
And heart thrice my size!

My name is Daphne,
Strategically selected.
I rhyme with laughing,
And although once neglected,
I emerge quite triumphantly,
A happy, laughing Daphne!

I am the youngest of three dogs in our family. We never go anywhere alone—always together. Bear, a yellow Labrador mix, is the oldest of our trio at thirteen years. Sasha, who looks like an all-black Border collie type, is nine years old. She was the eternal puppy until I came along five years ago.

Now I fill that role with more energy than even most puppies do! My story begins in 1996, the year of my birth. Not much is known about my earliest puppyhood, except what can be pieced together. I was born probably in February and somehow found my way to the streets of Savannah by the time I was about four months old. At that tender age someone had put tar on several areas of my torso and hind quarters to cover up patches of mange. Every variety of worm known to puppies thrived on me. I was so severely malnourished that my head was disproportionately large in comparison to my emaciated frame. Somehow I don't like to think this was intentional—I had a hole through my left front paw in the webbed portion between the first two claws. I must have stepped on a nail in my travels between dumpsters in my ongoing search of sustenance for survival.

My existence was miserable! I was always hungry. I drank from puddles in the street, dirty and nasty tasting as they were, and I was always limping and in pain with my holy paw! The patches of tar didn't bite anymore, but I don't think they did much for the problem. I still had mange, and I just itched interminably. Whenever I could, I would stop and lie down to cross my front left paw over my right and lick it to make it feel better. I did this so consistently that it didn't infect. Even so, it bothered me awfully and was always distressing. To this day I am often found with my front legs crossed in this fashion. Back then I don't think I gave a thought as to what would happen to me. I simply lived from dumpster to dumpster—from itch to scratch!

One unsuspecting, sultry August morning, I was dabbling on Drayton Street, scavenging for whatever I could find when a group of teens discovered me. Alarmed at my nonchalant regard for danger, they scooped me up. Drayton, I later learned, is one of the fastest one-way streets in Savannah, and probably a sure one-way ticket to the nether world for one such as myself. How lucky I was on that now-famous occasion!

It seems that once these young folks had me among them, they were at a loss as to the next step. There I was, an undernourished, filthy, mangy, flea-bitten bundle of six months. They now had a closer look, and it was pretty sad. What to do, what to do?

They carried me into the executive offices of the DeSoto Hilton Hotel on Madison Square to ask big sister Antonia, who was in the middle of a crucial business meeting. They knew she would be the most sympathetic to my cause, and besides that, she would know what to do!

Well, Antonia was horrified! How was she to remain professional and deal with this uproarious entrance? Sympathetic though she may have been, this was the absolute limit! She took one look at me and ordered us all out! I was to be given a bath straightaway, and she would deal with us later!

I think this must have been my first bath in life, and it felt so good! Rub-a-dub-dub, they scrubbed and they scrubbed. Lo and behold, I began to change color! I went from gun-metal gray to tawny brown. All I can say is, Antonia had the right idea! When she finally did come home, it was dinnertime and although I was considerably cleaner than found, I was not fit for inside anyone's home for a vast number of reasons. So I was consigned to the back porch, where there were French doors allowing me to see in. Although I couldn't be with my new friends, it was the next best thing. I became impatient, however, and wanted to be where the action was. I noticed a covered grill just under the kitchen window overlooking the sink on the other side. The next thing they knew, I had climbed up onto the grill and was peering in at them from my new vantage point. They thought I was very clever and actually, I did too! The next morning proved to be very beneficial. We went to the vet and returned with a full roster of medications and procedures to be administered for my better benefit. There were still, however, some major obstacles to be overcome before I would be happily ensconced.

As well meaning as Antonia and the youngers were, they could only take my case so far. In order to find a real home, I needed the approval of Mum and Dad, or be placed elsewhere. Mum was the doglover and already had Bear and Sasha. Dad didn't even like dogs—still doesn't! Mum felt she was at her limit with two dogs and didn't even look kindly on the challenge of considering what to do with me. She knew full well that she had a soft heart and didn't even afford herself the luxury of really looking at me—I mean seriously looking at me.

Then the unexpected happened. It turned out that my visit to the vet was incomplete. I never thought I would count my holy paw a blessing, but in a strange way it was. The vet never noticed my injury. When Mum did and showed it to Antonia, who realized that the hole actually went through to daylight on the other side, they were horrified! Off to the vet I went for a second time. Mum drove while I nestled between the front seats looking up at her. For the first time she really looked down at me and began stroking me softly. I knew she was thinking. She was sad. Her watery eyes said it all.

Thank God, Antonia wasn't exactly stupid! She knew and selected my name with great intent. Daphne was

Mum's original name, given her at birth. When she was several days old, they changed it. Consequently Daphne as a name waited for a second chance. I was and needed that chance, and Mum knew it!

The rest is history as they say. History, however, has a way of repeating itself. A little Tidbit is on the horizon. "Tibby" is another waif in similar straights as I was five years ago. Let's hold the good hope that the fates will look kindly on her as well.

DAPHNE

SAMMY ("SAM")

Sammy is a tricolor collie who was born in Brussels, Belgium, in June 1993. He was the runt of a litter of seven and literally left to die. Luckily a wonderful lady, Christianne, took him in and nursed him back to health. At the age of eleven months, Sam came into our lives.

Sam's original name was Romeo. Although he is gorgeous, the name didn't quite suit him, so my son Eric named him after the then not-so-famous Sammy Sosa.

It took a while for Sam to really bond to us. He always went back to Christianne when we went away. She has a small farm, with horses, dogs of her own as well as dogs she boards, cats, and at least one goat. When I took Sam there, he was so excited that it was like taking a kid to camp and not even waving good-bye. He moped around the house for days after I picked him up.

Belgium is a place where dogs are welcome in restaurants, cafés, and stores, but not in the supermarkets, though even there you would often see the elderly ladies with their little dogs in the seat of the shopping carts. We lived in the city, and I did many errands on foot, so I would often take Sam with me.

At the end of 1999 we returned to live in the United States, and decided to live in Savannah, Georgia. Sam went to Christianne while we were packing up. I picked him up the day before we were to leave. I had him groomed at the usual place around the corner, but then we couldn't go home. He was very agitated and nervous. Poor guy, he had no idea what was happening. We said our good-byes to the Cat Lady, who always had pieces of chicken for him; and to the shoemaker, Danny, at the kiosk. And we had our last coffee with Christophe and Natalie, who owned the restaurant across the street.

Not only had Sam never been on a plane before, but had never been in a cage. The vet gave me a mild tranquilizer that wore off long before the plane took off, but it helped to get him in his cage. He looked so sad. We arrived in Atlanta ten hours after takeoff. We had to go through customs. Sam arrived, cage and all, in the customs area. He absolutely would not look at me at all. Luckily customs is pretty easy and fast in Atlanta, but unfortunately I had to turn him over to someone else to get him up to the baggage area. And, also unfortunately, in U.S. airports dogs are not allowed out of their cages until they are outside. When I finally was able to get him out of the cage, he still was not very happy to see me. He was one unhappy, confused collie.

One and half years later Sam is very happy. Savannah is a great dog place, maybe that's why we chose it. I still speak French to him, so he doesn't forget, or maybe it's so I don't forget. His cage was in the garage until just today, when I gave it to our neighbor and friend Allie, who has just acquired a new puppy, Thor. She can use it for training. Sam, needless to say, was happy to see it go. And if I should ever need it back, which I doubt, I know where it is. JACKIE SIRLIN

HOBART
STUMPF-PIRALLA
("MAUSI-POOH")

Hi, my name is Hobart, I am two and a half years old, a mix of golden retriever and husky, and one of the lucky dogs that have a mami who loves me and cares a lot.

When I was a little six-month-old doggie, I got lost and could not find my way back to where I lived, so I had to fight to find food and shelter in a very scary world full of cars, strange noises, unfamiliar neighborhoods, and people I had never seen before.

I ended up at the porch of a little restaurant where three other dogs lived, and the nice owners gave me food and took me in. They also gave me my name, Hobart. I think that they named me after their kitchen equipment; not very flattering.

Because the two restaurant guys were very busy and already had to take care of their three other dogs, they could not keep me, and so they introduced me to all their friends. One day a very sweet girl came and took me for a walk in the park. I really liked her. She talked to me the whole time during our walk, and she also played with me. I was on my best behavior that day, and it must have impressed her because she took me to her home and became my mami.

218

I could not believe my luck at first, and was very shy and careful in the house; but both of my new parents let me check out everything and told me that this house and the yard was now all mine. My parents bought me toys—squeaky things and bones I had never had before—and I got my own bed, a big nice red pillow by the window, where I can see everything that goes on in the neighborhood.

There are things I do not like that much, especially those visits to the guy my parents call "vet." He always pokes me or checks me out. This is quite annoying.

I also hate when my parents leave me at the "dog hotel" and go places alone. I like it better when they take me on vacation, which we do at least once a year. Then I get to play for a whole week at the beach. The beach is my favorite, and I am really good at catching that round flying thing they call a Frisbee.

Mami even bought a new car for me, so that I have more space and lots of windows to look out. I really love to ride in the car since this usually means fun places to go to, like visiting my girlfriends at their house in the countryside.

My everyday duties include watching the house while my parents are at work. I also help Mami with the cleaning and carry the vacuum cleaner for her so that she has her hands free to pet me and get those good-tasting treats out of the special box.

My papa is not home as much as Mami, but he always takes me out to play ball in the park during the evening, we have a lot of fun together. As I told you already, I am so lucky to have found my parents.   HOBART

219

JOEY SUSSMAN

I was born December 27, 1997, into a bichon frise show family in Birmingham, Alabama. I lived with my mom, Grandmother Tootsie, and five brothers and sisters. I had a great time traveling to dog shows and learning how to strut on a leash, to stand for grooming, and to use the outdoor bathroom only. When I was five months old, my owners realized that I was going to be too small to show and decided to sell me.

There is a human expression: "Every dog has his day." My day was when my mom-to-be, Amy, walked through our door. During the morning I had been groomed, so I was a knockout—snow white and fluffy with a smile on my face. I was in Savannah within the month.

My new home is great. I must admit that even after five years I have not mastered the parlor floor stairs. Amy has to carry me down. I have full run of the main floor and can sit on the furniture. (In my old house that privilege was reserved for Tootsie.) It took two chairs and a sofa, but I finally learned that furniture is for sitting, not for chewing or digging. I have an abundance of stuffed toys and squeakies, and cannot go to sleep

220

without my teddy bear. I go for walks five times a day. The good part about being carried down the stairs is that it allows me to scope the block before hitting the street. I like the fact that most of our neighbors speak to me first. One even jokes, "Here comes Joey and his walker." I look up and smile when they talk; it ingratiates me with them.

I also love the tourists. There is a game that I play—How many can I get to notice me? It is much easier since the bichon won the Westminster Dog Show. Now people recognize me for what I am versus a pretty poodle. Since we live near Mrs. Wilkes's, the people smell great when they reach down to pat me—just like fried chicken.

It has not all been perfect. There have been adjustments. When my mom leaves town, I stay with my human grandparents. I used to fake illnesses in order to try to get my mom to remain home. The first illness was acting like I was hardly able to walk. After examining me and not finding the cause, my vet and Mom decided to wait until Mom returned to do additional tests. Of course by that time I was *cured*. The next time, when I saw my things being packed, I instantly developed an ear infection. Off again to the doctor's office, where I was diagnosed as a faker. The vet did say that I was smart to use a different illness, but Mom was not happy. I have not pulled the stunt again.

In all, my life is wonderful. I have my dog friends (Max, Rosie, and Lucy) and my cat friend, Orlando, that I see on my walks. Most of all, I have a smart mom who took only five years to train me to do everything that suits me. JOEY

221

BELLE TARSITANO

If cats are natural liberals (pure elitists, motivated by the belief that everything belongs to everyone equally, and especially to themselves), then dogs are natural conservatives. Dogs love, even crave, order. Dinner, for instance, should be at precisely the same time daily, and served in the accustomed dish and in the established way. When supper time comes, the average dog will be found sitting patiently at the ready, like a customer in a fine restaurant, waiting to be served.

Our dog, Belle, is more conservative than most. Born ten years ago in a wood lot near Cusseta, Georgia, the offspring of a black Labrador mother and a just-passing-through father, she has matured into a great lady. The gray hair that has gradually filled in her eyebrows and developed around her muzzle gives her the exaggerated dignity of a grand dame. If she were a human being, she would be the sort of woman that Groucho Marx loved to torment in his movies.

No one in our family, of course, would dare be so irreverent with our Belle. We were teaching our children to dance, and she was quite content to watch silently as we waltzed. When we started a polka, however, she was on her feet in an instant, in the middle of the floor, and chastising us loudly until we stopped. We thought, perhaps, that this was a figment of our imagination, so as an experiment we returned to the waltz. She stopped barking at once and went back to her place to watch. She has never let us do the polka since, which she apparently finds too gauche to permit in her home.

We even know Belle's religion. She is an old-school Episcopalian, like the rest of her clerical family. When evening prayers are said, she will wait her turn with the children for a goodnight blessing. Belle is also very patient about being dragged off to the church for animal blessings every October on the Feast of St. Francis, but when she gets there her demeanor is pure Episcopalianism. The other dogs may introduce themselves to one another (you get the picture) and offer up their lusty "Amens" during the service, but Belle does automatically what any other lifelong Episcopal lady would do. She finds a place for herself in the equivalent of the back pew, says her prayers, and goes home.

Her home, as for any true conservative, is the center of her universe, and that universe has clear boundaries. She knows the difference between the mailman and a salesman, between a guest and a stranger, and she greets them appropriately. She can be fierce when she thinks that a limit has been crossed without permission. And she has a ritual of her own that she performs when she needs to go out at night.

Before she moves out into the yard, she pauses at the patio to bark. "Here I come," she announces. "You mind your business, and I'll mind mine." It must work, since for the last ten years, peace has reigned.

THE REVEREND DR. LOUIS R. TARSITANO

TOBY TIDE TEEPLE ("TOBY")

Toby Tide is my name and tennis is my game. Well, it's not quite tennis as most know it, but I do have a certain obsession with a tennis ball. From my earliest days I was easily entertained with the game of toss and retrieve. Everyone who came into my yard was quickly absorbed in my favorite activity. At the age of four I can go forever. It wasn't always the case. When I was a mere pup, I would tire easily and drop into a shady spot on the lawn for a quick nap. But now you should see me go; it takes more than one healthy human to keep up with me. Oh, they try to get out of it, but with my hallmark beagle bark I can usually persuade one or more to be my partner. Sometimes they try a diversion by hiding the ball; you know the old "out of sight, out of mind" psychology. But I am a tenacious kind of canine. When they hide that ball, I just nose-open the utility room door, go high on my hind legs, and get a fresh ball off of the window ledge. Then I need to really let them know who is in charge with my mighty bark. Those folks come running quickly to let me out—rescue me is what they think—but I know that they are just trying to put an end to my commanding voice.

My commands extend beyond these mere humans. When that ball is poorly thrown and lands in the pool, you should just see how that ball scoots around to the side of the pool at my barking commands. And you should see those humans jump into action when I do my magic act of making the ball disappear into the skimmer and bark it back into reality. I've got them behaving quite well after all these years. The best trick I may have taught them is to execute the proper toss to get the ball to bounce just off the edge of the cement so that I can perform my incredible vertical jump and snag that ball in midair. Now that one really wows the crowd!

It's really quite easy to keep these folks entertained. One night they had a sitter keeping me while they went out of town. Sometime, about 2 A.M., I got the call of nature and that kind sitter was more than willing to take me for a visit to the yard; like I said, I do have a command of the barking thing. Boy, was she in for some late-night entertainment! A stray pair of white panties that had dropped from the laundry found its way into my mouth, and we were off on a merry chase; what a sight that was, she in her pj's, and me at top run-and-dodge form.

My run-and-dodge game is not always at top form. There was the time that I thought it would be nice to explore the neighborhood beyond my yard. Unfortunately my escape route had not been well scouted, and I ended up in the dog pen of the neighbors. He was not the neighborly kind, so you can well imagine that it was not a friendly scene. So much for visiting. On other occasions my roaming was much easier, although you would never know it as you watch my family scampering through the neighbors' bushes and yards to bring me home.

Over the years I've worked on extending my interest in sporting activities. I am actually a very good swimmer. My preference is to ease into the pool on the steps at the shallow end, take a few laps, and make a grand exit by climbing the ladder mounted at the deep end of the pool. This is another little act that seems to keep visitors to my yard in amazement. They have been known to place my tennis ball in the middle of the pool just to see this act. They seem to be quite starved for entertainment.

I've made my share of mistakes, like the time I chewed up a brand new bathing suit. My most dangerous mistake in terms of keeping my happy home was the time I ate a pearl bracelet. I paid for that one in more ways than one.

All in all, my life thus far has been a good one. I truly won my place in the family during the evacuation for Hurricane Floyd. I traveled like a real trooper for all those hours to Macon. There was that one little problem when I tried to once again explore the neighborhood where we were staying, but I guess all's well that ends well, 'cause they did not leave me in Macon. They brought me back to Savannah, to the yard that I love best. Home sweet home!

TOBY

DUNE

Oh my gosh—I was chosen! Off I went to Jones Street. That was to be my home and even my workplace for a while. From the first day, I was *at work*. It was all so new to me—a family, an office, people coming and going. I loved it. I was carried around like a baby by Carrie, my new sister. She was home for the holiday (Christmas) and was aware that there was little time to bond. *Bond* we did. It happened at the beach—Tybee, that wonderful place where Dogs receive hundred dollar tickets for just "being"—yes, it was there where my family named me "Dune" 'cause I loved playing in the dunes.

Back at home and the office, the temporary location of Cora Bett Thomas Realty (she's my mom and official boss), my name became a household word. Home-and-office combination was a great place because I was always able to attract attention from the agents and customers coming and going, plus I could steal into the handbags and chew on the lipstick, glasses, or whatever had that irresistible scent.

It didn't take long for me to realize I had responsibility. This is the picture. It was much like that

228

"Designing Women" on TV. I was blond and so were all of the women sales team and so was Gregory, the only other guy helper at the time. I'm not sure how long it took me to fully grasp my position in the company, but it did require a bit of patience and higher education. Before I knew it I was at this fancy boarding school named the "sophisticated puppy"—it is run by Uncle Mikie—a one-on-one training for the very special canines in the world. I'm hanging on the walls with the best of the best. Uncle Mikie writes to me even now. While I was at school, I received many postcards and notes from my family and friends. They were under the mistaken opinion that I was homesick and lonely. I loved school. Uncle Mikie asked why I *never* barked. I answered, "I've never had to ask for anything." In order to be a good guard dog, I needed to develop a deep bark, he said. Well, I took it under consideration and graduated with honors without the bark.

It was *cool*—I was the head dog, so to speak. I was in charge of the "girls," you know. Keeping them happy and calm. Like the day Patricia, my favorite, was upset by one of her buyers who was mad because he didn't get the property he bid too low on. I've learned so much; I could give a course now on how to buy property. That's another article another day that needs to be in the financial section. Anyway, to help her that day I simply ate her glasses, chewed on her lipstick, and, before you knew it, she had forgotten all about the other. Mission accomplished. I had my place in the office—it was the club chair perfectly positioned so I could be the official greeter and properly sniff out the bad guys. As it happens, we've never had a bad customer. I, of course, am *always* "on duty." It's my responsibility to protect my girls—along with Gregory's help—and to keep them happy and calm and naturally to do my part of the selling. It was a lot to do for such a young guy. My mom and boss is a taskmaster, and that's the way the household runs even after hours. My sisters and brother don't mind; they get me to help with their chores. It's all good. Especially the kitchen stuff and the birthday cakes. I've eaten several entire cakes that were left on the kitchen counter. I *own the counter*. Seems to me it is mine for the taking if it is there. After all, my nose cannot resist. There seems to be a big deal commotion when that happens, but not for long. I've never quite figured that one out.

Now back to the bark thing. My dad said I needed to be more mocho. Whatever that word means. It's not part of my vocabulary. He said guard dog. Now keep in mind, I'm handsome and blond and pretty sexy—you got the picture, a lover not a fighter. Well, this guard stuff just isn't my bag. Noisy barking is not dignified, and the ladies I hang with would not like that. "Dune, Dune, do you hear that? What is it?" I'd be asked. "Who cares?" I'd think. Guard Dog is not my handle. Dune Dog is my name, and I'm a lover, not a fighter.

Okay, you got the picture—I'm in charge of most everything, even on Jones Street home. There is action there too, such as students walking by who come in to see me, and the horses pulling the carriages and tourists around. The horses are my cousins by marriage, so we speak a special language no one else can understand. They tell me what silly comments some of the tourists say as they go by our house. They comment on the former owner, Joe Odom. He was a main character in the famous book *Midnight in the Garden of Good and Evil*. I wish I had known Joe; my sisters and brother liked him so much.

Well, well, well. Before you know it, we were moving to the big office on Oglethorpe Avenue. I'll *never* forget *that* day. Charles, who helps in the office too—doing lots of things like cleaning and gardening and smiling and moving stuff around—well, he stepped into an open paint can and spilled it all over the new carpet. It was some sort of paint that didn't come out. I was nervous. When I get nervous I get hungry, so I ate a lipstick; it was the only thing in sniffing site. I got it all over the carpet too. The *only* good thing about that day was that I took some heat off of Charles. He thanked me.

I missed home and the kitchen being near. But soon the food came to the office, and I soon knew my place, or places—front door, back door, and on my Mom's sofa looking onto the center office. Often I keep one eye open as I sleep, just to stay in touch with my girls.

I've participated a great deal in the *big* deals. My very favorite is when we sold Harry Barker a house and a store. Harry is a noisy shelty, but quite the busy dog. He's very busy. He's on line and has a catalog too. Anything a canine could ever desire can be purchased there, and his mom is drop dead good looking. It's special to have been Harry's realtor.

Now to tell you about a couple more of my better customers. Hunter belongs to Steve and Russ, who buy investment property, renovate it, and then give it back to

Joan and me to sell. So they are one of our best customers, and I in particular like to assist them. So as you see, my position is extremely important.

Property management is another division and a story in and of itself. It is really intense over there. I need to do a lot of calming in that department. Clarence and Jackie work in the maintenance division, and Clarence walks me. He is my best friend. Clarence knows when the stress of the women is just too much for a guy, and we hang together at the cemetery or Forsyth Park. He's a cool dude, and he tells me what it's like in his life. We share guy stories and visit with the guys who sleep in the park. Their smells are outrageous. I can hardly decide. Clarence knows how I love to do that, so he lets me. Do not tell my mom.

Monterey Square and Madison Square are my digs, my neighborhood. Nicky, my buddy, is multicultural, so he knows more than I do about some dogs. We were babies together downtown. We're wise and older now. Nicky lives in that cool house on Bull and Gordon streets—the one with the iron balconies. Nick and I want to hang out on the balcony the way Sage gets to do at his home on the square. Sage's mom and dad, the Adlers, really talk our language. They are fun.

I have my own card at the front desk, and I've been promoted canine assistant to the sales manager, Gregory, who has been with the company from day one like me. Our responsibilities have grown, and we are a great team. He will share the sofa sometimes when he's weary, so I share, even with Patricia, who remains my favorite agent. That sofa has gotten pretty full these days as my mom saved the life of a basset hound, a beautiful girl by the name of Bella. Now get this. She was at the doctor's office the day I was diagnosed with that awful Lab disease, arthritis. She was living at the humane society, and we all know what that means. So home she came with me. I like that; I've got her in training at the office and at home. She's a quick study, but she's rather insecure. She bellows and barks when my mom leaves, and stands at the door so sad. I've had to take her into Patricia's office for comfort.

Back at home on Jones Street, Bella is still meeting and greeting the neighbors: Savannah, my old friend Labrador, just moved back from living in Macon, wherever that is. She's happy to be home again, and she brought a baby boy, Gus, with her. We love Gus and I love to kiss him. Now Bella likes Gus and Savannah too, but not like me. Hatcher, who lives next door, and we all pretty much own Jones Street. There is a fancy dog across the street. Her mom owns a nice dress shop, and she works every day too.

You see, downtown is a place to live and work and play, and it's cool to be Dune, to be famous for being the best realtor canine on the East Coast, and to live in the *best* historic city in the world. Aren't I good? Call me at any time or e-mail me at *dune@corabettthomas.com* or just give me a bark so I can tell you all about my life-style in our beautiful historic Savannah. It's Dune's life, my life, and it's a *good one*.

DUNE

SANDPIPER'S FURST ROMANCE ("ROMAN")

Downtown Savannah business owners, as well as the usual working-persons lunch crowd, are well used to seeing the eighty-five pound golden sashaying down Broughton Street with a stuffed macaw toy (or platypus, depending on what was easiest to grab) hanging out of his mouth for his daily constitutional. With the way tourists smile and elbow their buddies, you would think that Roman was part of their tour.

Roman came into my life in April 1995, eighteen months after I had lost Gophor, my thirteen-year-old companion golden. I attended a dog show in Perry, Georgia, and stood ringside and cried as I watched the eighteen goldens gaiting around the ring for the breed competition, looking like some spectacular golden fireworks display. I realized how hollow I had been since losing Gophor and made up my mind that I was ready to wrap my arms around another golden boy. As incredible luck would have it, a well-known and respected breeder had three twelve-week-old boys at the show. In very short order I had picked out Roman, and cried again as

234

I carried him back to my car. He was truly the most beautiful puppy in the world!

Roman not only immediately cured the hole in my heart, but he has worked on the heart strings of others as well. Roman took a therapy dog test, and was certified with Therapy Dog International in 1996. That meant that he could visit patients at hospice and in nursing homes. One of the partners at the law firm where I work had his dad in an assisted-living community. That was Roman's first outing—to visit all the folks at Savannah Squares. As young as he was, Roman loved needling his way through a sea of wheel chairs and visiting with all the patients. He is far more outgoing than I am. We would go into someone's room, and he would purposefully walk up to every bed and chair and slip his head under a person's hand. Whether or not they could pet him didn't matter. He just stayed there wagging up at them. At one point he visited with a woman who had had three pin strokes in as many days and was not really cognizant of what was going on around her. Roman paid a lot of attention to her, and before we left she was looking at him and *talking* to him. The nurses told me that she had not spoken since her strokes.

Roman's other accomplishments include making a commercial for a local pet cemetery (very tasteful!) and sitting in for Jody Chapin, who did the weather at that time for WTOC, Channel 11. And I mean sitting in. Roman was with me at the station one morning to promote a local dog-obedience class. During a commercial break the newscaster thought it would be funny when they returned to the air if Roman could be sitting in Jody Chapin's chair. I had about ten seconds to get him up in the swivel chair and to keep him there, sitting next to the newscaster. Somehow or other he jumped into the chair, I threw some treats at the newscaster to keep Roman's attention, hollered stay, and got out of the way just in time! He stayed sitting in the chair for that entire news segment. The television crew actually put his name on the screen right next to the newscaster's name! It was so funny!

Roman not only brings joy to my life, but to his coworkers' lives as well. Back in 1996 Roman joined me at work several times so we could do some therapy work at lunchtime. I just forgot to start leaving him home and nobody complained, and so began his nine-to-five life. Surely one of the highlights of his day is when someone has saved him a piece of their breakfast or lunch. That though has created a monster, for recently he stole a partner's lunch from right off the kitchen counter!

Lunchtime brings with it his daily constitutional, usually a walk down Broughton Street, over to CVS, across the street to where a bistro keeps a bucket of water on the sidewalk for dogs to catch a quick cold one, then through City Market and back to work. He absolutely cannot take this walk without his macaw toy. If he can't find a toy when we're on our way out, he's likely to pull a file off the shelf to take with him! He's wonderful about stopping on his walk through downtown to visit with tourists, who usually tell me that they want to pet him and think about their dog that they left home while they vacationed. I see many of them hanging off the trolleys and carriages taking his picture as he makes his way down the street with his toy dangling from his mouth.

When I take a day off work, coworkers ask, "Where's Roman?" Then they say, "Oh, is Roman's mother out today?" At the end of the day, when it's "quittin' time," Roman dutifully expresses good-night to Susan, the woman we work next to, before he waddles out the door for home, the ever-present stuffed toy hanging out of his mouth.

CAROL THOMPSON

BO

I first saw Bo with his mother walking Jefferson Street, where at that time I was parking my tour buses. Bo was only about six weeks old, cold, and starving. That was January 1996, and it was freezing in Savannah. 1996 was one of the coldest winters in Savannah in a long time. I would not get Bo and his mother out of my mind. I began buying dried dog food and putting it out for them. As all small animals do, Bo was constantly in the street. I watched with horror. I just knew that he would be killed by a speeding car. Bo's mother, a large black dog who was very street wise, began biting Bo on his right hind quarter, trying to keep him out of the street. His right hind quarter was all chewed up by the constant biting of his mother. I could not get close to either dog. But I continued to put out water and dried food.

By now, Bo was approaching eight weeks old and still very sick. I had been talking to him from across the street, and trying to get him to come to me, so far, with no luck. I saw Bo's mother less and less. She was beginning to leave Bo for long periods of time. One morning I was at the garage getting ready for the day's work,

238

when Bo, the little puppy I had been trying to get near for weeks, walked slowly over to me and laid down at my feet. He was so weak he could hardly stand up. I just bent down and scooped Bo up in my arms and rushed him to the vet.

As I was putting Bo in the car, he just kept looking at me with the saddest eyes. All the way to the vet's office I was talking to Bo and trying to reassure him everything would be all right. When we arrived at the vet's office, I picked up Bo and carried him in. Dr. Lester took one look at Bo and told me that he was not sure that Bo was going to make it, but we could try. Needless to say, after spending close to nine hundred dollars on surgery for Bo's hind quarter, mange, and deworming, Bo did make it, and today Bo is a cherished member of my family.

We had all talked about eventually getting a dog, but not just any dog. Now we have this dog of many mixed breeds. When my children and I walk Bo downtown, people will stop us to ask about Bo and what breed of dog he is. We did not know what breed Bo was, nor did we care. We thought Bo was just beautiful. We decided among ourselves that we would tell people Bo was a Red Jefferson Hound. That sounded very distinguished to us. And since Bo's coat was a very glossy red, and since we found him on Jefferson Street and he looks like a hound, that sounded good to us. It was amazing the number of people who knew all about the Red Jefferson Hound and would carry on long conversations about the breed with us. This got to be a joke with my family.

Bo is always at my side when I am at home. When anyone knocks on our door, Bo is always there to protect us from strangers. He has turned into the most wonderful guard dog. He would never let anyone hurt his family. Bo and I take long walks in the early morning as the sun is coming up and reflect on the day. It is always fun to see Bo running in the wet grass early in the morning or late in the evening as the sun goes down.

Today Bo is five and a half years old, and you could not ask for a better pet. Bo knows that I saved him, and every day he shows his love for me and my family. We could have spent a lot of money buying some expensive breed of dog, but never would we have experienced what Bo has taught us about love and reaching out to help an animal who is suffering and would have surely died without human intervention.

PAT C. TUTTLE

WYLLY WOODALL ("WYLLY GIRL")

I had just recently moved to Savannah when I met Mr. Tippins and his little brown puppy, Tilly. Barely ten weeks old, the sight of this beautiful, skinny, and one-of-a-kind mix immediately erased my years of dreaming about owning a Lab. I told him that if I ever got a dog I think I would want one just like his Tilly. Mr. Tippins told me of how his wife rescued this pup from the Veteran's Expressway. Tilly was starving, dehydrated, and abandoned to the fate of death by heat exhaustion on a hot, summer day in June. Mrs. Tippins brought this puppy into her home, made it part of her family, and nursed it back to health. Tilly was immediately embraced by the Tippins family, with the exception of their ten-year-old dog, Boogie.

Three days later I received a phone call from the Tippins, and my life changed forever. Boogie and Tilly were not getting along. They asked if I would be interested in having Tilly. "Yes," I replied with no hesitation. All I remember saying to them was "yes" and asking if I could come get her now.

Before I continue with my story, I think that I need to supply the reader with some details. I had moved from South Carolina and been in Savannah for three weeks. This was my first apartment by myself. I had always grown up with a dog, but never had any responsibility in raising the family dog. I was about to start a new job. Also, I had no clue as to the financial aspect of owning a dog or about maintaining a dog's health. Of course all these details didn't enter my mind when I accepted the responsibility of taking Tilly, but the Tippins were wise and thought about all of this. The Tippins not only explained to me the importance of loving an animal and raising one, but they guided me, helped me out financially, and were only a phone call away.

Their loving kindness has greatly blessed my life and Wylly's. Not only did the Tippins consider Wylly a part of their family, but they embraced me as well. I suppose you are wondering who Wylly is. I renamed Tilly and gave her the name Wylly after a family that opened their home and heart to me. Not to mention Wily Coyote because my Wylly will not stop at nothing when it comes to hunting squirrels.

For nearly four years Wylly and I have been inseparable. I love her dearly. Often I don't know how I could love her more, and she finds a way to open my heart wider. Wylly has continually taught me the importance of unconditional love, patience, and selflessness. She never ceases to amaze me. For example, Wylly loves to pull me to her favorite hunting ground, Forsyth Park, when I tell her it is playtime. Yet if I give the leash to my four-year-old niece, Mary Katherine, Wylly proceeds to the park like an old woman at a snail's pace. Also, Wylly loves to chase squirrels and has caught her fair share (thirty-two), but Wylly will stop within five yards of Mrs. Davidson when she is feeding the squirrels. Wylly sits and shakes until I rescue her or until Mrs. Davidson "shoos" her away. Wylly is smart and knows that Mrs. Davidson's squirrels are off-limits. She also knows that Mrs. Davidson will feed her scooby snacks if she behaves. Wylly is my best girl.

I have grown as a person as Wylly has matured. Wylly has been a great teacher of life. She is like my child. I love everything about her right down to her multiple-colored toenails. Often I just watch her and am amazed at how beautiful she is, inside and out. My favorite is when I come home and she is sitting halfway out my parlor-floor window, with an excitement on her face and the wagging tail that Mama is home. It also makes me very proud when the walking tours stop by our house on Jones Street and everyone talks to the dogs. (Wylly now has a brother, Winston. It took us three years before Tony and I decided we could love another dog as much as we love Wylly.) When she is happy, I am happy.

I look forward to reading *Savannah Dogs*. Savannah seems to be an animal friendly town. I can name numerous dogs and describe their personalities, but wouldn't be able to tell you their owners' names. Just this morning the daddy of Beau (black poodle) encouraged me to write. I always forget his name, but it's obvious that he loves his dog, and it makes me like him more as a person. The conversations between pet owners at the park or the cemetery is what I believe adds to Savannah's charm. Sorry to ramble, but one more thing. Now that Wylly has a vizsla brother, Winston, it is very difficult not to mention them both in one sentence. Thank you for reading this, but more important, thank you for recognizing how important dogs are in the lives of Savannahians.

AMY WOODALL

SAM

My person says that I am a boulevardier. It must be true, because I am happiest when we go for a walk around the city. We go to the most wonderful places and see lots of friendly people. Just a block from home are fancy shops, and the people give me a biscuit should we drop in. The postman in our neighborhood has biscuits for me too. If I see the truck, then I must track him down to say hello. It's especially fun to walk to the video store and the book store. Not only do I get biscuits, but they make a fuss over me.

In Savannah we have lots of squares that I get to visit. This is important, because I have carefully marked places in each off them saying: "Sam was here and will return soon, so leave me a message." I really like to know all the news, especially from the girls.

It's a full-time job calling on my friends, marking the streets and squares, and meeting all sorts of new people who come to Savannah. Lucky for me no one knows what kind of dog I am, so they have to ask my person. She says, "Savannah Setter," and adds, "A very rare breed found only in the downtown area." By that time the people have given me a pat and said great things like

"What a wonderful dog!" It's true; and I've had a chance to give them some extra special dog love, which will really help their day. Meeting, greeting, and giving out lots of affection to any one wise enough to let me is what I do best.

Now, my life wasn't always so great. In fact it was pretty scary. Only six weeks old, I was taken from my mother, brothers, and sisters, and dumped in Monterey Square. A storm had left five inches of snow on the ground. It was almost higher than me. It was lonely and cold, but I knew what to do—find a person to take me home. She came along just as I had hoped she would. She put me in her jacket and home we went. There two other female persons thought I was cute and wanted me to stay. The big male person said something about no more pets. It got noisy for a while, but I figured it would work out, so I ate a shoe, tore up the newspaper, wet the rug several times, and moved in. Life's been great ever since.

If you come to Savannah—and I hope you do—I'll be sure to greet you in one of our squares.

SAM

FLOWER
("FLOWER POT")

FLOWER'S DIARY

Monday: Still small, some days being a corgi can be so annoying! Can't see out of the car window, my neck hurts from looking up all the time, and my underbelly gets filthy from being so close to the ground!

Tuesday: Fantastic walk today! Was told four times how adorable I am. This is always much better than being asked what happened to my tail! The mailman remembered my treats, and I was really close to catching one of those fiendish skateboards!

Wednesday: Picnic in Pulaski Square. Hooray! One of my favorites for snacking!

Wednesday afternoon: I am supreme! I am wonderful! I surpass all dogs in my brilliance! I alone rescued a helpless baby bird! Would have missed her altogether if she hadn't been sitting next to some lovely sandwich leftovers underneath a bench I was investigating. "Oh, Flower, look what you found. What a good dog!" I think a parade or at least a medal is in order.

Wednesday evening: Hold on just a minute, this is not acceptable! I found this bird, me, the brilliant one! She is mine! Why have they put her in some foul box on a table higher than Mt. Kilimanjaro? They can't even hear her properly, for being so big their ears are disproportionate and useless! I have taken over the job of bird alert officer.

Thursday: My back is killing me! I tried desperately to get a took at my bird, but fell backwards into a table knocking over a book, which landed on my head! A golden sympathy moment, however, using my best devastated and hurt look, they moved the box to the floor. Yes, I am using my looks to get what I want, but it works for me and I can't help it.

Friday: I think they have lost their minds! They are putting *my* bird outside in the backyard! I suppose there is some logic to this; perhaps she'll get bored of hopping and fly.

Friday afternoon: Well, she did get bored and decided to go visiting; somehow she got out of our yard and went into the restaurant next door. I could hear all the cooks making a big fuss and feeding her cornbread. The injustice, I'm the neighbor who deserves such hospitality!

Friday evening: Thinking I'm never going to see my bird again, I call out my "Come back to me, I can't live without you!" yelp. It worked! The amazement of it all! My bird *flew* over the fence! I wasted no time in telling the entire city of Savannah! When my two big ones came into the backyard, she really put on a stunning air show for them. I was so proud. She knows how to work an audience, a trait she must have inherited from me!

Saturday: We are all going somewhere in the car. Hope it's the beach! Not the beach! Some place with a lot of trees, which is always nice.

Saturday evening: So this is heartbreak. I can't believe they let her fly away from me! She'll never be able to hear me from our house all the way out there! I have eaten an entire box of biscuits all by myself. This is just too tragic, I can't go on!

Sunday: Watering day! Definitely the perfect cure. I can't think of anything more therapeutic than attacking the sprinklers, not to mention the added beauty benefits of mud!

Sunday afternoon: Excitement! Have found huge frog in our fishpond! Brilliant me again!

FLOWER

DOVE

Dove, my blue Doberman, and I have been through a lot together, as has her extended family—friends who invited us to their home in Ohio for a week's vacation. On our first evening we took a long walk with Dove's pal, Keely. When we returned, Camper the cat streaked across our path. The temptation proved too much, and Dove gleefully chased Camper across a large lawn and into the woods. When Camper headed for a busy road, I knew a tragedy was about to happen. A large SUV, traveling at a speed of over fifty miles-per-hour, shattered Dove's back left leg. The force of the impact pushed her under the van causing a large area of third-degree burn as her side met the pavement.

With Dove in shock and near death, I knelt beside my beautiful dog and sobbed uncontrollably. But Dove's guardian angel appeared in the form of a neighboring vet's daughter. With cell phone in hand she reached her father on the golf course, and he met us at his office. The IV kept Dove alive while we drove to the animal hospital. Her age, robust health, and an excellent team of surgeons saved her life.

Several weeks of intensive care followed the installation of four pins and iron (metal?) fixators that ran from knee to ankle, through bone, on both sides of the leg. This elaborate and painful structure was necessary to hold the leg together because four inches of bone had been destroyed. It was promised that with time the separation would actually grow together to fill the space.

What began as a long anticipated vacation became a nightmare. When I left Ohio to return to work and flew back on weekends, my friends became responsible for Dove's care. Nursing was difficult and time-consuming. Painfully thin, Dove had no appetite. We rejoiced when she ate a little ice cream, but she turned her head away from the stews that simmered on the stove especially for her. A variety of medications were needed throughout each day, but the pills rolled in peanut butter were soon rejected. How pathetic she looked dressed in a white T-shirt to protect her injured side and a white athletic sock pulled over her bandaged leg.

Despite all, she retained her sweet and loving personality. Unhappy left alone in the first-floor den, she begged to join the action in the kitchen, which had been barricaded because of the three entrance steps forbidden in her condition.

After a month we were allowed to bring her to Savannah. On the long drive back she lay across a van seat, her head in the lap of her human seat-mate. Home, however, did not mean our home; climbing the long flight of stairs to the parlor floor was out of the question. Once again our friends came to the rescue, and we set up camp in their living room. The neighbors became accustomed to our slow walks, but tourists asked about her leg and the strange iron rods that held it together. Dog owners often stopped to observe, "This must be Dove. . . ."

I do believe Dove became somewhat of a celebrity, although we would have much preferred the renown that comes with a blue ribbon for the best of show in the Westminster Kennel Club!

DIANE LESKO

ARANTXA ("GIRLIE")

My name is Arantxa. Never guess the woman I live with plays tennis, would you? She was living with a bunch of male beings and really wanted another female to pal around with. The man of course was male; and there were two male dogs, two male cats, and one male rabbit.

My mother was living with a friend of my companion when the lady told her I was coming. My companion visited my mother when she was pregnant with me to make sure I'd be the type of girlfriend she'd like.

Sure enough, after I was born my companion came to see all of us together. We were placed on a rug and allowed to crawl around. None of us had our eyes open, so we had to go by smell. I was the smallest in the bunch, and I knew she wanted my bigger sister, so I had to make my move. I crawled as fast as my little legs would allow towards her. I finally made it to her leg, where I was able to get one paw up on her knee. I was home free after that. She announced that she had been chosen, so the search was over. Boy, was I relieved. Now all I had to do was last it out with the litter till she could come for me.

The day she finally came we were in the backyard playing with Mom, and of course I was the last in everything, even eating. The boys I lived with were so glad that I was going to a home by myself. They had been defending me until now, but I think they were getting tired of baby-sitting the runt.

I rode to my new home in my companion's hand. I was pretty small. Couldn't even maneuver one stair. She was wonderful. She took two weeks off from work, and played and held me constantly. She even made me a hot-water bottle to take long naps on so I wouldn't miss my mom. I had a new friend, Buster the bulldog, who liked me right off. He even let me bite his face and chew on him whenever I liked. He never scolded me. As I grew I started slipping off to the neighbors' houses to play with my friends I had made. Blondie, the cocker spaniel, lived on the river, and her people would let her out if I scratched on their back door. Sonny, the shelty, lived right next door and was always good for a game of chase.

I live in town now, but still have lots of places to walk and smell. My companion takes me twice a day to different places so I can investigate. There's a bird in the house, and I really don't like it. There are some rabbits outside in a cage. I'm not allowed to have anything to do with them either. I'm happy where I am. My companion comes home at lunch, and we spend a lot of time together.

ARANTXA

254

HAMPTON

My name is Hampton, named after my mommy's favorite place in the universe. When I've hit her nuclear buttons, she calls me Hamptonite. You can call me the long name, but I certainly won't answer. Won't even blink an eye. Just Hampton will do.

I don't usually go around imparting the wisdom of my five months as a Shiba Inu in books. But I'll make an exception for you today.

I don't hang out with other Shiba Inus. In fact, I'm quite rare here in Savannah. Quite honestly, pound pooches are my best buds. I find them healthier. They shed more, which gets me off the hook with my mommy, who goes around the house lighting funny smelling candles and sweeping up my hair. No matter how healthy they are, pound pooches are usually worse about stinking and shedding, so when they come over to play, Mommy realizes just how lucky she is.

Mommy has been rubbing my head and whispering into my ear a lot lately. She's begging me to give her some words to type into that machine she keeps in the family room. How many literary Shiba Inus do you think there are in the world? Not many, I wager. But I

255

live in a household of books, magazines, and newspapers and lots of dialogue bouncing all over the place. Coming into this family as a teeny-weeny pup, I was bound to be a dog of deep thoughts and few barks. I'm observant. In fact, I'm brilliant. And I have the varied experiences of my months to share, and so I shall.

Essay writing is more difficult, I believe, when one is extraordinarily intelligent, for how can I pick and choose from the breadth of wisdom harbored between my adorable ears? Yet as those very ears are stroked, they twitch in arousal. My brain is stimulated. I'm inspired. I am suddenly aware of the topic I wish to address here today—FOOD, of course. But not just any food. I would like to speak of food mixed with medicine.

Younger, less experienced canines should know that there comes a time when your mommies will mix medicine with your food. This is not pleasant, and there are ways to avoid this disgusting dietary supplement.

Approaching your dinner bowl, eye the contents carefully. Be alert for little pieces of powdery tablet. Your mommy will break the white tablet—right in front of your eyes, as if you're totally blind and stupid—and will attempt to hide the pieces under portions of your food. Shove the food around ever so gently, and you'll unearth the chalky pieces. Grab them with the barest bit of your mouth and spit them on the floor beside your bowl. Never let them touch your tongue. This is not difficult once you get the hang of it, and you'll rejoice in your mommy's ballistic reaction.

On occasion your mommy will open a capsule and sprinkle the bitter powder on your food. Again she will mix and sift and stir, thinking she's disguising the

256

terrible taste. Never. Refuse to eat. Sniff the bowl; move back a few feet. Lie down. Look at your mommy soulfully, your eyes saying, "How can you do this to me?" After a while she'll worry that you're starving to death and will pitch the powdered stuff and give you something clean to eat. The eyes. The eyes. Never underestimate the power of your eyes.

Finally, never let your mommy force your mouth open and shove a monster capsule down your throat. My mommy thinks she can do this—clamp my mouth shut with one hand, stroke my throat with the other hand, and, voilà, the medicine will go down. If you practice, you can manage to shift the pill over between your gums and your cheek. You can tell when your mommy thinks that the pill has successfully gone down because she smiles in a relieved way. She releases the grip of her hands. That's when you run into another room and spit the capsule on the carpet.

There's one more technique to spoil this provoking practice of contaminating good food with medicine. This method actually works better than the previously mentioned practices. Do this only as a last resort: Go ahead and eat the foul stuff.

Then vomit. Not one little pile, but several. In fact, if you can manage to run from room to room depositing a trail of medicated vomit in strategic places, you will have achieved your goal. Your mommy will pitch the medicine in the garbage pail, and you'll get well from whatever was initially ailing you, entirely on your own—the way my healthy pals, the stinky pound pooches do.

HAMPTON

 **HACHI**

Skin and bones. Covered with weeping sores. Abscessed eye. Heartworm, tapeworm, hookworm. Collapsed trachea. Swayback. Bad feet. Unable to bark. Bad teeth. Indeterminate age, but very old. Living out of trash and garbage cans.

We found him standing over his dead companion on the berm of President Street. Cars were passing both dogs by, and we thought of doing the same. But it was Thanksgiving weekend, and here was a creature that had absolutely nothing to be thankful for.

We turned the car around and tracked the animal through the Oak Tree Townhomes. It was easy to pick him up and put him in the car because he was too weak to protest. It was a short trip to the veterinarian, but even at that, the odor from the dog filled the van pungently.

Naturally the waiting room was full at Central Animal Hospital. Beautiful comments from the other waiting patients buoyed our spirits greatly. "My God, what happened to that dog?" "Is that a dog?" "Can he walk?" "Is he contagious?" Suddenly all the waiting animals had been pulled closer to their masters, and our hound was

258

hurried into the first empty treatment room. Fastest service we've ever had at the vet's.

Dr. Cochran said that he was the worst specimen she had ever seen. "The kindest thing would be to put him down right now. He probably has heartworm and every other imaginable thing wrong with him." So we debated for a few minutes. Check it out, we told her. We at least want him fed all he can eat for dinner so he can arrive at dog heaven with a full stomach. We waited for the test results.

Of course she was right. He did have everything possible wrong with him. But he looked up at Joe with his one good eye, and the matter was settled. Dr. Cochran said it could cost at least eight hundred dollars to save him because heartworm damage took a long time to repair and all his sores would require constant care with iodine washes three times daily. The vet couldn't even keep him over the weekend because they were full up for the holiday weekend. So he went to Jones Street and our carriage house.

During the morning walks to Chatham and Pulaski squares, he was quite a hit. He liked the trash can in Chatham the best because it sometimes smelled of chicken bones. Truthfully, he never saw a trash can he wouldn't investigate. Going down the center of Forsyth Park delighted him because the trash cans were lined up.

His name is Hachi, which means "eight" in Japanese. He is our eighth dog, and was named by a Japanese friend. We often wonder where he came from. Garden City? Miami? Air Liquide Park? Did he ever hunt coons? Did he ever hunt anything? Was he dumped after hunting season? Did he wander away by accident? We only know that we didn't steal this valuable black-and-tan coon hound. Who would?

Hachi graciously accepts all other dogs, cats, and people. He buries all food dishes, shoes, boots, and anything else made of leather because he never wants to be hungry again and maybe he can chew on the leather later when hunger returns. (We have dug up two high-tie boots, four thong sandals, one golf shoe, three New Balance walkers, and twelve leather work gloves.) Now, twenty-one months later, he has gained forty-one pounds and the sores are healed; but the swayed back, bad feet, bad teeth, congested heart damage from the heartworm, and the sore eyes remain. All this and then the final insult to a dog of the streets—castration!

The old hound is in his heaven now on our three-acre place on Wilmington Island. He can roam at will and sleep, sleep, sleep. He doesn't even waken when the raccoons run across the yard. The only thing he hears for sure is the clink of the dog food bowls and the rise of the moon. He bays at the moon and jumps with all four feet off the ground to greet Mother Luna. It is a treat to watch our Hachi . . . our Lazarus.

JOE AND EILEEN HERDINA

BAILEY MAY BELL

One time I ate a pork rib whole and almost punctured my intestine. Another time I ran so much I wore the pads off my feet and couldn't walk for a week. Needless to say, I've gotten to know my vet fairly well. Her name is Lesley Mailler, and when she told the humans I live with (Bill and Sharon Bell) that I had hermangeous carcinoma causing a five-pound tumor on my spleen, I figured it was no big deal. I assumed I would get a shot or something and that I'd be out chasing squirrels the same day. I figured wrong.

As Dr. Mailler filled Bill and Sharon in on the details, my paws began to sweat. I heard words like "surgery," "serious," "big," and the scariest word of all—"die." I've got to tell you, this is the only time I have ever envied anything about a cat. You see, rumor has it in the canine world that felines have nine lives.

The night before my surgery I was given a fresh can of tennis balls and, for dinner, a huge smoked turkey; and they took a bunch of pictures of me with Ann. Ann is Bill and Sharon's baby girl, and she is my favorite of all the humans. Now just because I'm a golden retriever

261

doesn't mean I'm dumb. All that attention could only mean one thing—the humans didn't think I would survive my surgery.

The morning of my surgery I said my good-byes and jumped up on the table at Dr. Mailler's to be put to sleep. Next thing I knew I had a very peaceful feeling and was floating in a dark tunnel moving toward a very bright light. As I got closer to the light, Lassie (my hero from the TV show) appeared and told me to go back, it was not my time. He said I had unfinished business on earth. There were more tennis balls to chase, mailmen to terrorize, smoked turkeys to chew, and squirrels to harass. Most of all, he said my humans needed me and would miss me too much if I didn't come back from the surgery.

After the surgery I found out that Dr. Mailler had removed my spleen along with the five-pound tumor that surrounded it. My recovery was slow at first, but now I feel like a puppy again. I was only given a fifty-fifty chance of living more than six months, but it has been nine months and all is well.

I do miss my spleen, but am very happy to be feeling well again and to be able to play with Ann. What's a spleen anyway?

BAILEY MAY

MULLIGAN ("MULLY")

On February 15, 1998, a friendly brown dog followed my friends and me as we played nine holes of golf at Bacon Park Golf Course. Later we went back to the clubhouse to make arrangements for our next game. The dog came up to the door and wanted to come in with us, so I let it in. I petted the dog and remarked to the manager how friendly it was. He explained to me that this female dog had been abandoned and was being fed by the guys out in the golf-cart garage. She had delivered two puppies out on the course, and both had been adopted.

"She sure is a friendly mutt," I remarked.

"You better say good-bye to her," he replied. "This is my last day here, and this is her last day. This course has been leased out to another operator. They take over tomorrow. Me and that dog leave today. I am going to take her down to the dog pound this afternoon. She can't stay here."

My wife, Gloria, and I had agreed that we would never have another dog because we travel a lot and it is too inconvenient. However, one of my golf partners,

263

who just loves all animals, persuaded me to take this mutt. He pointed out that if I did not, the dog was doomed. No one would adopt an unspayed female at the dog pound.

So I took the dog and named her "Mulligan" ("Mully," for short). A mulligan is a second shot that is granted to a fellow golfer by his friends if he has had a particularly bad golf stroke.

Mully is the friendliest dog I have ever owned. She was perfectly house-trained before she was abandoned. She was under such stress while living out on the golf course that she did not bark until about a year after I brought her home. The kids in our neighborhood like her so much that they sometimes have to stand in line to take their turn in petting her when I take her for her walk. Mully loves every minute of it.

SAM HOLLIS

264

ROBIN HOOD

There is a little dog named Robin Hood. Robin is a very happy puppy. He has big eyes and always smiles. He loves his home. He has a little boy to play with him, and Robin has a big truck he rides around in. From his seat in the truck he can see all the people and the other dogs in the town. Robin likes riding in his big truck because suddenly he is the tallest dog in all the land.

You see, Robin is a corgi, the kind of dog the Queen of England has. Corgis are sort of funny looking. They have tall ears that stand way up like a fox's. They have smiles that stretch from ear to ear. They have long bodies, but no tail. And the funniest thing is that they have very short legs. Robin's legs seem to be shorter than most. Even Wilhelm, his younger corgi brother, is taller than he is.

Robin loves people. He especially loves people who feed him food. And since Robin has a tendency to be a little, shall we say, wide around the girth, he's developed an interesting way to beg for yummy giblets of food. Robin's short and plump condition makes it a little hard for him to move around and do any sort of tricks for begging. And it takes lots of energy and hard work to look directly up at the food he's begging for. So he's slowly evolving. His eyes are slowly moving higher on top of his head. This way it won't hurt so much to hold his head so high for extended periods of time. The effect is amazing and renders his patrons helpless against his charm, cute looks, and eerie sense that they've just given food to a flounder. Robin enjoys his winnings from a begging so tactfully done.

What Robin probably wishes for the most, other than food and his big truck, is that the cats would respect him a little more. After all he is a DOG and they are just CATS, but they don't seem to register that *He* is supposed to antagonize them. Instead what happens at the most awkward moments, when people are watching or, worse, when other dogs are watching, cats stroll right up to him and use his stocky body as a rubbing post, just as if he were the leg of the person who was thinking about feeding them. No, instead they use Robin Hood as an object of affection and purr loudly to show everyone they mean business.

Robin, however, doesn't let this get him down. You see, Robin Hood is Dale's favorite pet. And Dale is Robin's favorite person. She takes him with her wherever she goes. They go to the stable to teach children how to ride horses. They go to the grocery store to buy the family food. They go to the drive-through at the bank. Robin wishes they'd have doggie treats there at the window. They go to the sandbar and swim in the river. They do absolutely everything together.

Maybe this is why little Robin feels like the tallest dog in all the land.

DALE THORPE

Cody Hooks

Like many dogs, I have a pretty nice life. I have parents who love me. I eat regularly, go for walks, and sleep indoors. Things are definitely good. Or, so I thought...

A few months ago, my life was turned upside down. My parents decided to sell our home. As any realtor worth his salt will tell you, dogs do not help sell a house. In fact, the mere presence of a canine can turn many buyers away. A dog scent in the air, a pee stain on the carpet, the occasional gnawed baseboard—all are detrimental when trying to close the sale. In order for our home to be ready to show at a moment's notice, my brother and I had to go.

My parents knew that asking anyone to take two dogs was just too much. So they strategically plotted to ship us to separate locations. As a result, I am now in the custody of my paternal grandparents.

I only thought life was sweet. Until I moved in with my grandparents, I had no idea what the good life really is. For fellow dogs reading this story (and I'm sure there are many of you), I would like to share some important

267

lessons I have learned about grandparents and why you should move in with them . . . immediately.

Grandparents don't work. It's true. They stay home all day. Which means I can go outside whenever I feel the urge. I always spend the day with someone. And I haven't spent the day in the kitchen since I moved in. In fact, I'm pretty certain my grandparents don't even own a dog gate.

Grandparents like to eat. Food is plentiful at my grandparents' house. Not just dog food, but all kinds of people treats. Since grandparents never throw anything away (yet another important lesson), leftovers often end up in my bowl. I never knew that I liked grits, eggs, or biscuits with syrup. Since I began sitting at grandma's table, I must admit that I have put on a few pounds.

Grandparents keep the same hours as dogs. At my grandparents', our motto is "Early to bed, early to rise." We wake up at 6 A.M. and go to bed by 9 P.M. On most days we find time for an afternoon nap. And no one gets upset when I need to potty during the night. Grandma is up in a flash. None of that "Cody, go back to bed."

Grandparents don't care if you sit on the furniture. This is a shocking revelation. But I've given it a lot of thought and have discovered the answer. Grandparents keep all of their furniture covered. Every sofa, chair, and bed in this house has a blanket or quilt over it. So, technically, I'm not sitting on the furniture.

Grandparents don't expect you to always be a good dog. Grandparents understand that you are a dog. You can bark at squirrels. They don't find drooling offensive. Baths are optional (or at least not required on a weekly basis). You can shed all over the house. And you don't have to perform a trick in order to get a snack.

Grandparents love unconditionally. You've probably heard this about us dogs. But it applies to grandparents. No matter where I go or what I do, they will always love me. And this is probably the best lesson of all.

As the saying goes, "All good things must come to an end." My parents' new home is almost ready, and soon I'll be leaving my grandparents'. But I'll take with me the memories of what a dog's life should be.

CODY

CHEWBACCA HOUGH ("CHEWY")

My name is Chewbacca. I think I am about seven years old. My friend Holly from Save-A-Life rescued me from death row at the pound. In other words, I am a "throw-away dog." Holly let me live with her and her other dogs until she could find a permanent home for me. Holly and her friends at Save-A-Life gathered in the park with all their foster dogs so that people could get to know us a little better, and hopefully find humans that would love us.

Charlotte noticed me right away because I reminded her of their "God-dog," Christy, the neighbor-dog who visited Charlotte and Bill regularly. Charlotte was look-ing for a surprise birthday-present dog for Bill. Holly agreed to put me in layaway for two weeks (until the Big Day), then delivered me to my new home.

Now I live with my humans, Charlotte and Bill, and Maggie and Katie, my cats. My human brothers, Darren and Kevin, go to college. I cry whenever they come home to see me. I get quite emotional sometimes because when someone leaves me I am never quite sure they will ever come back. Being abandoned will do that to a dog. But I don't dwell on the past. In fact, whenever I go out into my backyard in the sunshine I am so happy that I roll over on my back and then kick my feet up into the air as I scratch my back over the soft cool grass. Charlotte calls this doing the "happy dog." Bill often rolls on the floor with me as we play "croco-dog." I pretend that I am a crocodile about to gnaw Bill's arm off, and he grabs me from behind and wrestles me down to the floor like the Crocodile Hunter. It's a great game. Neither of us looks very dignified, but we don't care. Maggie and Katie think we are stupid.

I have many endearing qualities that make me especially desirable. For one thing, I am infinitely happy to see everybody. I love dogs, cats, and children (especially babies). I have only two enemies: golf carts and remote-control cars. I hate those things and will make every effort to catch them if I can. So far I haven't been successful, but I keep trying. I'm not crazy about thunderstorms either, but for those I hide under the bed.

My ancestry includes a Border collie and a springer spaniel. So as a result, I have a built-in desire to herd things—anything, but especially my cats. I like to keep an eye on my pack. One day a bad neighbor cat (one that wasn't so lovable) came into our yard and tried to attack Katie. My ears went up as I sprang from my deck and chased him out of the yard. Then I proceeded to "round up" Katie by nipping the back of her legs all the way back to the house. In retrospect, I'm not really sure that she really appreciated it because when we got to the door, she hauled off and slapped me right across the nose. It didn't hurt.

My life is pretty good these days. I am lucky to have

a good home, and Bill and Charlotte believe they are lucky to have me. Adopting a "throw-away dog" can be very rewarding for everyone, especially me.

CHEWY

Barben's I'll Make You Famous ("Henna")

My name is Henna. Actually I have a long, fancy name—it's "CH Barben's I'll Make You Famous JH, CGC"—but nobody calls me that. Mom and Dad just call me Henna, and that's how they introduce me to everyone. I am a vizsla, and recently became a princess. A vizsla is a Hungarian pointer, and we are incredible dogs. You don't have to take my word for it, just ask any other vizsla. I know I am a princess because Mom says I have a "title" and that I come from many, many generations of "titled" dogs. That's why there is a "CH" in front of my name. Dad likes to point out that I also have a "working title" (that's the "JH") and have many of those in my ancestry as well. I don't know about those working titles—it sounds very blue collar to me—but I guess they're okay since Dad seems very proud of them. After all, many famous individuals came from working-class backgrounds.

I was born at my Grandma Barbara's house in Atlanta. Many other vizslas live with Barbara (I'm not supposed to call her Grandma; it makes her feel old), including my dogmom, Sabrina. She's a princess too, and also has a long, fancy name. My mom and dad first came to meet me when I was just eleven days old, but I didn't get to go home with them until I was eight weeks old.

Although I was born to be a princess, I still had to work for it. When I turned six months old, Mom started taking me to dog shows. I love going to dog shows! They are so much fun, and I often get to see Grandma (oops, I mean Barbara) at the shows. She is always happy to see me, and lets me kiss her on the face and steal treats out of her pockets.

At dog shows there are hundreds of dogs, and we all want to be princesses. There is only one person who gets to decide who becomes a princess—the judge. The judge is a very important person, and we all do exactly what the judge tells us to do. We enter the ring, and trot around it to demonstrate that we are graceful and co-ordinated. Then we have to stand very still to show that we have good posture. The judge comes over to admire us, and will pet us, rub our ears, and feel our muscles. It's very important to remember to brush your teeth before going to a dog show, because the judge will check that too! After admiring everyone, the judge decides who is the most graceful, has the best posture, and strongest muscles. Quite often, that's ME! After the judge picks me, I get to have my photograph taken by a professional photographer.

At the last dog show we went to, the judge chose me over all the other female vizslas, and he gave me other prizes as well. I must have been really beautiful that day, because Mom was hugging me and laughing, and Barbara gave me a big kiss—right on the mouth!—and told me I was her "seventy-fifth home-bred Barben Champion." I don't know what all that means, but I'm pretty sure that was the day I became a princess.

HENNA

PETER RUSSELL ("PETE")

My name is Pete. It used to be Peach, but was changed for obvious reasons. I am thirteen years old. We think. None of us can remember when I was born, but I am getting old. I live in downtown Savannah in a big old house with a big old garden. I live with another dog, three cats, and my masters. Don't mind the dog too much, although she is bossy at times, but I really don't care for the cats. I try to ignore them, but sometimes they just won't leave me alone. I used to chase them, but my mistress said that was not allowed. Doesn't seem fair.

I am a pound dog. Mainly yellow Lab. Some chow? Some setter? I don't know, and since I'm not interested in finding my birth masters, I guess we'll just have to say I'm mixed-breed. I think I was lucky to have been adopted by my master. Someone else wanted to adopt me, but my master just kept coming back to visit, bringing me gifts, and the pound staff succumbed. My masters and I have been together ever since.

My masters say I am spoiled. I mean, really! Just because I bark to alert them my bone is stuck under the couch? And they say I am fat. I say I'm just big boned. At my age, eating is one of my few pleasures. When it is windy, my masters allow me to sleep on their bed even though they complain I'm a bed hog. Don't get me wrong, I'm not a wimp, but I've found my fear of wind makes a good excuse for special attention. My masters also complain about the holes I dig in the garden, and they say I shed enough hair to make a fur coat in one week. Yet they give me rawhide treats and take me for rides in the car.

At six o'clock every morning, my master takes me to Forsyth Park to meet his walking group. When it is time to go, I dance around and show off to the Saint Bernard who lives with me because she can't go. Mostly I run around the park to my favorite spots, looking for dead squirrels to roll in and puddles to get muddy. There is a big one by the tennis courts I can always count on. I then rejoin my master and listen to all the new gossip. Sometimes one of the walkers will give me a pat, but I'm usually too smelly and muddy. When we get home, I get a hosing down. It feels great. I have my master well trained.

I also love to swim. When I go swimming, and if the tide is running, my mistress makes me wear a life preserver. I am so embarrassed. I mean really, have you ever seen a Lab who couldn't swim? But she won't listen. I just try to pretend that there is nothing strange about the orange blob that strangles me and hope that there are no other dogs around.

I limp now—arthritis, you know—and I recently had major surgery. The agonies of old age have set in, but I'm feeling quite fit at the moment. All in all, I like a dog's life, mine, at least.

PETE

SPARKY BRENNAN

How much is that doggie in the window? Yes, that's me. Sparky Brennan. Cutest dog in downtown Savannah. Boy, I wish that I had a doggie bone for every time someone sees me and says, "What kind of dog is that?" Or, "He looks like a teddy bear." Or, "Oh, how cute!"

I am a soft-coated wheaten terrier, born in Scottsdale, Arizona, six years ago. I was adopted by my family when I was five months old. I flew on a plane to Savannah; and when I was greeted by my new family at the airport, they immediately fell in love with me. They laughed at my big black nose and thought I was so adorable. My family still laughs at me all the time because I'm not very coordinated. You might say I have four left feet. But, hey, it gets me a lot of hugs and doggie treats.

My job around the house is chief of security. Modesty aside, I think I do a fine job.

My favorite hobbies are attacking the broom or vacuum cleaner (much to my owner's annoyance) and going for rides in the car. Any car will do. Just shake those keys and I'm there—ready to go. So I guess you could say I'm a car enthusiast. I manage at least one ride a day. I attribute my good fortune to my family's complete and utter lack of organization.

To make a dog's life even better, Alex, the sixteen-year-old, who just happens to be a good-looking chick, takes me with her sometimes when she goes out at night—for security purposes, of course.

So that's old Sparky the dog you see all over town, living the high life.

SPARKY

SHERLOCK BENEFIELD

Wrong. Dogs don't like water, right? Just like oil and water, they don't mix . . . usually. That's what I thought too, before Sherlock came to live with Pepper, my seven-year-old schnauzer, and me.

Sherlock was a victim of divorce, and the sale of his home. His owner and her two small children had to move to an apartment; and this arrangement just wouldn't accommodate an active nine-year-old, wire-haired fox terrier who, at his advanced age, was forced to find a new home.

Sherlock had such a happy face and bright brown, button-like eyes that were full of excitement. His bark was more of an "Oh Oh" than an "arf arf." He surprised me one day by standing on his back legs and "dancing" when he wanted a cookie. After that, I was always a soft touch for the dance routine.

Sherlock and Pepper had a big, fenced-in backyard, where they ran and played together, barked, and slept. In spite of having access to a clean screened-in porch, I would often find both of them dirty from having dug a hole to sleep in. One day Sherlock was wet and dirty.

How did he get wet? It had not rained. Soon the mystery was revealed as I watched Sherlock wade into the water-garden and lie down with only his head visible! A fox terrier who loved the water? Fox terriers are not water dogs!

Time and time again he did this—to my dismay at not being able to keep his white fur perfectly white—and also had occasional intestinal disturbances on account of his drinking of nasty water. But he sure looked happy in or around the water.

Once, when my mother was visiting, she was relaxing in the bathtub and had her eyes closed a few moments. She got a big surprise when she opened her eyes and found herself almost nose-to-nose with Sherlock, who was poised to hop over into the tub with her!

A couple years later we moved. No water-garden at our new home. A kiddie pool of clean water didn't interest him. Getting a bath every couple of weeks was the closest he got to water now, and he never seemed to mind.

In January 2001 Sherlock became sick and, despite veterinary care, he died at the age of twelve and a half. I miss my Sherlock so much. He was pure joy, and full of energy, surprise, and love.

CAROL BENEFIELD

DICKIE, DARLING ("D-D")

A few days after the death of my sixteen-year-old Momma Dog, I received a telephone call from the manager of the Chatham County Animal Control facility telling me about a "special" little dog that was due to be destroyed within the next forty-eight hours, and that the dog looked remarkably like Momma Dog. (Momma Dog had been a pound-rescue many years previously.) The manager wanted to know if I would be interested in adopting her. My heart was still aching from my loss, and I had several other dogs and cats. I did not feel that the time was "right" to adopt somebody else. I told her that Save-A-Life would try to find an available foster home in order to save the life of a "cute little fawn and white dog, approximately six months of age."

I contacted Pam Chumley, a Save-A-Life volunteer, and asked her to try and find a foster home within the next forty-eight hours.

No foster home became available. The day arrived when time was up for the little dog. I received a frantic call from Pam early that morning, telling me that the manager of the pound had reluctantly put the little dog into the gas chamber, and just as she closed the door, the dog started scratching hard on the glass panel, looking at her intently, as if to say, "No, not me . . . not me." At that point she pulled the little dog out and then called Pam to *please* come and get her.

"Did you go?" I asked.

"Yes, but I can't keep her here." (Pam had five children, one of whom was a six-month-old baby. And, of course, she also had pets of her own.)

I was in a quandary. Obviously this little dog was not meant to leave the world at this time. I did not have too long a period of time to worry about the situation, because within an hour Pam was on my doorstep—with the little dog in her arms. She was the image of my Momma Dog—except for the different coloring!

The first words from my husband were, "You know, we do not need another dog." Pam responded by asking if we would please just foster for a few days, promising that she would find her a good home.

We had the little dog spayed immediately, and started house-training her. What should we call her? When the Queen of England does not know somebody's name, she has a habit of calling them "Dickie, Darling." So we followed her example—she became "Dickie, Darling."

Almost three months passed. One day, when Pam was at our home, my husband reminded Pam that she had promised to find a good home for "Dickie, Darling" in "a few days." She responded, "That is right. And I did!" So Dickie, Darling became ours. Of course, we were already completely smitten by then!

Over the years Dickie, Darling has been a wonderful

dog. She was a bright, spirited youngster at six months. She loved to play chase with Belle, our old Afghan hound, and would snuggle up in her bed with her at nighttime. They would roll and play together. Our other dogs and cats also accepted little Dickie, Darling. She seemed to understand that it was their home first, and was never aggressive toward them in any way. In fact, as they began to pass away from old age, she mourned for all of them!

Dickie, Darling is always the first to greet people when they come to our home. Her little tail wags as hard as it can. She likes to get into people's laps, but never forces the issue, and is generally quite content just to lie at one's feet and look up in an adoring manner. She is sensitive, loving, gentle, obedient, intelligent—more reasons enough for her life having been saved! I often wonder who her original owner was, and why the owner never came to look for her.

At seventeen and a half years of age, Dickie, Darling is very gray around the face, has very few teeth, and is partially deaf. Her eyesight is also failing. She still, however, is enjoying life at this point. The occasional limp occurs, and she will look at me as if to say, "What is wrong with me?" But the next minute she is digging into her toy-box looking for her favorite toy to throw around. Of course, at her age, she now has to have several small meals a day, and her food has to be mashed up for her with warm broth. I find that we also have to go on many more "mini-walks" each day. She is a great communicator—just gives me her special look, and I know that she is either hungry again or else she needs to "go" again!

I am looking forward to having her with me for some time yet to come, and feel grateful for the seventeen-plus years we have already spent together. Her undying love, devotion, and appreciation will be hard to replace. What an honor to have her in my life. What a loss it would have been without her. Just hope that when I reach her age in human years, I will be as gracious as she.

Stay a while longer, Dickie, Darling. Gosh, I am *really* going to miss you!

DEBORAH J. FRIEDMAN

MAXINE

Woof!

My name is Maxine. I was born in Long Island, New York, six years ago. I remember it so clearly; I was just a little puppy. Six weeks after I was born, I took a long trip to Savannah, where my great life began with the Maleki family. Now I am a true transplanted Yankee. I have so much fun here, especially with the four Maleki boys. When they are out playing, they somehow include me in their games. Sometimes they get in trouble, but mostly we have a great time and everyone is happy. My favorite games are fishing, crabbing, and shrimping (unlike fetch-and-catch). Those boys are so good at it. They are out on the river all summer long. I love to see their catch jumping up and down on the dock. I enjoy playing with and eating the bait fish. During the school year, I wait patiently for the boys to come home from school to play with me. For all this fun, I have a few responsibilities—including the guarding of the homestead and making sure all strangers know I am there at all times.

I am the type of dog that has an intimidating appearance, but often have been accused of being a Lab trapped in a Doberman's body. I have to let you know a secret. I am deathly afraid of thunder and lightning or any other very loud noise. Not too long ago, the boys and their friends set off fireworks on the Fourth of July and scared me to death. Now the boys know my secret, and I know their secrets too! Yesterday one of the twin boys broke a large dining room window. So far, no one has confessed and I am keeping my nose out of this one! I see the boys coming. Got to trot!

Woof, woof!

MAXINE

SYRR RUN'S QUICK CHASE ("CHASE")

Greetings! My formal (AKC) name is Syrr Run's Quick Chase, but you can call me Chase. I am a three-year-old male boxer. I live on Tybee Island beside the marsh. My family includes Ted and Jan, retired adult humans, and me. Our family gets to spend a great deal of time together, and I go everywhere with them.

Let me get my bragging out of the way. I was born at Syrr Run's Boxers in St. George, South Carolina. I am brindle with a white chest, a long white stocking, and four white paws. If I say so myself, I am a very striking boxer, and many humans have told me so. Both my sire and dam are AKC champions, and, in fact, back four generations there are only two non-champions!

Why do they call me Chase? When I was a baby I had some health problems and fell behind my littermates in size and strength of leg. Since I spent my early weeks "chasing" to catch up, my breeder began to call me Chase. By the time Ted and Jan were ready to adopt me, I considered that my name. I was a member of the "Q" litter, and "Quick" was a natural addition to my name.

Because I got a slow start, I was small for my age. A show-quality boxer male has to be big and strong, and my breeder didn't think I would measure up. She was willing to let me be adopted by folks looking for a pet. Ted and Jan were looking for a female puppy because they believed a female would be smaller and easier to raise. I demonstrated to them, however, that I wanted them to adopt *me*. I did this by sitting close to Jan in the whelping box and making eyes at her while she talked with the breeder. They adopted me.

I must admit that I didn't stay the small male I was expected to be. I grew in size and spirit, and in my opinion matured to show quality. Jan tells me all the time how beautiful I am! I have been a handful to train and civilize, but least you think it impossible, I did get my Canine Good Citizen title. I have always been trained with treats and petting, and have learned well. I am actually very easy to train, as I am very smart, but sometimes have to act up just to keep them on their toes. I have my moments when Ted and Jan refer to me as "dog out of control," but they tell me I keep their lives from being boring.

I am not *all* play. My vet refers to me as a very contemplative dog. I spend a good part of my time trying to understand my world. For instance, each morning, when I first go outside for my walk, I stop on the top of the stairs to look, listen, and smell in all directions. Living on the marsh makes this a joyous experience and the beginning of another good day.

I live like a king and am so lucky to be part of such a loving family. We have a lovely life together. One thing I know is that the boxer breed is special, and I am a special boxer. I am very friendly and love people and am always looking for folks to pet me. However, to me, Jan and Ted are tops!   CHASE

BELLA

Bella is . . . definitely a "Savannah Dog!"

To me, she has the energy of a marsh sprite or a tree fairy, like a creature that would flit through the mucky reeds or dance in the woods around the moss-laden live oaks found here. She actually looks like a moss-fairy, with her scrappy, mussed-up, grayish-black hair, and ears that stick out for miles, dripping on the ends like the thready stems of Spanish moss—every twitch an expressive clue to what she's thinking or feeling. And her snappy brown eyes sparkle with her endless curiosity and mischief—a joy to behold! She loves the beach at Tybee, she loves oysters, and she's very social, like any proper Savannahian would be. And she's a good sport, as those who have seen her in her hot-pink feather boa at brunch about town can attest.

Bella is . . . a companion and a snuggle-bunny who sleeps with her head on my pillow, and keeps me toasty in the winter, like a warm, live teddy bear that snores. It's *her* bed, really. She just lets me squeeze in.

Bella is . . . a gift, because it is she who is responsible for instigating certain important changes in my life. In fact, the mere adoption of her was the impetus for me to finally change my residence—something for which I was experiencing inertia to put into action. I wasn't even planning on adopting a pet. But there she was, in the very last cage of the very last row at the Savannah Humane Society. There were four other people on the list to adopt her, but Providence moved, and Bella was mine!

Bella is . . . a teacher. Although she's only four, she recently had a stroke, which suddenly left her paralyzed and unable to move the right side of her body. It was pitiful and scary, and I was going out of my mind because it was something I couldn't control. Imagine that! But with weeks of physical therapy Bella has made a miraculous recovery! And through this experience, Bella, again, has instigated movement in my life, by showing me how truly lacking I have been in attending to my spiritual life. When this happened to her, I turned to prayer like never before and realized that my fear would not have been so great had I cultivated a more active sense of faith. An important awareness. And by continuing to personally administer to her physical therapy, Bella has taught me that it takes consistency and action to truly love and care for oneself. In taking care of her, it has taught me a little about what it means to take better care of myself.

So, as Bella and I continue to love and learn from each other, I am expecting that there will be more lessons—and I will be the curious student. Bella, to me, is more than just a dog. But out of all the dogs she could be, I'm glad she's a Savannah one. And I'm glad she's mine.

ALYSON BEASLEY

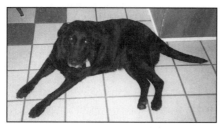

LADY DOG
("LADY")

Lady Dog is our seventy-pound black Lab. Sweet, lovable, and friendly, she has a healthy appetite for everything except raw vegetables. Lady is especially found of hallah, the twisted egg bread we eat at Friday dinner in honor of the Sabbath. Lady has learned the Friday evening ritual. After I light the Sabbath candles, chanting the blessing softly, family and guests gather around the table singing a hymn welcoming the Sabbath. We bless each of our sons. By this time Lady is positioned at my husband's side, waiting. He continues with Kiddush, the prayer over wine that ushers in all holidays as well as the Sabbath. Sensing what is coming next, Lady shifts her weight from left paw to right paw and back again. The embroidered hallah cover is lifted from the bread. The proper prayer over bread is recited, and a piece of bread is dipped into salt and passed around the table for all to share. The fresh-baked smell wafts downstream to Lady's nose, the organ that clearly governs her body.

The next slice of hallah is for Lady, and she knows it. Lady is normally quite docile, rarely barks, and seldom growls. But if the hallah doesn't come her way fast enough, she does both, as if to say, "It's my turn now—hurry up. It's *Shabbos* [Yiddish for 'Sabbath'], where's my hallah?" Perhaps she's actually the incarnation of a Talmudic scholar and knows that by Jewish law the hunger of one's animals takes precedence over one's own. After consuming her initial allotment of hallah, Lady sits down next to the diner most likely to continue to feed her more hallah. When Grandpop Bernie was living, he was the generous one. Since his death, Lady posts herself by Pop-Pop's chair. She knew to stay away from Mom-Mom, who chose to ignore the salivation and low-pitched growling. Lady also avoided the small children as they were frequently intimidated by her size and large canines, and were not likely to offer handouts.

We usually purchased our hallah from a local caterer. Standard sized, baked in a rectangular pan, the loaf fit nicely onto the special olive-wood cutting board on our table. Occasionally a guest might bring homemade hallah, which tasted and smelled infinitely better. One *Shabbos*, our guests brought a magnificent loaf; easily twenty inches long, it hung over the board and extended off the table as well. My husband raised the hallah and recited the blessing. He replaced the loaf and started to cut—with a knife—from the right-hand side. Lady approached the table and began to cut—with her teeth—from the left-hand side! Before we could stop her, she had removed a nice chunk of the bread! At least she had the good sense to wait till after the blessing. We should have scolded her, but we were all convulsed with laughter. I removed the hallah, estimated the contamination, cut it off, and we resumed our dinner. Fortunately our guests had a pet of their own, and they accepted this rather unsanitary incident as part of life in the Sacks household.

DR. LINDA SACKS

KUDZU SHELL ("KUDZ," "ZULU," "KUDZU KINS," "KUDZU-FACE")

Okay. There once was an alpha mom. And her name was Blake. She had a lot of great friends who went to college with her. But she was still a little lonely because she didn't have the one relationship that she needed most. And then a little puppy-doggie named Kudzu was born. And when Blake's professor told her that he had a litter of grandchildren and that she could have one, she was very . . . upset. What? Why would she be upset? Ever since her favorite family-doggie had passed away, she had wanted a doggie in order to form a family with just her; not her mother's or her father's, but just hers.

But she was upset because she didn't know if she could care for a puppy as much as she needed to. She was curious, however, about a puppy that had been described as a huge white German shepherd–small spaniel mix, so she went to see it.

This is where I come into the story. I was hanging around with my brothers and sisters, kind of toward the back. (Compared to me, the rest of the litter was a little bit hyper.) So when Alpha Blake picked me up, I was surprised. The others were cuter in that puppy way of being cute (although I did turn into a very handsome dog, in that baby-swan-not-as-cute-duckling revenge that some of us are lucky to have). So I met my alpha; and she told me that she loved me. And then I was hers. So, during the fifteen months that I have been alive, I have stuck with her pack. She is alpha, and sometimes I listen to the other humans with her, but I know that I'm really second in command.

I really liked Sewanee, the Mountain where we stayed for a year. The police didn't make us wear attachments to our alphas. So I ran around with other dogs while we waited for our alpha moms and dads to get out of the buildings that they called "classes." But after a very strange week called "graduation," we moved to Savannah. I love the hunting ground that Mom calls the "park." The outside rodents with big tails are much slower than they are on the Mountain. One of my first days here, I actually caught one.

I was so surprised to catch a rodent that I dropped it, which was very embarrassing. Luckily no dogs saw it, and Alpha Blake pretended not to notice. So I kept practicing, and I killed one the other day. It was my biggest accomplishment, except the protection of my home from what Mom called the "landlord." He was a man who, unannounced, frequently came over to our house, so I had to chase him away a lot. Mom didn't want to bring the rodent home to eat. I have no idea why not. She made me leave it, but I have been intent on killing more now. How nice it is to have a large hunting ground for the dogs plus all of the small ones in the city. Savannah is a nice place for doggies. Next we'll work on taking back the beaches.

KUDZU

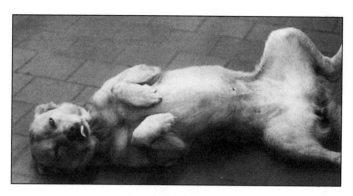

AMOCO

Where does one start when referring to man's, woman's, best friend? Noooo, it's not like the relationship with your spouse. It goes off on its own tangent—creates with it a unique set of values, strange demands, and un-requited desires by both participants. The relationship between dogs and their owners is pure love.

As the owner of two mongrel dogs, and under direction to limit my discourse to only one of my canine buddies, whom do I leave out? Simba, the 125-pound, mix black Lab, or Amoco, my thirty-pound, Chatham County common cur? Both have interesting and diverse "tails" to tell, if only they could tell it themselves. Thus I have been cast as both benefactor and narrator. Here is Amoco's tale.

Simba was nearly three in human years when I came upon the mutt that became known to all as "Amoco." On a miserably cold and rainy November morning, I was descending from my truck when I spotted a small, wet fur ball sticking its cold, wet nose out from under a Dempsey Dumpster. The dumpster was located behind the old ice cream factory on Forty-first and Montgomery streets. It had been raining for days, and the small depression under the dumpster was full of water. This was Amoco's home. The drenched puppy whined and cried when I approached it, but then tried to bite me when I extended my arm. Imagine the nerve of this little creature, turning down a perfectly good, half-eaten Quarterpounder with cheese! Again I tried to coax the freezing cold, wet, little puppy from its haven under the dumpster. She would have none of it.

The next day I again had business with the repair shop behind the ice cream factory. The rains had ceased, leaving behind the bitter cold, pushed by the harsh November wind. Again there was the puppy, still cold and still wet. The depression under the dumpster was still full of water, and there was puppy, snug in her haven, water and all. I ignored the puppy's whine as I went about my business. On the way out I quizzed the shop owner about the creature under the dumpster. He only offered that it had been there for several days. Again I approached the muddy little fur ball. But this time I was armed with a sausage biscuit from the table of Mrs. Wilkes. I was not to be denied. The dog's milk teeth bared, snarling and snapping at my hands. I reached within the confines of the dumpster depression. Grabbing the hapless creature by the scruff of her neck, I endured the hardship of her terror as she squirmed and fought me to the truck. We soon settled into the warm confines of my pickup truck while the starved little creature devoured some of the best eats in town. Now I had two mouths to feed. How was Simba going to react to his new roommate?

After numerous trips to our favorite vet, Amoco

settled into a daily routine. She had been abused and was slow to gain confidence and trust, but with Simba to guide her we have all become close friends. The question arose immediately, What kind of dog is Amoco? Pure mutt, right? We have all seen these mongrel dogs, well past their glory days, curled up under the front porch of a house. Might even be a pack of them, fox-like in looks and demeanor, as they prowl their domain, sniffing for scraps of food. We drive on by, giving them faint notice and little else. What was revealed at the vet caused even more questions than answers. Seems that Amoco's DNA is similar to those first dogs to cross into America, via the Bering Straight, some eight thousand years ago. So my Chatham County common cur might have more than just a little lineage behind her. No matter her origins, she will always be my good friend and companion.

BROTHER LOGAN

HERCULES

This little ball of teeth and fur came into our family on Valentine's Day 1997. He was a little over five weeks old and the runt of the litter. We picked him out of the entire litter of the cutest Jack Russell terrier puppies you have ever seen. He was so bold. He walked right up to my son and sat in his lap and claimed us as his. He has been a very loved member of our family ever since. We named him "Hercules," a name truly fitting this little mighty might.

He has the energy of five dogs combined and is extremely intelligent. He has trained us well. Every morning we are greeted with a wagging tail and a big lick, I mean "dog kiss." It is his way of letting us know that sleep time is over and Hercules time has begun. Every evening we are greeted by him at the front door—tail wagging, unconditional love, you can't beat that.

Sometimes, when we are distracted, he will quickly divert our attention back to him by leaping up from the floor, snatching whatever it is we are holding, and running off so we will chase him. And chase we do. He is like a greased pig, and this task usually involves calling reinforcements from the rest of the family. He is still small enough to get behind the sofa or under the bed, just out of reach.

When we are reading or watching television, he will jump up into our laps and roll over for that all-important belly-rub. He will not be denied. We managed to find an indestructible little red ball that he likes us to throw so he can catch it. We are exhausted long before he is. In our attempt to end the game, we will sit still with our hands folded on our laps so we can no longer catch the ball. This will not do. He will jump up on our laps, taking his paw and opening our hands to place the ball in our hands. He has this look on his face like, "How many times do I have to show you this before you get it?"

He loves to go for his afternoon walk. He just bounds down the street, ears bobbing and tail wagging, like he is king of the street. The children on our street all love him. When he goes by their front yards, they usually stop playing and run to him and yell, "Hercules, Hercules." They pet him and play with him. They love him and he loves them. This little bundle of energy has brought much love to our family.

KATHY BUCHOLZ

300

DUNCAN LEE

Hi! I'm Duncan Lee, and I want to tell you, life is good. This is especially true for me, considering how close I came to not having one.

My story starts in the Effingham Animal Shelter, where I was given my *first* chance to find a new home after being left there because I had been too much trouble for someone who didn't have time to care for me. Being a devilishly handsome dude, it didn't take too long for someone to notice me and decide that I would be a great playmate for their little boy. I knew I was up to the job and really tried to show how well I would take care of the lad. Unfortunately I seem to have gone about doing so in all the wrong ways. Every time I tried to play with my new buddy, he would run away or start screaming. Great, I thought, he really wants me to chase him; and I always managed to catch him. My new mom didn't seem to understand what was going on, and blamed *me* for being too rough and aggressive! No one would believe that he really wanted me to chase and grab him! Why else would he run and squeal like that? I couldn't figure it out, and wasn't getting much help from anyone else either. All I knew was that he wanted to play chase, I did, and then got yelled at for it. Go figure.

This behavior pattern soon earned me a trip to the Humane Society in Savannah. Everyone at the shelter recognized how great I looked, and they had the world's largest supply of tennis balls for me to chase. This was perfect! I wanted to claim everyone there as my human. I liked them even more than my boy at the last home. It wasn't long, and another family decided that I was going to be the perfect pet for them. I was determined to try even harder to please this time. They had children too, and I was not going to let this chance go by without letting them know how much I enjoyed them.

Well, they didn't seem to appreciate me and my efforts any more than the last people did. Every time I caught one of their children for them, everyone got upset. Pretty soon my new family started yelling at me. I thought they wanted me to try even harder, and they just decided I was being too aggressive. I tried even harder, and all that happened was everyone got even more upset. So, it was back to the shelter and I was homeless again.

Now I was really confused, but being back at the shelter wasn't all bad—lots of people to play with, and those tennis balls were great. This time, however, instead of letting me play the way I wanted to, I kept finding that when I caught one of the people with my mouth, I ended up biting myself too. It didn't take very long to realize that it was not very pleasant being on the receiving end of my own enthusiasm. People didn't like me holding them with my mouth! I did it as a puppy and they thought it was cute, but now that I'm grown up, no one likes it anymore. It didn't take long to learn what my mistake was. Why didn't anyone tell me this before? So here I was, homeless again.

Every time I went to catch one of the people at the shelter, they let me know it was considered bad manners to take their hand in my mouth! They were pretty persistent about it too. I finally figured it out (most of the time, anyway) and was content to let them pet and hug me, instead of me having to claim them. After that it didn't take long for me to attract a really nice lady who saw that I was both cute and pretty well mannered. *At last*, a real person of my own. All that was left was a trip to the vet for my shots and to be neutered, whatever that meant.

End of story, right? Not quite.

It seems that my new companion had another companion of the same species, and this companion decided to surprise her with a special Valentine's Day present. You guessed it, a new puppy. Now I know I'm a good-looking guy, but how was I going to compete with that? I never got the chance to find out. As I sat at the vet's clinic waiting to go home, she called the Humane Society and told them she couldn't take me, and would they try to find me another home?

Now for the good part. When the Humane Society found out what was going on, they sent the boss to pick me up. We got in his truck and I realized this was the same guy who convinced me not to show people I loved them by biting them. Did I feel sheepish when I found out that it was back to the big house, *again*! I mean this time I hadn't even had a chance to screw things up.

Well, he looked at me, I looked at him, and we decided enough was enough. I've been his buddy for almost two years now, and it looks like this is going to work. I have two cats of my own, and get to go to lots of events to visit with other dogs and kids, and even get to visit new friends at the shelter and schools a couple of times a week. So, like I said, life is good. This is especially so when I think about how many others like me still need a chance. I had four, and needed all of them. Some of us take a little longer to figure things out, but we can learn if *you* give us a chance.

DUNCAN

NORBECK ARABIA ("PATCH")

My name is Norbeck Arabia, but I go by "Patch." I was born on April 27, 1998, in the town of Biggar, between Edinburgh and Glasgow, Scotland. My father, Park Brecks Breeze, is a black, hunting English cocker and a field champion. My mother is Norbeck Megan, a blue roan cocker. After the normal weaning period, my breeder turned me over to Harry Shaw, a well-known trainer of spaniels, who lives in nearby Leadhills, Scotland.

For the next two and a half years I lived with Harry and his wife. My daily routine consisted of walking (really running) the grouse moors. I mostly chased rabbits, but I was especially partial to grouse whenever I could find them. I lived in the kennel with three other English cockers and two springer spaniels. If I flushed three or four really big hares, Harry would let me sleep in the house, which made the other springers and cockers very jealous.

When I turned two, Harry took me to several field trials and I rewarded him with first- and second-place performances. In November 2000, when I was showing real promise as a field champion, a Southern gentleman phoned who was looking for a top hunting companion. Well, to paraphrase the conversation, "Money talks and dogs walk." On November 9, 2000, Harry introduced me to this Southern gentleman in Suffolk, England. I showed my new owner that I was an experienced champion retriever, and that I could handle pheasants even though I only weighed twenty pounds.

Oh, I would miss the words and poems of our famous Bobby Burns and the beautiful Scottish moors that I covered each exciting day; but the time had come for me to travel across the ocean to the United States and be part of the renaissance of the English cocker as a gun dog. I would learn to flush upland birds and retrieve doves and waterfowl. Incidentally, I am not the first English cocker to arrive in Savannah. In 1999 my new owner's son had flown over to Scotland and picked up "Sooty," a five-year-old English cocker spaniel. Sooty and I get together every so often and discuss war stories about Harry.

When I arrived in Bluffton in November, two experienced Brittany spaniels, Gussy and Winnie, welcomed me. They immediately let me know that they had seniority in the kitchen and during sofa time with my new owner's first lady; however, it didn't take me long to convince them that I could keep up with them on our two-mile hikes and romping through the quail woods of lower South Carolina. Not only did Winnie and Gussy welcome me to the "low country," but so did the *Savannah Morning News*, when they took a picture of me and ran it in their December 30, 2000, edition of "People over 60 who can make a difference in Savannah."

I could go on and on about myself, but I want to finish by telling you about a special "doggie" doctor who saved my life last month. As I was taking my normal morning walk with Winnie and Gussy, I was struck by a cranky reptile while trying to bury a stick. Since good Scottish hunting dogs are trained not to bark, I did not make a sound. As the day progressed, however, my ear had swollen to the size of a softball. My owner rushed me to Dr. John Schoettle, who diagnosed the bite as one from a large diamondback rattlesnake. He gave me expert care, injecting me with 500 cc of anti-snake venom. Thanks to Dr. Schoettle, I am back to my original energetic self—minus some hair on my right ear. My owner and I are committed to helping Dr. John build some doggie parks in the Savannah area. These are badly needed so that owners and their dogs can have quality times together in fenced areas.

I am off to Alaska to hunt ptarmigan and shoot ducks in Saskatchewan. When I come back I can be found on Charlton Street, and anyone who would like to help with Savannah Dog Parks, please give me a bark.

PATCH

JJ
("J-Bird")

It's spring cleaning at the Perigard house, and the whole family is involved. My room is on today's agenda, and at noon we're moving along quite swiftly. We saved the biggest task for last, my waterbed. As anyone who owns a waterbed knows, they are fun to sleep on and even more fun to move. One must drain the water first, then disassemble and move, then reassemble, refill, and heat. So now the whole family's attention is focused on bringing the hose through my open second-story window to drain the water.

Throughout this entire day, as during any other day, our three-year-old yellow Lab–golden retriever mix, JJ, is milling around the house. We haven't had her for very long, and she has had two previous owners in her short life, so training has been tricky. Her prior owner had intended for her to serve as a guard dog, but this dog would lick a stranger to death before she would harm one. Also, she has no bias when it comes to attention; to her, any attention is good attention. Her combination puppy mentality and string of past homes has left her a little fearful and disobedient, to say the least. However, the furthest thing from our minds during this process is our bullheaded dog. So my parents and I are hovering over my depleting bed, and my dog is planning her secret escape.

JJ has been in my room all day, but is now being what we call an "underfoot dog." All dogs are underfoot dogs, even if only occasionally. You're cooking or talking on the phone, and your dog is at your side, begging or bugging you, for any spare attention you may have—as if you pay no attention to them whatsoever. The bed is taking a while to drain, and JJ's solicitation of attention is getting worse. After tripping over her twice and nearly stepping on her a third time, my aggravated stepmother screams, "JJ, *move!*" In a moment of panic, and taking the advice quite literally, JJ turns and jumps out the second-story window! We all rush to window expecting to see an injured dog, whimpering for our help, but she is nowhere to be found. Not only was she all right, but she didn't even break a fingernail! Her cunning escape has earned her the nickname "J-Bird."

THE PERIGARDS

309

SYDNEY

As soon as my leash is on and I'm out the front door, I'm ready. I know they're out there waiting for me.

Suddenly I'm no longer the lazy creature lounging on the couch. I'm a boxer on a mission. My eyes scan the sidewalks to the treetops and back again, searching for any sign of a bushy tail. It's a tough job, this squirrel-hunting business, but someone's got to do it. When I'm on the scent of one of these rascally rodents, I'm more than just a dog. I'm a sleek white tiger, a crouching tiger, if you will. Those squirrels don't stand a chance, not when I'm around.

You see, the squirrel isn't the smartest nut in the tree. Those beady-eyed creatures think they can sit on the sidewalk as I approach in super stealth mode and dart up a tree at the last minute, but I'm too crafty for them. With my long pink tongue flapping in the breeze, I charge, dragging my person along behind me. (I know she secretly loves to chase squirrels as much as I do.) But while some lesser squirrel-hunting dogs might just stop at the bottom of the tree, I keep going. I run up the trunk like a crazed cheetah. Maybe I don't always make it to the top, but I think the squirrels understand that I mean business.

What's that? You want to know how many squirrels I've actually caught? Well, let me think . . . there was that day in Colonial Cemetery. Oh, what a great day that was! I found, er, I mean, I caught, this squirrel. He was just kind of lying there on the ground. He made it so easy I almost didn't bother with him, but what the heck? A squirrel's a squirrel in my book. So I picked him up in my mouth and galloped back over to my person, who was standing with a group of other humans. I couldn't wait to show her what I'd gotten. So why was everyone looking at me in horror? I was just doing my job. I thought they'd be impressed. But they're people, and as I always say, you'll never figure *them* out.

Well, I think I'll go chew on a pig's ear for a while and plot my next attack. I know the squirrels think they can outwit me, but I'm always two steps ahead of them. As long as I'm on patrol, no Savannah squirrel is safe.

SYDNEY

311

CAESAR'S PALLAY HAHN ("CAESAR" OR "BUB")

Hello. My name is Caesar, and I am an oversized, short-haired, miniature Dachshund. I live with my parents and two Yorkshire terriers. At two years old I am the baby of the family. I cry when my parents come home, I am so excited. Yippee! I try to not jump on them, but I am so happy, I have to nibble on their ears.

I love to eat, and you can tell by my size that I am not lacking when it comes to getting enough. I have to eat by myself as I would eat my share of the dog food and the Yorkies'. If they forget and leave out the Yorkies' food, I run straight for their dish and eat as fast as I can, hardly taking a breath. I know what it means when people say "breakfast and dinner." I run for my room (the laundry room) and get behind the gate. I know that if I am behind the gate I will get my chow. I used to try to get behind the gate even when it wasn't in position because I know I will get fed if I am behind the gate. My parents don't give me people food, so on occasion I must help myself. One day I jumped onto the kitchen table to eat three miniature Payday candy bars and half a granola bar. My mom heard the wrapper rustling and came running. She found me in the middle of the kitchen table. Busted! What could I do, but the "happy-to-see-you-mom tail wag." I am very clever. If there is anything to be found, I will snoop it out. I also like to eat soap, shred paper, and take Kleenex out of the garbage to chew. I once found some gum in the purse of my mom's friend and started to chew. I had such minty fresh breath after that.

I love to be around people and always sit on someone's lap or with them on the couch, but always under the covers. Even when it is hot, you will find me buried deep under the covers. I can get under the covers by myself when I have to, but I prefer to wake someone to lift it for me. I have my parents trained well!

A favorite thing is to play chase with my thirteen-year-old sister. I don't really want to catch her, just make her run. I act like I can't catch her and she gets wild, and I start running circles around the living room furniture. I also like to wrestle-play with my three-year-old brother. I usually get the best of him. I am double his size and can throw my weight around. I insist that male Yorkies are not supposed to wear ribbons in their hair, so I bite it out every time my mom tries to put his hair up. It works great to pull him around too.

The most favorite thing I like to do is ride in the car. If the front car door is open, I will jump in and go to the far back side of the car so that my parents can't get me. They will either work hard to get me out or take me for a ride. Dad usually takes me for a ride. I have left my mark all over our windows with my long nose. It is rare that a suitcase is packed without my help. It either makes a nice bed or I will take out those things that my parents pack, which I feel aren't necessary for the trip.

Last year I was in the Wiener Dog Race. I was just about the biggest boy there. I wasn't sure what I was really supposed to do, so I watched some of the others first, then I took off running. I can run pretty fast, but I didn't win the race. At least I didn't come in last. My parents take me for long walks around our neighborhood. I consider myself in training for the race this year. Come watch. I love to show off for the people of Savannah.

CAESAR

THE TASMANIAN DEVIL ("TAZ")

There are probably a lot of reasons why people tag their dogs with the names they do—their dogs' looks, their personality, they remind them of some other pet or person they know. Whatever the reason, dog owners look at the furry little face and say, "That's a fido," or "Hey, killer," or "Ooh, my little fru-fru." Not us.

For the first two months of our little five-pound toy poodle's life, he was nameless. I know. Shame! Shame! But during those two months he was earning his name. And believe me, we tried several names, but for one reason or another none of the names that we tried stuck or did him justice.

He was born on April 24, 2000. He weighed twelve ounces, and would fit in the palm of your hand. He was mostly white with a tint of apricot, and of course had the sweetest face. We tried "Rusty" because of his color. But, no, color could change. We then tried "Dusty" and "Fluffy" because his hair was so thick and curly. But after his first puppy cut, it just didn't seem to fit. Our next attempt was "Bogart II" after our previous poodle, but

315

my wife, Judy, said his personality was just not loving enough to be a Bogart.

During the whole time that this process was going on, our little fur ball—who by now I was calling, oh, "No Name"—was busy earning his own name.

I mentioned earlier his first puppy cut. On that day, when Judy picked him up, the groomer mentioned how cute he was and what a handful he was. Everyone dismissed it as "Oh, it was just the first haircut" thing. When he went for the second cut, everyone was sure. It was not just the first haircut thing. In fact, that day we received a note from the groomer stating that he definitely was a handful, that we needed to work on getting him calmed down some, and, by the way, there was going to be an increase in the groomer's fee. We still are not sure if that was an across-the-board increase or a nuisance fee.

Each day you could see his true identity being revealed. This cute, cuddly, little fur ball, who had never barked, now started to exercise his lungs and stretch his legs. He was four and a half pounds of lightning speed. He tore through the house going "ninety to nothing," stopping only for food, drink, or an occasional nap. "No," "Sit," and "Stay" were not commands to him, but rather challenges. If we said, "Do you want a beating?" he just rolled over with a look of "Okay, hurry and get it over with. I have mischief to do."

By now there was no doubt what his name would be. We joked about it for a while, but soon realized it was no joke. Ladies, gentlemen, and other pets, let me introduce our dog—The Tasmanian Devil.

PAUL AND JUDY GANEM

316

Dudley
("Putti Dog," "PD")

Riley and I first encountered Happy Fluffy Putti Dog on our daily walk to Forsyth Park. PD came bouncing up to us, all floppy drippy tongue and orange fluff, wanting to play with Riley, my lumbering Bouvier. Because PD was wearing a green collar, I assumed that his human must be off in the park somewhere. But when this scene repeated itself a third day, and as PD was becoming decidedly less fluffy and more meager in appearance, I realized that he was either irretrievably lost or abandoned. As even the normally very reserved Riley had grown fond of this funny mix of chow and who-knows-what-else, we agreed that PD should move in with us.

PD, however, had other plans. Though apparently enjoying his newfound domesticated bliss, PD was literally not to be fenced in. I discovered him missing only a few days after he came home to live with us. I posted flyers about town and ads in the paper, which quickly proved effective. I received a call from a man at Cyrano's Lounge on MLK, Jr., Boulevard. It was the middle of the day, but it could have just as well been night inside the smoky cave of Cyrano's. There at the end of the bar amidst a cluster of Cyrano's veterans was Putti Dog. Somehow he had managed to thoroughly ingratiate himself amongst the patrons, as everyone was busily feeding him treats. It was as if he was an old friend of theirs fresh out of the slammer, regaling his fascinated bar buddies with his adventures from the inside.

Our reunion, however, was to be short-lived. Not more than two days had passed when I discovered PD had snuck out through the back gate again. Again I posted ads and flyers. I received a phone call, this time from a woman at the old Crossroads bar (now Bar Bar) in City Market. When I arrived, I found him circulating about the woman's and her partner's pool game, once again lapping up treats from sundry patrons. Reportedly, the indomitable Putti had made several attempts to breach security at the entrance to Crossroads, and finally had succeeded in sneaking in amidst a distraction of some sort.

Increasingly puzzled, I brought PD to his would-be home once more. I began stuffing Putti with a veritable smorgasbord of treats in a crude attempt to obviate a third departure. The next few days were an orgy of rawhide, doggy biscuits, and cold cuts. In retrospect, I believe he thought I was rewarding him for his roving ways. This because I soon discovered him missing a third time. By then I had grown quite fond of him and was consequently more determined than ever to find him. In addition to posting the usual ads and flyers, I conducted a thorough search of the local lounge and bar scene. His buddies hadn't seen him at Cyrano's, nor had anyone at Crossroads. I called the pound several times, but each time a surly woman's voice informed me that nowhere was an orange fluff dog in evidence.

On the third day I was becoming frantic. He had never been missing this long. After three days the pound puts a dog to sleep if he is unclaimed. I decided that I should go in person to find out for myself. I arrived at 4:45 P.M. The pound closes at 5:00 P.M. The gate had been closed. Heart pounding, I maniacally banged on the gate to get someone's attention. The night security man approached, and he reluctantly agreed to allow me a quick look about the place. I tried as much as possible to walk around the entire perimeter of the pound. First I walked around as far as I could on the right side, then on the left. Just as I had turned to go, I heard him! A characteristic Putti Dog yelp! He was in the last cage, in a corner obstructed by boxes. Only a small but excited Putti nose was visible. Elated, I explained to the night security man that I had found my dog. He explained that if he indeed was my dog, I would have to go to the police station to pay a fine for PD's lack of shots and identification. Only now it was past 5:00 P.M., so I also had to pay twenty dollars to the night security man to stay open. An additional seventy-nine dollars later, I came back with a receipt from the police station and was promptly reunited with a lively and tail-wagging Putti Dog.

MICHAEL BROWN

319

GIZZIE GILBERT ("LIZZIE'S GIZZIE," "GIZZIE")

My name is Lizzie's Gizzie; I prefer, however, to be called just Gizzie. I was born in Savannah, Georgia, on June 15, 1990.

I was born to two very handsome apricot Lhasa apsos, aka, Mom and Dad. I was the only girl in a fine litter of six fur balls that could be mistaken for gremlins. We were such a handsome litter that my mom's owner sold us and put us on display at the pet shop in Oglethorpe Mall. That is where my life really began! I was on display in the glass container because of my ultimate beauty for only three days. I noticed a young couple come into the pet store—Steve and Dawn Gilbert, who looked at all of the wonderful pets. I knew that I had to do something quick to get their attention so that I might be a candidate to go home and become their little pup. I quickly rolled over on my back with all four of my chubby, furry little paws stuck straight up in the air. (Boy, did I feel like a dork.) But, hey, a pup's gotta do what a pup's gotta do to find a good home. Well, that did it! Dawn and Steve started laughing, and then said, "What an adorable ball of fur!" Boy, were they naive. A wise old pup of six weeks like me, however, knew exactly what she was doing. Not to my surprise, the deal was done and I went home to live with this nice couple. I got another great surprise when I got home. They also had three boys: Cory, Chris, and Neil. I was delighted—three more people who not only thought that I was the cutest little gremlin that they had ever seen, but also marveled at how I could drink water after midnight, and at how I never complained about "bright lights."

The years passed, and I was very happy with my family. They fed me, groomed me, and took me on frequent trips to the "Pup Parlor" and to that dreaded man who gave me shots. I grew into a fine, mature Lhasa apso. I have but one addiction that I would like to admit. I must speak frankly about it. I have this addiction for, well, it's very hard to admit it, but okay—Pepsi. There, I've said it. I like nothing in the world better than begging my mom and dad or my three brothers for a bowl of ice-cold Pepsi. Like I said before, a pup's gotta do what a pup's gotta do.

I hope you like my picture. I admit, I have lost my girlish figure from too much Pepsi. Okay, I had a weak moment last Halloween with one of my "Beary good Buds." Those Halloween parties can certainly make a pup want to change her profession. Anyway, I could certainly "see" my life more clearly, and I must admit, I'm the happiest pup in all of Savannah!

GIZZIE

321

 **DIXIE**

Dixie wasn't anyone's dog, she was everyone's dog. Born on mill property fifteen years ago, she spent thirteen years there. She was a little dog—maybe twenty-five pounds in her prime—with a beguiling brown-and-black face and a delicate air that belied her toughness—a canine "steel magnolia."

Her job, as she defined it, was to greet the company's employees each work morning with a little dance and a self-taught "smile," to welcome visitors in a restrained but cordial manner, and to know and defend every inch of the rambling buildings and land. On her own, she did perimeter checks and sounded the alarm with a surprisingly deep bark if something was askance. She wasn't a chronic barker, so when she shouted, we knew to come look. When the company first contracted with off-duty Chatham County Police Department personnel to provide security in the evenings, the officers wanted to know how to maneuver around the perimeter and through the maze of buildings. They were told, "Follow the dog." They did, and she showed them everything they needed to know.

Dixie welcomed the company in the evenings, and the sixteen officers who made up the security roster fell in love with her. She didn't make a nuisance of herself, she didn't require a lot of hands-on attention, she just was the soul of the place. She was the constant around which we humans orbited.

As time went on, Dixie's ability to defend her turf began to wane, and in her thirteenth year she took a brutal beating from a pack of dogs who strayed onto the property. She was old and weak by then, and her wounds were terrible. Her vet, my husband, and I all agreed that Dixie's days at work were over. She was now a "retired dog," and so she came to live at the O'Grady-Brannen Canine Beach Camp and Convalescent Home, where four dogs and one boarder were already in residence.

It's always interesting to watch the dynamics of a dog group change when a new dog is added. Dixie came in as an old, wounded dog of imperious bearing, and she moved, like a dowager queen, right to the head of the line. She indicated to us that she'd like her bed to be where she could observe the whole household—by the television, in the living room—and clearly communicated to the other dogs that she would tolerate their presence in her world, but they were not to expect to become chums. Such was her power that our motley crew accepted the new arrangement and accorded her utmost respect.

In her final two years she received, as though it was her due, all the privileges reserved for elders. She reveled in upholstered furniture, air conditioning, and regulated meals. She discovered the luxury of being brushed, the pain-stemming qualities of steadying hands on tender, aching old bones. She wasn't crazy about getting baths, but, oh, she loved the towel massage afterward!

To the officers who were left to patrol the compound without her, I became known as "the lady who got Dixie." I'd provide anecdotes of Dixie in retirement, but every now and then I'd just bring her to work so they could visit with their old pal. Some officers even left me their business cards with instructions to call them if I brought Dixie to work on a day they weren't scheduled so they could come see her!

Dixie died in her fifteenth year—her body just gave out—but the number of people who believe she was one of the most remarkable dogs they've ever known guarantees that she'll live forever, in lore.

KATIE O'GRADY

If you have lived in Chatham County very long, you probably know someone who met Dixie. She was around so long, and people never forget her. Police officers, truck drivers, railroad folks, the UPS and Fedex drivers, they all knew Dixie and so many of them spoke of her to others.

When Katie called a couple of years ago to say Dixie was coming home to recuperate, I knew she would never leave. It's just that way around our house. Remember the song "You Didn't Have to Be So Nice"? That's the way we are with dogs. Dixie was so badly hurt it seemed she might never be whole again, but over the months she became stronger and stronger. We were very lucky to have her for the years we did. I know there are people who will always remember Katie and me best as the folks who took Momma in. That was Dixie's other name. The cops all knew her as Momma.

To the very end Dixie, or Momma, always had the energy and desire to respond whenever Katie came home. She never lost her hearing and would struggle up, to be at the door before Katie's Volvo pulled into the driveway. A few months ago she could still dance a little jig, the last day she just wagged and smiled.

Some dogs are never wrong about people; Dixie was one of those dogs. I'm very proud to be married to someone she loved so well.

LYNDY BRANNEN

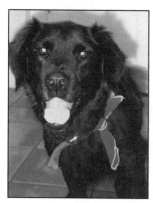

Lucy

This is the story of love at first sight—a classic tale of "dog meets girl." Unlike my other dog, she does not have a bookstore as a namesake. There is no answer to the question "What is her breed?" It is not her physical features that define her, unless "constantly wagging tail" is a breed characteristic.

She lived as a street roamer. Her territory was Park Avenue, between Price and East Broad streets, surviving on garbage and the kindness of a young teenage boy. On a slow, hot, muggy day in 1996, I was conducting field work with my friend Elizabeth, a colleague at the City of Savannah and a dyed-in-the-wool animal lover. As we stood behind a boarded house on Park Avenue, surrounded by junk, knee-high weeds, and dirt, I glanced down to see a creature nearing me, at about knee level. It was a black dog—evidenced by the remaining tufts of hair on its feet and head, and the strip of fur along the spine. The rest of her body was nearly hairless and raw with mange, with the outline of her ribs clearly visible. Street dogs are usually vicious, aggressive, wild. As I stood frozen, heart racing, uncertain, this creature took a few steps closer . . . and licked me on the shin, assuring me with a wagging tail. Then a look up at my face with a grin, her extra-long tongue hanging to one side. At about twenty-five pounds, no more than six months old, she was hardly a threat. Elizabeth said, "She would make a wonderful pet, she's so eager to please," then noted that this dog's life was guaranteed to be short if she remained on the street. As the dog's eyes met mine, I knew that we were in the paws of destiny.

From the house next door a wooden screen door slammed. A boy in his early teens at most, red T-shirt, jean shorts, nearly shaved head with a shaved-in part, "big-boned" but with soft features. He called her "Lady," for lack of any other name, and had been feeding the dog, and rubbing her down with motor oil to help curb her mange. This boy was the St. Francis of the neighborhood, but his grandmother wanted him to stop feeding all the dogs "so they would quit coming around."

With his blessing, Lady came with me. Being new at this "dog and girl" relationship, Lady and I bounced from the Humane Society to the pound, then connected with PALS before ending up at Dr. Kane's veterinary office. The dog was pronounced malnourished and sickly, but curable. Once home, I made a panicky phone call to my friend Kay, another animal lover and mother to Easy, a formerly abused eighty-pound male dog of unfathomable origins. Kay arrived with a heart full of love and head full of information, and a gift-wrapped Milk Bone to ease us through the newlywed stage. When told the dog was named Lady, Kay demurred. "It doesn't suit her." I knew she was right, and we sat in silence for a moment. As a name rose to my lips, Kay said it aloud: "Lucy." That was it. Lucy wagged her tail in acceptance of her name and her new home.

ROBIN GUNN

ZEB

My life was nearly perfect. A dog that was one of the top field-trial champions sired me. He had titles and awards from all over the country. My destiny was cemented when I was chosen to be trained as a field dog. I was taken to a home where there were seven other dogs training to be field dogs. I lived in the kennels, and at night I would dream of retrieving birds. By day I would actually train with birds. I would anxiously wait by the hunter's side until I heard the gunshot. I would then scan the horizon for either the sight or the sound of the bird falling from the sky. The hunter would give me the signal and off I would run, through the fields, sometimes having to swim into the pond to find my goal—the bird.

One day, after running six times, I was sent for the seventh run, and as I was returning to the hunter with the bird in my mouth, my hind legs collapsed. I could not bring the bird to the hunter. After a short time of rest, I was back up and ready to go, however my day with birds was over. All the hunters dismissed it as heat stroke or exhaustion. I felt fine! My life was birds! The next day, after running the same amount of time at

329

approximately the same distance, I collapsed again. What was happening? After one year of life and training, my career as a great field dog was over. I was taken to a top university veterinary school. I was poked and prodded. After running all kinds of tests, they still were not sure why it happened and when it would happen again. The doctors diagnosed me with EIC (exercised-induced collapses). No reason why it happens, no cure for it at the present time. However, my life at becoming a great field dog was over.

No one was sure where I might end up. One day, when all my friends were in the field, I sat in my crate and watched the activities. A strange truck drove up to the field and out walked a lady very unsure of her surroundings. I was taken out of my crate and was left to run with my friends. I was too busy looking for birds to notice that my crate was being placed in the stranger's truck. After a while I was placed in the stranger's truck and taken to what would be my new home.

My new home consists of a mom and a dad, with two other dogs—Krash (Border collie), my older brother, and Kimba (Keeshond), my older sister. Now instead of chasing birds I chase tennis balls. I also take long walks each morning with my mom and Krash. I have started to train for obedience trials. It may not be birds at great distances anymore, however it's nearly as good. At night, after my mom goes to bed and Kimba and Krash follow her, I sit by my dad and get all the attention. When it's time to go to bed, I now sleep at the bottom of Mom and Dad's bed and dream of chasing tennis balls. Now my life is perfect.

ZEB

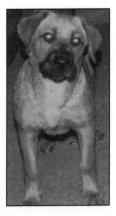

MISS JULIE BROWN VAUGHN ("BROWN")

After just getting settled in a new home on Hilton Head Island, South Carolina, Abby, my three-year black Lab and I were told to evacuate on account of an approaching hurricane. So, without further to-do, Abby and I headed to my parents country home in Jesup, Georgia, to wait out the revenge of the storm. Now you can already tell that I am a dog lover, but really this story isn't about my Abby. This is the story of a garbage-dump dog named "Brown" (short for "Miss Julie Brown," the name she acquired shortly after being found at the garbage dump as a pauper and later turned into a princess for sure).

Upon arriving at my parents' home, Abby and I were greeted by my sister and her beloved Miss Julie, a sixty-five pound, brown-eyed, honey-colored, mixed breed of a bulldog that my sister had discovered homeless as a pup eating garbage at the dump. Miss Julie had quickly adjusted to an indoor princess lifestyle with timely Southern grooming and some mighty fine country vittles served regularly on her own place setting of dog china. In other words, this pup came a long way baby in a short

331

period of time and needless to say was a playmate for my Abby.

After a reunion with my parents, sister, and pets, I returned to my car, gathered my luggage, and, with all hands full, opened the front door to have Miss Julie dart out the door unleashed and without the boundaries of a fence. She immediately ran the distance toward the dirt road that ran beside my parents' home, and within seconds began chasing a 240 Nissan automobile. My little sister was in pursuit as was my father, commanding Brown, as Miss Julie became known, to stop; but Brown ran on and on in what I am sure she thought was the most fun she had experienced in many months. There was no princess pup here, simply a born-to-chase-cars dog out of control as well as the car.

Moments later the small sports car stopped. We saw Brown get up from in front of the car and begin to walk back down the street toward us when much to our surprise the woman stepped on the gas and slammed into Brown, knocking our beloved Miss Julie Brown into the ditch. The shrill cry of Brown was mixed with the car's deadly engine as the driver sped away never even looking back.

Poor Brown, moaning and crying, was lying in a mass of blood. Immediately my emotions took second place and my experience as a nurse took over, directing my sister to call the vet, any vet, my father to bring the car around, and my mom to bring sheets to wrap her in. As I knelt beside her, her big brown eyes looked up to me with fear and for help beyond what I was empowered to have in me. Quickly, but gently, we gathered her onto a sheet and put her on the back seat of the car to take her to the emergency vet's office. As we prepared to go, my sister returned to say that she was unable to reach a vet by phone. It was then that I began to cry; and as I cried, my father began praying; and the more he prayed, the stronger I became; and I too prayed for God's divine intervention in this matter that at the moment seemed all too helpless and almost too much to ask for in a miracle.

Upon reaching the vet's office, Brown's honey-colored coat had turned to ashen blue as the blood continued to seep from his body. His beautiful brown eyes had closed, and his breathing was less than a whisper. I asked my father and sister to leave us on the bench outside the vet's office and try to find another vet in this small town. As I sat next to Miss Julie, I prayed for strength to be able to tell my sister that her dog had died, and I remembered my Abby back at home. Abby would sure miss Brown as we all would.

An hour had passed since the accident—the golden hour of trauma that usually reveals the outcome. I had to do something! I got up and began to beat on the door, thinking that maybe an alarm might sound and someone would come who could make this miracle happen. Suddenly the door opened, my adrenaline kicked in, and with super human strength I pulled her from the bench with the sheet. Just as I got to the door, this sixty-five-pound beloved animal stood and waddled through the door before collapsing again losing all bodily functions.

Okay, God, we made it so far, help me again. I gathered her with superhuman strength and placed her on the examination table. It seemed that Brown wasn't even breathing now, but I knew in my heart she was. Looking around the room, I gathered up what was needed to start an IV and attempted to gain an intra-venous access in order to begin giving her fluids when in walked two veterinarians, whom my father had located. They took over.

The night was long and, it seemed, without hope, but faith and love kept us as Brown was transferred to Savannah for several hours of intense surgery. Brown sustained three breaks in one leg, which appeared for a while might need amputating. She lost a lung, and her kidneys were damaged; but a miracle indeed was experienced by our animal-loving family. The power of prayer is the greatest of all.

Today Miss Julie Brown has recovered in spite of numerous surgeries and infections. She still likes to chase cars, but this time she chases them inside a huge fenced yard. My dad has clocked her at thirty miles-per-hour. Amazingly she has not one limitation, or so we have observed. She now weighs eighty pounds and may run like the wind, and she resides as the pauper-turned-princess in my parents' home. Some people may argue that cats have nine lives, but I bear witness to at least two for our Miss Julie Brown.

As for what happened to the driver of the little sports car—I confronted her and her explanation was without remorse. The lady said she thought the dog belonged to someone else. Intentionally hurting an animal is a crime. I was so angered by the response of this woman, I called the state's attorney, who advised me what to do. The woman was arrested; and although she did get out on bail, we later went to court over the matter and she was fined and put on one year's probation. She also had to pay for all medical expenses. While the pain and agony that Brown had to endure could not be forgotten, I hope this woman will forever remember to always brake for animals and to be especially kind as well.

GENIE VAUGHN

QUEEN ELIZABETH
OF SAVANNAH
("CHOMPS BELCHER")

On a beautiful Saturday morning in 1980 I received a phone call that led to the gift of a pet that became a dedicated and most-loved family member and friend to all who came in contact with her for the duration of her life.

Petless at the time, and with two children, ages six and ten years old, I can recall the day quite clearly. We had just moved into our home on Grace Drive and purchased a new vehicle. The lady who called identified herself and explained that she had spoken with my husband several days before at the airport. She was there for the departure of a relative who had adopted one of her seven English springer spaniel puppies born to her prized dam, Amanda Bounce McGlaun, and sire, Sylvan Grand Slam. My husband assisted her with the flight arrangements, and was so taken with the beauty of the pup, he asked if she had any other puppies for sale.

The lady's response was simply that she did not sell her puppies, and, yes, she indeed did have several remaining in her care that had not been placed. Quickly my husband provided her with our home phone number, never really expecting to hear from her, and asked her to call if the opportunity presented that she might consider our family as an adoptive family.

Now the call had surprisingly arrived, and I was being preliminarily interviewed as the mother in an adoptive family. This very sincere lady wanted to know the age of our children and how responsible they might be to pet care, had we previously owned pets, and if we had a fenced yard. I obviously answered correctly, and we moved toward the second part of the interview, where she would evaluate the children as well as myself as a sincere adoptive family. With directions to her home on Hilton Head and an appointment time, our ecstatic children and I set out in our new car to meet the pups and their owner.

Now I wasn't quite as excited as my children. During the ride there, I had time to reflect on exactly what damage a new puppy could do to both new car and home. So I quickly made the decision that this would simply be a Saturday outing to visit this charming lady and her puppies. At that point I had never even heard of English springer spaniels. Surely they couldn't be too cute, the kids would understand, and maybe we wouldn't even pass the interview.

Oh, was I ever wrong! My children exhibited their very best behavior and quickly attached themselves to this precious little liver-and-white puppy with long curly ears and a single white heart on top of its head that I soon learned was a trademark of springer spaniels. I too was quite smitten with this little animal.

After extensive instructions and paperwork promising to be a loving family that would provide only the very safest and best care to the little pup, I provided the owner with directions to our home, where she would follow up with us from time to time in the future.

By the time we arrived back in Savannah, the children had quickly come up with the name "Chomps," named for the staring dog in the TV movie C.H.O.M.P'S, which we had watched the previous evening. Our stop at the pet store to quickly pick up the immediate puppy necessities at a minimum cost turned into a bigger financial commitment than anticipated. Nothing too good for this new family member. As we inquired in the store for a simple collar and leash, we were bombarded with people asking where this wonderful pet had been purchased, if there were others, and what was her pedigree line. Several people quickly gave us a lesson in English Springer Spaniels 101. We left with our Chomps sporting a lovely blue top-of-the-line harness, collar, and leash to match; sweater; nourishments set for any princess; and, of course, enough reading material to guide us through the puppy phase.

We all knew at that point that we had been blessed with a beautiful gift for a pet, but little did I ever realize the joy this pet would bring to the Belcher household and to the many children and adults of whom she became a part in the years to follow.

Our entire family quickly embraced our new puppy, and the return love was tenfold. Even when we went to work or school, we hated to leave Chomps alone. We quickly set about choosing a veterinarian, having her immunized, and putting up a fence shortly before her previous owner came for a visit. Boy, was that a close one; but I must tell you that this lovely animal was reared and lived in our home, rarely going outside for anything other than the necessities or to play.

We arrived home one afternoon to find Chomps, around ten weeks of age, unable to get up. Having vomited severely, she was very hot. We quickly transported Chomps to our vet, Dr. Billy Sanders, who during the next sixteen years became our veterinary hero, but who was not given a lot of encouragement. There was a new virus attacking puppies—parvo. While it had not been reported in Chatham County, our vet was very knowledgeable about the severity of the illness. We left Chomps at the vet for treatment. The outlook was grim and sad, but with prayers and the wonderful treatment by our vet, Chomps recovered and was soon home, again happy and playful.

Chomps graduated at the head of her class in Paw Prints Obedience School. She became indoctrinated in tub baths, twice weekly; and with a simple clap-and-direct command, she would spring into the tub and sit waiting for her grooming. She became the mascot of all the children in the neighborhood. She dressed in costume for Halloween trick-or-treating; for Easter egg hunting; and for Christmas as Santa's helper and as a quarterback football player. All snapshots had our Chomps regally positioned out front. Chomps's name had stuck with everyone; and even when her American Kennel Club papers arrived, accepting her formal name as Queen Elizabeth of Savannah, she never knew it.

Chomps was the bed partner of everyone who stayed in our home, many of whom declared that she did not know that she was a dog. She would start with the first one in bed, staying with them until asleep, and progress with each to follow. Chomps always was lovingly referenced in Christmas greeting cards, letters, and conversations. Everyone wanted a pet like our Chomps.

We began to get calls from people who wanted us to think about breeding her and to consider their pet as the sire. At the age of two, and after we chose a worthy suitor, we proceeded with the pregnancy of our little princess dog. Just before Christmas, Chomps gave birth to eleven healthy pups. Since we had been told that Chomps would probably have only one or two puppies, her whelping box was too small; but the children and I caressed her head and offered encouraging words. What a litter—eleven little Chomps. The next day my husband and children built a lovely new home for Chomps's large family—a five feet long, three feet wide, two feet deep, painted-white, wooden home that bore the carefully lettered and stenciled "Chomps and Crew." The home was decorated with red Christmas bows. Friends and neighbors from all around visited, cuddled, and loved on every one of Chomps's children. And even with eleven pups there were not enough to go around. Some of our dearest friends, who became hooked on springer spaniels, have had several more since then; and we still receive Christmas cards from those who share our same love for the English springer breed. That Christmas—when Chomps and Crew lived under the Christmas tree in their home until the holidays were long gone—has become a legend among our family and friends. A year later, in the same box, Chomps again was bred with a select suitor. She gave birth to ten pups, with all the neighborhood children either watching in the room or peering in the windows. I am sure that all those who are now grown remember the birth of Chomps's two families.

After two pregnancies and twenty-one puppies, and against protests from many who wanted a "Chomps," we decided that Chomps should retire from puppy motherhood and simply return to being the mother that she had once been to all of us. So we scheduled an appointment for surgery with Dr. Sanders and proceeded through what appeared to be a successful and uncomplicated procedure. Almost ten days after the operation, however, I awakened in terror in the middle of the night to hear whimpering at the side of my bed. Our dear pet was in a pool of blood. Quickly I awakened my husband, scooped up her limp body, wrapped her in my bed comforter, and headed for the car. Meanwhile, my husband called Dr. Sanders. As I recall, it was a Saturday night, somewhere around 2 A.M., and as I arrived at Dr. Sanders' office, he arrived also.

There was a quick assessment, IV fluids were started with great difficulty on account of the severe loss of blood, Chomps was intubated, and I was instructed to breath for Chomps using the Ambu bag connected with oxygen. Dr. Sanders proceeded to open and explore the surgical site. He found that she had experienced a rare allergic reaction to the suture used as the sutures began to absorb after her surgery. Dr. Sanders quickly tied off the bleeder, stitched her up, and left for the Emergency Clinic several miles away in order to obtain blood. I continued to breathe for Chomps and prayed for her. It seemed like hardly any time elapsed before Dr. Sanders returned with blood and expertly transfused her. Some time around daybreak, I was told that that was about all we could do. Now it was left up to God's plan. Dr. Sanders advised me to leave her with him, but there was no way I could possibly do that. So although she was still unconscious, I wrapped her up and took her home, where my husband had prepared a place for her in front of the fireplace, where the warm embers of an all-night fire remained. The embers had a very calming effect on the tragic, tiring, and very emotional night.

Dr. Sanders had explained the risk of not knowing exactly what Chomps's mentality would be when or if she survived. But we were willing to take our chances and truly felt that love and prayers would make the difference. Indeed they did. Around noon Chomps stirred, opening her eyes to find the Belcher family and, by then, neighbors cheering lovingly. She had no strength to pick herself up, but we knew as she tried that she needed to go to the bathroom. So we gently carried her outside and held her up on all four shaky legs so she could urinate. It was then that I relaxed, knowing our prayers had been answered. It took several weeks for things to return to normal, but they did.

Chomps lived on exuberantly and with meaning for another thirteen years. She proudly shared in every event of our family. We recognized her royalty and pedigree as being from the line of Salilyn's Macduff; the picture of her great-great-grandfather Macduff had been on the front cover of *The New English Springer Spaniel* (1980) by Charles S. Goodall and Julia Gasow. Macduff was best in show at the National Specialty in 1959, and in his record that year he placed second as a show dog of all dogs in the country. He received the Parent Club award for "Springer of the Year" three times: 1958, 1959, 1969.

It's no wonder that Chomps and her puppies were such wonderful family members. We never chose to show this remarkable animal, but she was our prize for more than fifteen years and will always remain one of our family's warmest memories.

THE BELCHER FAMILY

SARAH MIRIAM PEALE NANGLE

I've been waiting around between dog treats for my people to write my biography, but they are always involved with painting pictures and setting type for books, so I find I must do it myself. Until they adopted me I always had to rely upon myself. I learned how to be good to avoid punishment. When I was abandoned I learned to forage around dumpsters for food and to endear myself to people so they would like me and help me take care of my puppies. I miss my puppies. Sometimes I smell a familiar scent in the air, but my puppies are never there.

After my puppies were born, I got very sick. I was living in a trailer park with the kind people who took me in. They were worried about me and took me to a doctor who said he knew how to make me better, but the medicine cost a lot of money. They didn't have a lot of money, but they did want me to get better, so they gave me to Save-A-Life. Save-A-Life did save my life, and I went to live with a man who had lots and lots of dogs and cats. One day, when I was feeling a little better, he took me to a parking lot and stood there with me on a leash. Lots of people came by to see me. I saw a man and a woman with gray hair get out of their car and come straight over to me. The woman said, "That's the dog I want," and I jumped up on her and wagged my tail, the way I always do. "See," the woman said, "she really likes me." That's how I came to be with my new people.

They took me home with them, and when they opened their front door, my heart sank. There was white wall-to-wall carpeting all over the place, and I was beginning to feel sick again. I found their bedroom and curled up on the rug next to their big bed. "See," the woman said again, "she really does like me. She's curled up on the floor next to my side of the bed."

Even so, I was afraid and I went back into the living room and was sick. They were dismayed and worried. "It must be the heartworm treatment," the man said. They cleaned up the mess and petted me and said it was all right, but I knew it wasn't, because I could feel myself getting sick again. They kept saying it was all right, but after what happened to me before, I knew it wasn't. Finally, they took me back to the doctor. I was so afraid and felt so sick. When I heard the doctor say, "Are you going to keep this dog?" I knew it was over; but the woman said, "What do you mean? Of course we're going to keep this dog." The doctor looked at me and said, "Sarah, you've got it made." I stayed overnight with the doctor and gradually I began to feel better. The next day I went back home with the white carpet people. They added "Miriam Peale" to my name because Sarah Miriam Peale was the first woman painter in the United States to support herself by painting pictures. Then they added their name, Nangle, because now I am part of their family.

The white carpet people feed me twice *every* day, and keep my water bowl full. In the summer they let me lie on the air conditioning vent. It smells funny in the studio and the floor is hard, but I get dog treats when I go in there, so I sometimes keep the woman company in there. She likes that. They both take me on walks and on long car trips to see another dog, Charlie, and his people in the big city. Charlie is in love with me. His people give me lots of dog treats too. Then we go to see two cats, Zuni and Hopi, and their person. Those cats need to be taught some manners because they are always getting up on tables, but we get along together pretty well considering they're cats. Visiting those other four-footers is the only excitement I get now, and it's plenty for me.

I am content and make sure my people know I love them by licking their legs and jumping up to greet them when they come home, which they don't like, but I just can't keep myself from doing it. At night I curl up next to their bed, where I feel very safe and go to sleep.

SARAH

KALVIN

On a February afternoon two years ago, I was walking home from Kroger when I heard something crying pitifully underneath some bushes on Gwinnett Street. After further investigation I tucked the ball of mud with two little eyes in the crook of my arm and carried him home with my groceries. Shivering after a rigorous bath, the newborn puppy looked at me for the first time. I called him Kalvin, and he wagged his tiny tail.

I worried about the possibility of behavioral problems because he had been separated from his mama at such a young age, and I wanted to make up for it in any way I could. I taught him about architecture, how to send e-mails, and all the ingredients that go in a quiche. He learned how to juggle, how to roll down the car window, and the names of all the different kinds of clouds. I knew Kalvin was uncommonly gifted, but it was not until a year later that I realized my dog was also a talented con-artist.

I was sitting in the living room of my house on Henry Street repeating my credit card number to a Bell South operator on the phone when my roommate rushed in screaming that Kalvin had just been hit by a car. Of course I ran outside, rushing to my pet with arms extended. Kalvin was surrounded by people, and according to the neighbors, only his tail end had been hit—"maybe a broken leg . . . could've been a lot worse . . . he's real damn lucky"—et cetera. I transported him to the car on a blanket and sped off. At the animal hospital I was struck by how calm Kalvin was. His mouth was foaming, but his eyes were clear and focused. Other than panting softly, he was silent and still as his body was examined.

The following day, after receiving instructions regarding his injuries, I was allowed to take my dog home. Poor Kalvin had broken the toes in his right hind foot, and they had set the foot in a bright pink cast. Kalvin hates pink! He also had to wear a retainer collar—a giant white plastic cone that looked incredibly uncomfortable, not to mention ridiculous. Kalvin hopped on his three good legs across the waiting room floor toward me, his eyes averted and head hung low, as if he knew he looked like some kind of weird space thing that had oddly chosen to present himself to planet earth wearing only one pink sock.

Naturally I had expected the process of Kalvin's recovery to move slowly at first, but because he had received no head trauma or injury, I imagined that with plenty of rest and good food he would be playing beach volleyball and riding his big wheel around the neighborhood in no time. As soon as I got him home I realized that this would not be the case. The doctor had stressed the importance of keeping Kalvin still, so as not to put pressure on his damaged toes. Kalvin refused to lie down; he paced back and forth from room to room relentlessly, stopping only to stare wild-eyed at the walls for a couple of hours every so often. He lost all desire for food and water and panted constantly. Worse, he could not fall asleep at night and began crying his head off as soon as I turned the lights out. I phoned the veterinarian, and he said to be patient; but after a week they agreed to keep Kalvin overnight to observe his behavior. Because I was so exhausted and emotionally drained, it was almost a relief to hand him over to someone else for the night, but at the same time I was terrified that something bad and unfixable had happened to Kalvin's brain, and that he would never be the same.

Late the next afternoon, the doctor called and asked me to describe again the behavior that had me so concerned. When I had finished he said rather vaguely, "This is very puzzling," and asked me to come to the hospital as soon as possible for an "experiment." I rushed right over, nervously imagining all the terrible things this experiment might entail. When I arrived the doctor took one look at my face and quickly began explaining that Kalvin was absolutely fine. His cast had been removed, and his toes had healed perfectly. He had raced around the yard with the other dogs for over an hour that morning, and he had willingly eaten three cans of dog food. My eyes began filling with tears because I thought he was suggesting that I was making everything up. He hastily reassured me, saying he had a hunch about what was going on, and he sent the nurse to retrieve my dog.

I could hear Kalvin running down the hall, but when he turned the corner and saw me, he stopped in his tracks. The hurt foot he had been running on moments before was instantly tucked up as if he could not bear to walk on it. Once again his eyes took on a wild look, as if he were staring intensely at nothing. I called to him, and

349

he swayed and stumbled forward like he might faint from exertion. Fascinated, the doctor handed me a can of food and instructed me to feed Kalvin. As I brought the food up to his face, Kalvin swooned again and actually collapsed to the floor, his "hurt" foot dangling in the air. He rolled his eyes back in their sockets and, with his tongue lolling, made horrid gurgling sounds in his throat. I burst into tears, thinking that my dog blamed me for letting him get hurt and wanted to punish me, and the doctor patted my back in sympathy. "The reason is quite obvious," he said gently, and with sane amusement went on to explain. "Kalvin is a little boy, and you are his mother. He has recovered physically, but his brain cannot process the events of this traumatic experience, and so he is suffering emotional damage. He is showing us that what he needs most is all the attention, babying, and love you can possibly give him."

Once I knew it was just a performance, and Kalvin was not dying after all, it became almost fun like a game. I fixed the most scrumptious meals and ate them on the floor, trying to feed him from my plate. Kalvin would pretend to faint. I would gasp in concern and pet him, letting the food fall near his face so he could slyly lick it up without me noticing. I stared at the walls with him, went to sleep with the lights on, and left his water bowl where I couldn't see him drink. I even carried him (he weighs sixty pounds) from room to room when he felt he couldn't possibly use his "hurt" leg. This went on for two weeks, and I became dismayed. Kalvin was not growing tired of playing sick as quickly as I was growing tired of playing nursemaid. I had to help him remember how much more fun it was to be a normal dog like he was before. With renewed determination I led him, limping extravagantly, to the car, and drove him to the beach. I almost felt sorry for him, watching him try his best to hobble convincingly through the thick sand. He stood at the water's edge, right hind foot hitched up off the ground, head drooping. I had to admit I was impressed with his dedication as an actor, but it was time to give it up. I reached into my backpack, pulled out my secret weapon, and launched it into the water. Kalvin's favorite rubber chicken bobbed up and down in the waves, and I knew it was all over. I looked at my dog, he looked at me, and in the next instant he was splashing through the waves carrying the chicken victoriously back to the beach. He ran right past me all the way to the car waving the chicken like a lunatic. When I reached him he was waiting patiently. He gave me the chicken, and I told him he was very, very good. He hopped in the car, rolled down the car window, and gave me a look that said, "I know, I know!" He's been e-mailing, cooking quiches, and playing beach volleyball ever since—just like any normal dog.

ANNA TROUPE

MINNIE
McQUILLEN
BEIL

It all began with a typical Saturday morning trek to Home Depot almost six years ago. As my husband and I entered the parking lot, we saw a huge hot air balloon looming over the grand opening of yet another retail establishment in the same development as our Home Depot of choice.

"It's a PETsMART," I exclaimed in a desperate effort to postpone the inevitable Home Depot excursion, adding the somewhat brilliant observation, "I bet they'll have pets there." Reluctantly my husband agreed that we could briefly check out the grand opening.

Upon entering the front door, a woman approached the same entrance with a grocery cart filled with five puppies. Two of them were white, two were brown-and-white combinations, and one of them was solid black. As I stopped to admire the woman's cart o' puppies, I was drawn immediately to the small black one. As I reached into the warm puppy pack to pick up the little black one, I asked if she had a name. "It's Minnie," she replied.

In my arms Minnie felt like the most perfect little puppy in the world. When she looked into my eyes, I knew that my husband, Deric, and my days of carefree irresponsibility were rapidly coming to an end. As I began the ever-important process of bonding with my newfound friend, Deric made brief passes by us in a manner that was absent any true interaction.

"Hey, Mary Ann, put the dog down and come look at these birds," Deric said as he passed by and quickly headed toward some other unexplored aisle. "I think there are some lizards and turtles over here," as he made another pass. And a few minutes later he made his final pass—the one that meant that it was time to go. "Come on, Mary Ann, we've got to get to Home Depot. Now put that puppy down."

"Oh, but she's so cute," I countered.

"All puppies are cute," Deric argued.

Having had twenty blissful minutes of Minnie's little heart beating against mine, I was reluctant to end this engagement. Deric was adamant, so I pushed the puppy onto his chest and announced emphatically, "Okay, we can return this sweet little creature to her life of abandonment, but you will have to put her in the grocery cart yourself."

Once on Deric's chest, Minnie looked up into Deric's face. It took all of thirty seconds, if that, for Deric to issue the following mandates. "Go get my dog a leash," he instructed me. And as soon as that was in hand, "Go get my dog some dog food" was the second instruction. Of course this second command required that I wrestle a forty-pound bag of food over my shoulder and lug it to the front of the store.

Once back to the front of the store, I could not locate my husband and his newly acquired companion. Then I heard Deric's familiar voice. "Here, we're over here."

Following the sound of his voice, I saw Deric and Minnie getting their picture taken. "I'm getting my picture made with my dog," Deric clarified, just in case I couldn't put this all together.

Well, the handwriting was on the wall from that moment on. I had the dog that I so desperately wanted—at least for the first twenty minutes—but she would be Deric's dog and dearest companion for the rest of her life. Lucky for me, they still let me hang around with them both.

MARY ANN BOWMAN BEIL

DUNCAN

My name is Duncan; I am a three-year-old Yorkshire terrier, aka alpha dog, and the center of the household. I was one of a litter of five born to Mandy and sired by Lovebubbles.

I'm sure I was the alpha dog of the litter as I think back on the day my new momma picked me out of the box. My three brothers and one sister were timid and stayed back in the box. Not me. She looked like a nice person, so I was up there on the edge of the box looking as cute as I could. And what do you know, it worked—she picked me.

I was taken to my new home on East Victory Drive, where I live with my brother, a golden retriever, Cheerio. When I first arrived there at one and a half pounds, it was pretty scary. I couldn't get up steps, make it from one room to another without needing some help, or walk through the grass; but now, ten pounds later, I am fearless.

My momma (as I refer to her) wanted me to be comfortable and confident regardless of where I was, so she put me through obedience and agility classes. I made a lot of friends; my best friend in school was Maddie. We were the smallest and needed to stick together.

I have a lot of friends; many are in this book. Minnie and I have hosted Christmas parties with other friends, celebrated St. Patrick's Day together, and enjoyed Forsyth Park, my favorite place in Savannah.

I enjoy the park so much that my family can't drive past it that I don't jump up and suggest that we stop. What could be more important? Next to going to the park, taking a walk, and my momma, the most important thing to me is play. My favorite sport—fetch. I have eight to fifteen tennis balls going whenever someone is willing to play. If I can't find a taker for that, tug-of-war or tag will do. I have a lot of toys. Each one has a specific purpose or game. Sometimes, however, an unknowing visitor will try to play fetch with "blue ball" (it's for tug-of-war), and they wonder why I won't chase it. One of my favorite toys that makes everyone laugh is a giant rubber turkey leg. It is great to shake. Sometimes I shake it so hard that my whole body spins in a circle. I've played with it so much that I'm on my fifth one in two years. My momma says that she hopes that they don't stop making turkey legs.

When I'm not enjoying Savannah or playing one of my favorite games, I'm snuggling. I give up the macho alpha-dog attitude and find the greatest comfort and confidence in being with and near my family, my momma especially. "The daddy" says he thinks we have a string connecting us to each other. She and I really connect. She sees my smile and her eyes light up; I see her and get all dreamy-eyed, and my ears flop. It's a good thing the daddy isn't jealous.

He really likes me too. He's put me on his payroll in

his cabinet shop, where I keep everything under control. I do neighborhood watch out the doors and tend to anything requiring my attention. I can always tell when the workday should be over and start making subtle suggestions that we head for home.

Once home, if my momma isn't there, I can't play or rest. I watch until she drives in and then run to greet her and give her lots and lots of kisses. My way of saying, I'm glad you picked me.

DUNCAN

KONDAHARS THE FINANCIER ("DOLLAR")

We acquired Dollar about three years ago when we lived at the Landings. We were restoring a house downtown on Jones Street and thought it would be a good idea to have a sizable dog. Dollar was three years old at the time, and was used as a confirmation dog. He apparently did quite well, but "broke"—meaning that he looked at another dog while being judged during a contest. He was expected to win, but didn't. Dollar is also a certified pediatric and geriatric therapy dog, and is thus excellent around children and the elderly. Apparently only a small percentage of dogs has the personality and aptitude for this certification.

Because of his training, he was actually afraid to look at other dogs at first. I thought he was a wimp. We have taken him to Coastal K9 three times a week for the last two years. This allows him to relate, run, and challenge other large dogs. Dollar is about eighty pounds, and oddly enough, he has become an alpha dog according to the trainer, Skip Brandon. His temperament, however, has remained affectionate and playful with both people and other pets. He lives in a home with two cats, two birds, and a small twelve-year-old female poodle. Actually she seems to be the boss in our household. Dollar is respectful toward the opposite sex and the elderly.

Dollar is a great athlete. His main agenda at Coastal K9 is to run for miles. As soon as he gets out of the car, he just takes off. According to Skip, other dogs will take a lap with him and then rest for one lap and pick him up again for the following one. Dollar just keeps running. Expectedly he is very muscular and has minimal body fat. His color is black, and people comment about his beauty virtually every time we walk him. Actually, in spite of his good disposition, people often prefer to walk on the other side of the street.

Dollar can be quite funny on the days that he stays home. He tends to run laps around the coffee table. But for the most part he tries to sneak up into Cheryl's lap, a difficult job for an animal the size of a small deer, or he just wants to be petted.

My opinion of the Doberman breed has completely changed from the usual one of a vicious unpredictable dog, to big pet or an affectionate lap dog. Is he protection? Most definitely! He seems to sense when someone is doing something wrong and will stand his ground. And who is going to test an animal with teeth like a miniature T. Rex? But all in all, one would have to be doing something pretty bad for him to act as mean as he looks.

RON AND CHERYL FINGER

MRS. HOPKINS' DOG

I'm the kind of fellow who loves other people's dogs. Never owned one myself, but that's all right—I've enjoyed others' canines.

The one I'm telling you about was a handsome beagle whose name I never knew, but whom I became quite fond of simply through our every-morning acquaintance-ship at the street corner. You see, I would walk to the corner each morning and wait for Wally Davis, my city editor at the time, to pick me up and take me to work. Since Wally was coming my way, it made sense for him to pick me up.

This beagle would always be at the corner, waiting for me. I would approach the corner and he'd start toward me, wagging his tail and otherwise extending a cheery greeting. I'd pet him and talk to him while waiting for Wally.

Each day, our comradeship lasted briefly because Wally would be there in three or four minutes. He would pull over, and I'd open the door and hop in, telling the dog good-bye, and the dog would then head southward to his own home.

Now, I knew where the dog lived, and I knew his owners—Mr. and Mrs. Bill Hopkins—but not well. We were just friendly "hello" kind of neighbors.

Well, one day Wally drew to a stop, I opened his car door, and the dog bounded into the vehicle before I did.

Nothing Wally or I did could budge that dog. Finally, I told Wally the dog lived just a couple of blocks away, so let's simply take him home. Wally whirled his car around and headed for the Hopkins house. We arrived there in short order.

I opened the car door, and the dog hopped out before I could and ran to his front door. I followed and rang the doorbell. After a brief wait, Mrs. Hopkins came to the door and began to thank me, but she never finished. The dog took over. He stood just behind her and growled menacingly at me, baring his teeth and making certain I knew he was in command. So vicious was the dog's manner that I backed to the car, keeping an eye on him.

Which goes to show, I guess, that a dog at home will protect his mistress and the house. The dog continued to greet me at the corner each morning, but darned if I'd ever take him home again.

TOM COFFEY